Praise for

BELIEVE ME

INTERNATIONAL BESTSELLER

"Imaginative, unusual, clever and fun."
—*The Times* (London)

"A dark and haunting thriller . . . A superb evocation of conflicted emotions, this never lets you guess what's coming next." —*The Daily Mail*

"An intense, stylish psychological thriller."
—*Good Housekeeping*

"Fast-paced . . . A solid pick from bestselling author Delaney (*The Girl Before*) for readers who enjoyed the paranoia factor in A. J. Finn's *The Woman in the Window* or the unreliable narrator of Paula Hawkins's *The Girl on the Train*."
—*Library Journal*

"The author produces a bobsled run's worth of twists."
—*Publishers Weekly*

"I so enjoyed it—what a twisty, exciting read."
—Sabine Durrant, author of *Lie with Me*

"Likely to follow its predecessor's path straight to the international bestseller lists . . . a compelling read . . . redefines the concept of an unreliable narrator . . . This rich, nuanced, highly literary take on the *Gone Girl* theme adds dimension and complexity to a trend that was in danger of wearing out its welcome."
—*Booklist* (starred review)

"It's one very gripping story that had me snagging late-night reading and early mornings wondering who I should believe." —*Bookreporter*

THE GIRL BEFORE

"A pitch-perfect novel of psychological suspense."
—LEE CHILD

"*The Girl Before* generates a fast pace . . . [JP] Delaney intersperses ethics questions on standalone pages throughout the book. . . . The single most ingenious touch is that we're not provided either woman's answers."
—*The New York Times*

"Riveting . . . Writing with precision and grace, Delaney strips away the characters' secrets until the raw truth of each is revealed." —*Publishers Weekly*

"[A] must-read." —*New York Post*

BY JP DELANEY

The Girl Before

Believe Me

BELIEVE ME

BELIEVE ME

A NOVEL

JP DELANEY

BALLANTINE BOOKS · NEW YORK

A Ballantine Books International Edition

Copyright © 2018 Shippen Productions Ltd.

Published by Ballantine Books, an imprint of Random House, a division of Penguin Random House LLC, New York.

BALLANTINE and the HOUSE colophon are registered trademarks of Penguin Random House LLC.

A hardcover edition has been published in the United States by Ballantine Books, an imprint of Random House, a division of Penguin Random House LLC.

The author published an earlier version of this story as *The Decoy* under the name Tony Strong.

Excerpt from *Casablanca* granted courtesy of Warner Bros. Entertainment, Inc.

ISBN 978-1-9848-1776-1
Ebook ISBN 978-1-101-96632-7

Cover design: Carlos Beltrán
Cover photographs: DreamPictures/Getty Images

Printed in the United States of America

randomhousebooks.com

9 8 7 6 5 4 3 2

FOR MICHAEL

You act with your scars.

—Shelley Winters

No man, for any considerable period, can wear one face to himself and another to the multitude, without finally getting bewildered as to which may be the true.

—Nathaniel Hawthorne, *The Scarlet Letter*

BELIEVE
ME

PROLOGUE

On the day of departure, guests are requested to vacate their rooms by noon.

By eleven o'clock the sixth floor of the Lexington Hotel has nearly emptied. This is Midtown Manhattan, where even the tourists are on busy schedules of galleries and department stores and sights. Any late sleepers have been woken by the noise of the maids, chattering to one another in Spanish as they come and go from the laundry room beside the elevator, preparing the rooms for another influx this afternoon.

Dotted down the hallway, discarded breakfast trays show which rooms still have to be cleaned.

There's no tray outside the door of the Terrace Suite.

Each morning, a folded copy of *The New York Times* is delivered to every room, with the hotel's compliments.

In the case of the Terrace Suite, the compliment has been refused. The paper lies on the mat, untouched. A DO NOT DISTURB tag hangs from the handle above it.

Consuela Alvarez leaves the Terrace Suite till last. Eventually, when all the other rooms are done, she can leave it no longer. Wincing at the ache in her lower back—she's changed a dozen sets of linen already this morning, and scrubbed a dozen shower stalls—she taps on the door with her pass card, calls "Housekeeping," waits for a reply.

None comes.

The first thing she notices as she lets herself in is the cold. An icy draft is blowing through the drapes. She clucks disapprovingly as she goes to the window and hauls on the cord. Gray light floods the room.

The place is a mess. She bangs the window shut, a little ostentatiously.

The person in the bed doesn't stir.

"Please . . . You have to wake up now," Consuela says awkwardly.

The sheets have been pulled right up over the face. Smoothing the body's contours, like something buried under layers of snow.

Looking around at the debris—a tipped lamp, a broken wineglass—Consuela has a sudden sense of foreboding. Last year, there was a suicide on the second floor. A bad business. A boy overdosed in the bathroom. And the hotel was fully booked: They'd had to clean the room and get it ready for the next occupant at five.

Now that she looks again, there are several things that seem unusual, even strange, about the Terrace Suite today. Who goes to bed leaving broken glass on the carpet, where they might step on it next day? Who sleeps with sheets covering their head? Consuela has seen a lot of hotel rooms, and the scene in front of her seems somehow unnatural.

Staged, even.

Consuela crosses herself. Nervously, she puts her hand

on the bedcovers, near where the shoulder must be, and shakes it.

After a moment, where her hand has pressed, a red flower blooms on the white linen.

She knows there's something wrong now, something very bad. She touches the bed again, pressing with just a finger this time. Again, like ink spreading through tissue paper, a red petal blossoms on the sheet.

Consuela summons all her courage and, with her left hand, yanks the covers back.

Even before she takes in what she sees there, her other arm is reaching up to cross herself again. But this time the hand that darts to her forehead never completes the gesture. It comes down, trembling, to stifle her scream instead.

PART
ONE
(FIVE DAYS EARLIER)

M y friend hasn't showed yet.

That's what you'd think if you saw me here, perched at the bar of this corporate-cool New York hotel, trying to make my Virgin Mary last all evening. Just another young professional waiting for her date. A little more dressy than some of the other women here, maybe. I don't look like I just came from an office.

At the other end of the bar a group of young men are drinking and joshing, punching one another on the shoulder to make their points. One—good-looking, smartly dressed, athletic—catches my eye. He smiles. I look away.

Soon after, a table becomes free near the back, and I take my drink over and sit at it. Where, suddenly, this little scene unfolds:

INT. DELTON HOTEL BAR, W. 44TH ST.,
NEW YORK—NIGHT

MAN
(belligerently)

Excuse me?

Someone's standing in front of me. A businessman, about forty-five, wearing an expensive casual-cut suit that suggests he's something more than the usual executive drone, the collar lapped by hair that's just a little too long for Wall Street.

He's angry. *Very* angry.

ME

Yes?

MAN

That's *my* table. I just went to the bathroom.

He gestures at the laptop, drink, and magazine I somehow managed to miss.

MAN

That's *my* drink. *My* stuff. It was pretty clear
this table's occupied.

Around us, heads are turning in our direction. But there's going to be no confrontation, no eruption of New York stress. Already I'm getting to my feet, pulling my bag onto my shoulder. Defusing the drama.

ME

Sorry—I hadn't realized. I'll find somewhere
else.

I take a step away and look around helplessly, but the place is busy and my previous seat has gone. There *is* nowhere else.

Out of the corner of my eye I can sense him taking me

in, running his eyes over Jess's Donna Karan jacket, the expensive one she keeps for auditions, the soft dark cashmere that sets off my pale skin and dark hair. And realizing what a stupid mistake he's making.

> MAN
>
> Wait . . . I guess we could share it.

He gestures at the table.

> MAN
>
> There's room for us both—I was just catching
> up on some work.

> ME
> (smiling gratefully)
> Oh—*thank* you.

I put my bag back and sit down. For a while there's a silence I'm careful not to break. This has to come from him.

Sure enough, when he speaks his voice has changed subtly—it's huskier, thicker. Do women's voices change the same way? I should experiment with that, sometime.

> MAN
>
> Are you waiting on someone? Bet he's been held
> up by the snow. That's why I'm staying an extra
> night—it's chaos out at LaGuardia.

And I smile to myself, because it's actually pretty neat, the way he tries to find out if this person I'm meeting is a man or a woman, and at the same time let me know he's here on his own.

> ME
>
> Guess I could be here awhile, then.

He nods at my now-empty glass.

> MAN
>
> In that case, can I get you another one of those? I'm Rick, by the way.

Of all the gin joints in all the towns in all the world . . .

> ME
>
> Thank you, Rick. I'd love a martini. And I'm Claire.

> RICK
>
> Nice to meet you, Claire. And, uh, sorry about just now.

> ME
>
> No, really, it was my mistake.

I say it with such offhand nonchalance, such gratitude, that even I'd be surprised to discover it's a lie.

But then, this isn't lying. This is *behaving truthfully under imaginary circumstances.* Which, as you'll discover, is very different.

The waitress takes our order. As she leaves, a man at the next table leans across and gives her a hard time about a missing drink. I watch as she sulkily tugs a pen from behind her ear, almost as if she can pull the customer's words out and flick them to the floor.

I could use that, I think. I put it away somewhere, deep in the filing system, focus my attention back on the man opposite.

> ME
> What brings you to New York, Rick?

> RICK
> Business. I'm a lawyer.

> ME
> I don't believe you.

Rick looks puzzled.

> RICK
> Why not?

> ME
> The lawyers I meet are all ugly and boring.

He matches my smile.

> RICK
> Well, I specialize in the music business. Up in Seattle. We like to think we're a little more exciting than your average criminal attorney. How about you?

ME

What do I do for a living? Or do I think I'm exciting?

To our mutual surprise, we're flirting now, a little.

RICK

Both.

I nod at the waitress's departing back.

ME

Well, I used to do what she does, before.

RICK

Before what?

ME

Before I realized there are more exciting ways to pay the rent.

It's always in the eyes—that slight, almost imperceptible stillness as an idea dawns behind them. He turns the possibilities of what I've just said over in his mind. Decides he's reading too much into it.

RICK

And where are you from, Claire? I'm trying to place that accent.

It's Virginia, damn you. Hence the way I rhymed the *law* in *lawyer* with *boy*.

                    ME
I'm from . . . wherever you want me to be from.

He smiles. A wolfish, eager smile that says, *So I was right.*

                    RICK
I never met a girl from there before.

                    ME
And you meet a lot of girls, right?

                    RICK
I do combine my business trips with a certain
amount of pleasure.

                    ME
Before you fly back to your wife and kids in Seattle.

Rick frowns.

                    RICK
What makes you think I'm married?

                    ME
              (reassuringly)
The ones I go for usually are. The ones who
know how to have fun.

Certain though he is now, he doesn't rush it. We sip our
drinks and he tells me about some of his clients, back in
Seattle—the famous teenage idol he names who likes under-

aged girls, and the macho heavy-metal star who's gay but doesn't dare admit it. He tells me, with a hint of emphasis, how much money there is to be made doing what he does, drawing up contracts for those who are temperamentally unlikely to abide by them, requiring the services of people like him at both ends, the making of the contract and its eventual dissolution. And finally, when I look suitably impressed at all that, he suggests that, since my friend clearly isn't going to show, we move on to someplace else, a restaurant or club, whichever I'd prefer—

RICK
(softly)
Or we could just get ourselves some room service. I'm staying right upstairs.

ME
Room service can be expensive.

RICK
Whatever you want. You choose. A bottle of Cristal, some caviar . . .

ME
I meant, room service can be expensive . . . when I'm the one providing it.

There. It's out in the open now. But don't react to what you've just said, don't smile or look away. No big deal. You do this all the time.

Just ignore the hammering in your chest, the sick feeling in the pit of your stomach.

Rick nods, satisfied.

RICK

I'm not the only one here on business, right?

ME

You got me, Rick.

RICK

If you don't mind me saying, Claire, you don't
seem the type.

Time to confess.

ME

That's because . . . I'm not.

RICK

So what type *are* you?

ME

The type who comes here to take acting classes
and gets behind on her tuition fees. Every couple of months I go out, have some fun . . . and
the problem goes away.

On the other side of the lobby, a family is checking in. A
little girl, about six years old, all dressed up in a coat, knit
hat, and scarf for her trip to the city, wants to see what's
going on behind the desk. Her father lifts her up, placing
her feet on her elephant-trunk suitcase, and she sprawls
across the counter, excited, as the manager issues the key
cards, handing one to her with a smile. Her dad keeps one

hand protectively on the small of her back, making sure she doesn't slip off. I feel a familiar tug of envy and pain.

I push it from my mind and get back into the conversation with Rick, who's leaning forward, his voice lowered, eyes bright—

RICK

And how *much* fun are you looking to have tonight, Claire?

ME

I guess that's open to negotiation.

He smiles. He's a lawyer. Negotiations are part of the game.

RICK

Shall we say three hundred?

ME

Is that what they charge in Seattle?

RICK

For that you get quite a lot in Seattle, believe me.

ME

What's the most you've ever paid for a woman, Rick?

RICK

Five hundred. But that was—

                          ME
                   (interrupting)
Double it.

                         RICK
                      (stunned)
Are you *serious*?

                          ME

No, I'm not. I'm an ordinary girl out to have
fun—and that's why I'm worth a thousand dollars. But if you've changed your mind . . .

I reach for the bag, deliberately casual, hoping he won't see
how much my hand is shaking.

                         RICK
No, wait. A thousand's . . . fine.

                          ME
What's your room number?

                         RICK
Eight fourteen.

                          ME
I'll knock on the door in five minutes. Don't
make eye contact with the concierge.

He stands up.

RICK
(admiringly)
That trick with the table was pretty neat. Picking me up right under the noses of the bar staff.

ME
You get to learn these things. When you're having fun.

When he reaches the elevator, Rick looks back. I give him a nod and a tiny, secret smile.

Which dies as soon as the doors close, obscuring his view of me. I pick up my bag and walk to the street exit.

Fade out.

Outside, it's finally stopped snowing, the fire hydrants along the sidewalk all wearing white toupees of snow. A short way down the street a black town car is waiting, its lights off, its engine running. I pull open the rear door and get in.

She's about forty-five, Rick's wife, with the kind of jaded but expensive looks that suggest she was probably part of the music scene herself once, before she started hosting Rick's business dinners and bearing his children. She's sitting next to Henry on the backseat, shivering despite the warm air gushing from the heaters.

"Everything okay?" Henry asks quietly.

"Fine," I say, pulling the little video camera out of my bag. I've dropped the Virginia accent now. In my ordinary, British voice, I tell the wife, "Look, I'm going to say what I always say in these situations, which is that you really don't have to watch this. You could just go home and try to work things out."

And she says, as they always say, "I want to know."

I hand her the camera. "The bottom line is, he uses prostitutes regularly. Not just when he's away, either. He talked about paying up to five hundred dollars back in Seattle. And he just offered me a thousand."

The wife's eyes fill with tears. "Oh God. Oh *God.*"

"I'm really sorry," I say awkwardly. "He's waiting for me in room eight fourteen if you want to go and talk to him."

Her eyes might be full of tears, but they also blaze with anger. *Remember that.* "Oh, sure, I'll talk to a lawyer. But it'll be a divorce lawyer. Not him."

She turns to Henry. "I'd like to go now."

"Of course," he says smoothly. As we get out of the car—Henry to get behind the wheel, me to go on my way—he discreetly passes me an envelope.

Four hundred dollars. Not bad for an evening's work.

And after all, Rick was a scumbag. He made my flesh crawl. He was arrogant and aggressive as well as a cheat. He deserves everything his wife's about to throw at him.

So why, as the town car pulls away through the dirty gray snow, am I left feeling so sick and disgusted by what I just did?

2

So now you're wondering who I actually am and what I'm doing here in New York. My backstory, in other words.

    Name: Claire Wright
    Age: 25 (can play 20–30)
    Height: 5'7"
    Nationality: British
    Eye color: Brown
    Hair color: Flexible

Those are the facts. But you aren't really interested in those. You want to know what I *want*. Because that's rule one, day one, the very first thing you learn: *It's what you desire that defines you as a character.*

I was telling Rick the truth—that part of it, anyway. I want to be other people. I've never wanted anything else.

In any list of the top ten acting schools in the world, around half will be in New York City. The Juilliard, the Tisch, the Neighborhood Playhouse, to name just some. All teach variations on the same approach, rooted in the work of a great Russian actor called Constantin Stanislavski. It's about immersing yourself in the emotional truth of a part until it's a part of you.

At the New York acting schools, they don't teach you to *act*. They teach you to *become*.

If you're lucky enough to get through the initial round and be invited to New York to audition; if you're lucky enough to be offered a place; if acting has been your whole life ever since you were eleven years old, a little girl escaping the drabness of successive foster homes by pretending to be someone and somewhere else . . . then not only are you one in a thousand, you would also be crazy not to accept.

I applied to the Actors Studio course on an impulse—Marilyn Monroe studied there, and she grew up in foster care too—auditioned on a weird conviction that it was meant to happen, and accepted in a heartbeat.

They even gave me a scholarship. It paid some of the tuition fees. It didn't pay living costs in one of the most expensive cities in the world.

According to the terms of my student visa, I could work . . . so long as my job was on campus. *Campus* was Pace University, a cramped modern block adjacent to City Hall and the Brooklyn Bridge. Not many opportunities for part-time employment there.

I managed to get a waitressing gig at a bar in Hell's Kitchen, sprinting there three evenings a week after class. But the owner had an endless supply of young women to choose from, and it didn't make sense to let any of them stay too long. That way, if the IRS or Immigration came checking, he could always claim their forms were in the mail.

After two months he told me, not unkindly, it was time to move on.

One of my teachers, Paul, suggested I talk to an agent he knew. I found the address—a narrow doorway in a pre-war block zigzagged with fire escapes, right at the end of 43rd Street—and walked up three flights of stairs to the tiniest office I'd ever been in. Every surface was piled high with headshots, scripts, and contracts. In the first room, two assistants sat either side of a cramped single desk. I heard my name being called from the second. Sitting behind another desk was a small woman rattling with oversized plastic jewelry. In her hand she had my CV, which she was reading aloud while simultaneously waving me to a seat on the other side of the desk.

INT. NEW YORK AGENT'S OFFICE—DAY

MARCIE MATTHEWS, a tough New York agent, is reading my CV.

MARCIE
Stage school. London School of Dramatic Art—
for one year. A TV walk-on. A couple of European art-house movies that never got released.

She tosses the CV aside, unimpressed, and stares at me critically.

MARCIE
But you're pretty enough. Not beautiful, but you could play beautiful. And Paul Lewis tells me you have talent.

ME
(pleased but trying to be modest)
He's such a great teacher—

MARCIE
(interrupting)
I still can't represent you.

ME
Why not?

MARCIE
No green card, for one thing. Which means no
union membership. Which means no work.

ME
There must be *something* I can do.

MARCIE
Sure. You can go back to England and apply for
a green card.

ME
I . . . can't do that.

MARCIE
Why not?

ME
It's complicated.

MARCIE

No, it's not. It's depressingly familiar.

She reaches for a vape and clicks it on.

MARCIE

I emailed a couple of colleagues in London about you, Claire. Know what they said?

ME
(miserably)
I can probably guess.

MARCIE

The kindest was "a little intense." Mostly, it was "stay away." And when I went deeper, the word *tumult* kept cropping up.

She raises her eyebrows.

MARCIE

Care to explain?

I take a deep breath.

ME

Tumult . . . That was the title of my first studio movie. My big break. Playing the love interest opposite . . . Well, I guess you already know his name. He's famous and good-looking and everyone knows he has one of the happiest marriages in showbiz.

I look at her defiantly.

> ME
>
> So when he fell in love with me, I knew it was the real thing.

> MARCIE
> (snorting derisively)
>
> Sure.

> ME
>
> That was before I heard the phrase they use on movie shoots. DCOL, darling. Doesn't Count On Location.

> MARCIE
>
> And?

> ME
>
> And after four weeks his famously beautiful wife turned up on set with his three famously beautiful kids in tow. Suddenly the producers found excuses to keep me out of the way. I was stuck in a sound booth, redubbing lines I'd already done perfectly first time around.

> MARCIE
> (nodding)
>
> Go on.

ME

That's when I started hearing the rumors. That
I was a crazy stalker. That I'd threatened his
wife. The same PR machine that spun his movies was now spinning *me*.

I'm fighting to hold back the tears. I know how naïve I must
sound. But the truth is, I wasn't inexperienced. You don't
come out of foster care some blinkered innocent.

But you do come out desperate to love and be loved. He
was the most beautiful man I'd ever met; the most passionate, the most poetic. He could recite every love speech in
Shakespeare like it was written just for him.

Moral: Never fall for anyone who prefers to speak someone else's words.

I don't tell Marcie about the other stuff, though I suspect
she knows already. How, deranged with adolescent despair
at the unfairness of it all, I went to his trailer and cut my
wrists open on the same daybed where we'd made love between scenes. How I'd wanted to show him that it hadn't
just been acting. That it had been *real*.

At least, for me.

ME

And that was that. Overnight, the castings
dried up. I'd committed the number one sin,
you see. I'd been *unprofessional*. It was a week
before my eighteenth birthday.

Marcie nods thoughtfully.

MARCIE

You know, Paul's right: You're pretty good. For a moment there, you almost had me feeling sorry for you. Instead of: What a dumb, self-destructive *fuck-up*.

She stabs the end of the vape at me.

MARCIE

The producers were right. Find yourself another career.

ME

I hoped America would be a second chance.

MARCIE

That was naïve of you. The days we took the huddled masses yearning to be free are long gone.

ME

This is the only career I've ever wanted. But I can't go on studying without some kind of work.

Marcie scowls and sighs at the same time. Tusks of vape smoke swell from her nostrils. Then, as if against her better instincts—

> MARCIE
>
> All right. Leave your details in the front office.
> There's a couple of crummy music videos com-
> ing up. But no promises.

> ME
>
> Thank you! Thank you so much!

I jump up and pump her hand overenthusiastically. As she
disentangles it, batting away my thanks with the end of
the vape, Marcie happens to glance down. Something in the
mess of papers on her desk catches her eye.

She reaches for it, re-reads it, looks up—

> MARCIE
>
> How would you feel about working for a firm of
> divorce attorneys, Claire?

> ME
>
> As an assistant?

> MARCIE
>
> Not exactly . . . Look, I'll be honest. The job is
> not great. But they need someone like you and
> they're prepared to pay well. *Very* well. Non-
> union. And cash.

3

As the town car with Rick's wife pulls away, I turn and head in the other direction. The streets are littered with icy slush and I don't have an overcoat. Snow works its way inside the toe of my right shoe.

Times Square is a riot of electricity and color. A single mime artist, braving the cold, entertains a ticket line. Billboards flash snippets of reviews: "MESMERIZING," "BRILLIANT," "EXTRAORDINARY." I pass under a street sign that says THEATERLAND.

Theaterland . . . If people were allowed to pick their own country, that would be mine.

Then I turn off Broadway, down a barely lit cross street. To where a weathered, peeling sign says THE COMPASS THEATER. People—students on dates mostly, taking advantage of the daily half-price unsolds—shuffle into the foyer. I go on a few yards farther and slip through the stage door.

Assistant stage managers, the runners and gofers of the backstage operation, are rushing around urgently with props and clipboards. I find the greenroom. It's been divided with a stage flat to create two makeshift dressing rooms, girls one side, boys the other. In the first one, Jess is putting on her makeup in a mirror she's sharing with three other girls, all of whom are trying to do the same thing.

"Hey," I say brightly.

"Hey, Claire." Her eyes flick to me, then back to her task. "How was it?"

I pull out Henry's envelope. "It was four hundred dollars. Now I just owe you another three."

Jess's dad, who's super-rich, has bought her an apartment in Manhattan. I'm supposed to pay rent monthly, but sometimes I get a little behind.

"Great," she says distractedly. "Actually, give it to me later, could you? We're going out after and I'll only lose it."

I must look hopeful, because she adds, "Why not watch the show and come along? You can tell me if I've nailed that feminine distress Jack's been going on about."

"Sure, why not?" I say casually.

Because even the company of actors in a bar is better than nothing.

"Three minutes," a stage manager calls, slapping the flat with his hand.

"Wish me luck," Jess says, smoothing down her dress as she gets up, eyes still on the mirror. "Break a leg and all that shit."

"Good luck. Not that you need it. And take the forest scene slower. Whatever your dumb-ass director says."

Within seconds the greenroom has emptied. I make my way to the side of the stage. As the house lights go down I creep forward and peek at the audience through a gap in the scenery, breathing in the potent, addictive smell of theater: fresh scenery paint, old stage dust, moth-eaten cloth, and charisma. That moment of power as the darkness settles, and with it, all the noise and bustle of the everyday.

For a beat, we all hang there, waiting. Then the stage lights come up, rich with color, and I take a step back. Snow tumbles through the air, glittering and soft—fake snow, but the audience gasps anyway.

The director's big idea is that this *Midsummer Night's Dream* takes place in winter. A gimmick, I'd thought when Jess told me, but now, seeing those fat snowflakes drifting through the air, settling like sequins in the actors' hair as they tumble noisily onto the stage, I can see how he's captured in one image the play's magical, otherworldly quality.

> THESEUS
> Now, fair Hippolyta, our nuptial hour
> Draws on apace . . .

I feel a sudden stab of longing. This is the forbidden kingdom, the dream from which my lack of a green card and my problems in the UK have banished me. The hunger is something physical, a craving so deep it knots my stomach and thickens my throat. Tears sting my eyes.

But even as the stage swings glassily to and fro I find myself thinking: *Next time you need to feel something in class, use this. It's gold dust.*

4

Four hours later we're all in the Harley Bar. Somehow, we always end up in the Harley Bar, a basement sweatbox with vintage motorbikes hanging from the ceiling, where the waitresses wear a house uniform of black bras under fraying sleeveless denim jackets. Springsteen blasts from the jukebox, so we have to yell—twenty trained voices coming down from a post-performance high, plus girlfriends, boyfriends, and hangers-on like me.

Jess and a group of us are swapping stories. Stories about acting, of course. It's all we ever talk about.

JESS

What about Christian Bale in *The Machinist*? He lost, like, a third of his body weight for that role.

ACTRESS 2

Or Chloë Sevigny doing a blow job for real in *The Brown Bunny*.

ACTOR

Define *real* in that context. No, I'm just saying.

ACTRESS 3

Adrien Brody in *The Pianist*. First he lost thirty
pounds and learned to play the piano. Then, to
know what it felt like for his character to lose
everything, he got rid of his car, his apartment,
and his phone. Now *that*, my friend, is commitment.

ACTRESS 2

Hey, I could do that! Oh, wait. Except I cur-
rently play a singing dancing chorus mouse in a
Broadway musical.

She does a little drunken mouse dance.

ACTRESS 2

Mousy mouse, mousy mouse, welcome to my
mousy house—

Across the room, the barman glances at me. A glance that
lingers just a little longer than it needs to.

The last time I saw that look was when Rick the scumbag lawyer offered to let me sit at his table.

But *this* guy is my own age, tattooed, cool, and skinny.
Despite the icy cold that blows in every time the street door
opens, he's wearing just a T-shirt, and the dishcloth he's got
tucked into the back of his jeans whisks around his butt every
time he turns back to the row of bottles behind the bar.

All of a sudden, I'm there. At the bar.

GOOD-LOOKING BARMAN
    Hey!

He's Australian. I love Australians.

ME
    Hi!

And for some reason I say it in my Virginian accent, the one
I used earlier with Rick.

GOOD-LOOKING BARMAN
    What can I get you?

ME
            (shouting over the noise)
    I'd love a martini.

GOOD-LOOKING BARMAN
    Coming right up.

He fills a shot glass to the brim with Jack Daniel's and slams
it down on the counter.

ME
    I asked for a *martini.*

GOOD-LOOKING BARMAN
    That's the way we make martinis in this bar.

He grins at me, daring me to complain. Nice smile.
    So I pick up the glass and drain it.

ME

In that case, give me a piña colada.

GOOD-LOOKING BARMAN

One piña colada . . .

He splashes a measure of Jack Daniel's into a glass, adds
another measure of Jack Daniel's, and finishes it off with a
third measure of Jack Daniel's.

I tip the whole lot down my throat in one long chug.
People crowded around the bar break into spontaneous
whooping and applause.

Applause. Now, there's a sound I haven't heard in a while.
At least, not directed at me.

ME

You'd better line me up a Long Island iced tea
while you're at it.

. . . which really ought to be a fade-out in this movie that's
always running in my head.

But it isn't. It's a jump cut, or a montage sequence, or
one of those other technical things, because then everything
gets messy and jumbled until suddenly I'm in someone
else's apartment on top of someone else's body, moaning.

ME

Yes, yes, omigod yes—

RANDOM MAN

Yes—

Ah, yes. Cast change. The good-looking barman, whose name was Brian, didn't get off till three. So I hooked up with a friend of one of Jess's friends instead. By that point I was too drunk and too high on the applause to settle for my own bed.

Though if I'm honest, it wasn't only the alcohol. Or the appreciative audience.

The feel of a warm body, and someone to hold . . . That's something I crave, after one of Henry's jobs.

Because if a woman can't trust the man who said he'd love her forever, who in this world can you trust?

And knowing it was me—my skills, my lines, my *performance*—that helped break up a family always makes me feel weird.

I'm not proud of that stuff I do for Henry.

But sometimes I am proud of how well I do it.

5

Next morning I take the subway back to Jess's, still wearing her jacket and not much else, ignoring the knowing looks from commuters. One of the exercises Paul makes us do involves going out onto the streets of New York in character and talking to complete strangers. Once you've done that a few times, you develop a pretty thick skin.

Ditto sitting in hotel bars and having married men hit on you.

That was one of the things that persuaded me to take up Marcie's suggestion, actually—thinking it might be good for my acting, as well as my finances. So Marcie hooked me up with Henry. Henry likes to describe himself as a paralegal, but effectively he's the law firm's in-house investigator. He arranged to meet me in a bar, which seemed an odd venue for a job interview until he explained what they wanted me to do.

"Think you can handle it?" he'd asked.

I shrugged. It wasn't like I had any other options. "Sure."

"Good. Go outside, come back in, and try to pick me up. Think of it as an audition."

So I went out and came back in again. And because it felt strange to be chatting up this gray-haired older man, it was easier to slip into a character. Just a voice and an attitude—a femme fatale from an old film noir; Lauren Bacall in *The Big Sleep,* maybe—but it gave me somewhere to hide.

I took a seat at the bar and ordered a drink. I didn't even look at the man two seats down.

Never hit on them directly, he'd told me earlier. *Make it clear you're available, but they have to proposition you, not the other way around. The innocent should have nothing to fear.*

Yeah, right. Because if there's one thing I've learned, it's that men's brains don't work that way.

INT. A DIMLY LIT NEW YORK BAR—DAY

Reflected in the mirror behind the bar, we see CLAIRE WRIGHT, twenty-five, as she plays with her drink, a little bored.

HENRY, a lean ex-cop in his early fifties, moves to the next stool.

HENRY
Are you on your own?

CLAIRE
(a smoky, languid drawl)
Well, I *was.*

He glances at her hand.

HENRY

I see you're wearing a wedding ring.

CLAIRE

Is that good or bad?

HENRY

It depends.

CLAIRE

On what?

HENRY

On how easily it comes off.

Her eyes widen at his audacity. Then:

CLAIRE

Now that you mention it, it has been getting a
little loose lately. What about you?

HENRY

Am I loose?

CLAIRE

Are you married?

HENRY

Not tonight.

CLAIRE

Then I guess it's my lucky night.

She gives him a look—frank, confident, direct. This is a woman who knows what she wants. And what she wants right now is some fun.

                    HENRY
              (breaking character)
Jesus H. Christ.

                     ME
Did I do that okay? I could try something different—

He loosens his collar.

                    HENRY
I almost feel sorry for the bastards.

Three days later, I sat in a quiet bar off Central Park and allowed a businessman to tell me he no longer found his wife attractive. Afterward, I handed his wife the tape, and Henry handed me four hundred dollars.

It wasn't a regular job—some months there'd be three or four assignments, sometimes none at all. Most of Henry's work was actually what he called spousal surveillance: following people around, trying to catch them in the act. "Most of our clients are women," he told me once. "Usually, they're correct in their suspicions. Maybe they've clocked their husband wearing a fancy shirt to the office, then texting later to say he's been held up. Sometimes it's just a new aftershave. Or they've already seen incriminating texts on his phone, and just want to know what the woman looks like. Men, now, they're more likely to be wrong."

Back when he was a cop, Henry worked undercover, and he clearly misses the buzz of those days. During the long hours in town cars and hotel lobbies, waiting for our targets to show, he passes the time telling me stories from past operations.

"You have to see the gray. Criminals instinctively know when you despise or fear them. So you gotta make yourself believe whatever *they* believe in. And that's the dangerous part. Not the guns or the beatings. Some guys, the gray takes hold of them, and they can't make it let go."

I tell him he's a method actor without knowing it, and swap him acting stories in return. Such as our very first class, where Paul had us do a scene from Ibsen. I'd thought my fellow students were pretty good. Then Paul made us do it again while trying to balance broom handles on our hands. Under the pressure of doing two things at once, we all fell apart.

"What you did that first time wasn't acting," Paul told us. "It was *pretending*. You were copying what you've seen other actors do—but it wasn't real to you. That's why you couldn't do it when you had to put your conscious minds to something else. I'm going to tell you just one thing today, but it's the most important thing I'll ever say to you: *Don't think.* Acting isn't faking or impersonating. The clue is in the word. Acting is *doing*."

Henry thinks this is all bullshit. But I myself have seen actors in a greenroom sneezing and snuffling with flu, only to have it dry up the instant they step on stage. I've seen shy introverts become kings and queens, the ugly become beautiful and the beautiful repulsive. Something happens, something no one can explain. Just for a few moments, you become someone else.

And that's the best feeling there is in the world.

. . .

Manhattan's looking like a movie set this morning. Steam vents have made melt holes in the snow, smoking lazily in the sunshine. Last night made a sizable dent in Henry's envelope, but I stop at a deli anyway to get bagels for Jess and me. When I come out, a bunch of kids are fooling around, throwing snowballs, so I scoop up a handful and join in. I can't help thinking, *Wow.* Here I am in New York, *the* New York, taking part in a scene straight out of a movie, and studying at one of the best drama schools in the world to boot. The script has a happy ending after all.

Is it just me who does this—who feels they're constantly watching themselves in the movie of their own life? When I ask my friends, most claim they don't. But they must be lying. Why else would you become an actor, if not to edit reality?

Even if I've just remembered that the scene playing in my head, the one with the New York snowball fight, is from that terrible movie *Elf.*

As I let myself in I catch voices from Jess's room. She's on a Skype call with Aran, her boyfriend, who's doing a commercial in Europe. I have a quick shower, check the jacket's not looking too bad, then knock on her door.

"Breakfast, rent, and Miss Donna Karan," I tell her brightly. "Any reviews?"

Every morning the first thing Jess does is check the Internet to see if anyone's blogged about her. She shakes her head. "Nothing. But my agent emailed—I have a go-see with a producer who saw the show last night."

"That's great," I say, trying not to sound too envious.

"And how was your night?" Her voice is carefully neutral. "I looked for you about two, but you'd left."

"Oh, it was good."

She sighs. "Bullshit, Claire. It was empty meaningless sex with a total stranger."

"That too," I say lightly.

"I worry about you sometimes."

"Why? I always carry a condom."

"I meant safe *life*. Not safe sex. As you very well know."

I shrug. I'm not about to get into a conversation with Jess about my love life, or lack of it. When all's said and done, she's got a family, and people with families don't understand.

I hang up the jacket and raid Jess's panty drawer for clean underwear. At the bottom, my fingers encounter something small and hard and heavy.

I pull it out. It's a gun. An actual *gun*.

"Well, Jesus, Jess," I say, stunned. "What the fuck is *this*?"

She laughs. "My dad made me get it. You know, just in case. The big bad city and all that."

"And you worry about *me*?" I say incredulously. I point the gun at my reflection in her mirror. "You gotta ask yourself, punk, does that color suit ya?"

"Careful. I think it's loaded."

"Yikes." Gingerly, I put the gun back and take out some red Alaïa leggings.

"Then again," she adds, "I might need to shoot the person who keeps stealing my clothes."

"There's three hundred and fifty dollars in the envelope. Well, three twenty, at least."

"Actually, that's something else my dad's getting a bit

weird about." Jess says it casually, but I pick up the underlying tension in her voice.

"Oh?" I say, equally cool.

"He's between jobs, so he's not getting a salary, and it's like this apartment is his pension or something. He kinda wants me to tell you to move out."

This is not good. "What did *you* say?"

"I said, what if Claire paid you all the back rent she owes?"

"Which is what—another four hundred?"

Jess shakes her head. "Seven. Anyway, he wasn't too happy. Said he'd think about it, but he'd have to be paid in advance from now on too."

I stare at her. "But that means finding *eleven hundred* dollars."

"I know. I'm sorry, Claire. I tried to argue, but he's got this whole thing about me being fiscally irresponsible."

"How long have I got?"

"I can hold him off for a bit. A few weeks, maybe."

"Great," I say bitterly, but I know it's not Jess's fault. My room is easily big enough for a couple, and the East Village location would be perfect for young professionals working in the financial district. Her dad could be getting a lot more.

There's a long silence. Jess picks up her playscript and starts leafing through it. "I have to go over this—Jack's given me a note. The forest scene still isn't nuanced enough, apparently."

"Want me to read lines?"

"Would you?" She tosses me the script and I find the page, though I probably know it by heart. You can forget *Romeo and Juliet:* Done right, this is the sexiest scene in

Shakespeare. And Shakespeare, despite most people thinking he's Culture and stuffy and not relevant anymore, wrote the best characters ever.

Jess starts.

> JESS
> (as Hermia)
> Be it so, Lysander: find you out a bed,
> For I upon this bank will rest my head.

She lies back, arranging her limbs for sleep. I go and lie down next to her.

> ME
> (as Lysander)
> One turf shall serve as pillow for us both:
> One heart, one bed; two bosoms and one troth.

Uncomfortable, she wriggles away.

> JESS
> Nay, good Lysander; for my sake, my dear,
> Lie further off yet; do not lie so near.

It's a classic example of where the words on the page say one thing, but the actor just *knows* the character means something else entirely. Lysander really wants to screw Hermia's brains out. And, despite all the beautiful poetry, he'll say anything to get what he wants. He's a man, right? And Hermia, although she knows she probably shouldn't let him sleep so close, fancies him back. She only wants him further away so she won't give in to temptation.

Text and subtext.

I get up on one elbow, looking down at her.

ME

O take the sense, sweet, of my innocence . . .

But even as I stare longingly into Jess's eyes, there's a part of me that's screaming *Eleven hundred dollars? Even Henry's jobs can't provide that sort of cash.*

Suddenly I'm faced with the prospect that this whole fragile fantasy is going to collapse around me like a stage set between scenes. No money means no apartment. No apartment means no classes. No classes means no visa. I'll have to limp home with my tail between my legs, to a country where no one will ever employ me as an actor again.

I drop my lips toward Jess's. For a fraction of a second, she's tempted—I can see the confusion in her eyes. Then she pulls away.

JESS

Lysander riddles very prettily.

Meaning, he's a pretty good kisser. And then he

tries to kiss me again, yada yada yada, and we're

back.

I roll off her bed. "Seemed pretty nuanced to me."

"You know," Jess says wistfully, "you're so much better than that jerk I'm really playing that scene against. I'm sorry, Claire. There's no justice."

Tell me about it, as they say over here. Meaning: Please don't, nobody's listening.

6

'll say this for the English foster care system: It makes you resilient.

I was seven when I lost my parents. One day I had a family: The next, thanks to a truck driver who was texting at the wheel, I didn't. My mum and dad both died instantly, the nurses told me later. I was in the back, in a forward-facing child seat that probably saved my life when it was thrown clear of the wreckage. I don't remember that, or anything else about that day. I've always felt bad about that. If you're going to spend a last few hours with someone you love, you ought to be able to remember it.

It was horrible enough coming to terms with their deaths. Then it sank in that I was going to lose everything else as well: my bedroom, my toys, all my familiar things. It sounds crazy, but in some ways, that was almost as bad. I wasn't just orphaned. I was uprooted.

There was a shortage of foster parents in my South London borough, so my emergency placement when I came out of hospital was in Ealing, on the other side of the city. And when, six weeks later, I was found my first foster family, they were in Leeds, 170 miles away. That meant moving school and losing my friends as well.

I was a middle-class girl, a Londoner, dropped into a school where the other kids had all known one another for years. They talked what seemed like a different language. They thought I was stuck up, or la-di-da as they called it. I quickly became two people: the person I'd been before, and whoever they wanted me to be.

I learned to speak exactly the way they did too. It turned out I'm pretty good with voices.

My new family were professional foster carers—as well as two of their own kids, they had about three foster placements at any one time. They were perfectly nice to me; kind, even. But ultimately, fostering was a business to them—a way of affording a better house, nicer vacations. They were professional, when what I craved was unprofessional, unconditional love.

The legal name for my new status was *cared for*, which was the biggest joke of all. Because pretty soon you realize that no one cares. No one cares if you do your homework. No one cares if you have friends or not. No one cares if you come first or twenty-first in your exams. Why should they?

I remember seeing one foster father, Gary, giving his birth son a hug. Still hurting from the loss of my parents, I went to join in. Gary gently told me it would be inappropriate for me to get hugged too. That was the word he used— "inappropriate." Like I'd made a pass at him or something.

That was when I finally realized I was on my own now. Once you get that feeling, it never really goes away.

It was when I went to secondary school that I first came across drama. I hadn't even known it could be a subject before then. I still remember the time Mrs. Hughes, the teacher, told the others to stop what they were doing and look at me.

"Watch Claire, she's a natural," she told the class.

Pretty soon it was all I thought about. I wasn't a child in care when I performed. I was Juliet, Annie, Nancy, Puck. I was princesses, murderesses, heroines, whores.

When we put on a play, and the other children's parents came backstage to tell them how brilliant they'd been, I had no one. It just made me more determined.

There was a performing arts academy nearby where some of the students had gone on to act in soaps like *Holby City*. When I told my caseworker I wanted to go there, she frowned.

"That's a private academy, Claire. The county council's not going to pay school fees for a child in care."

Gary promised he'd speak to someone at the council. A week later, I asked him what the answer had been.

"Oh," he said, clearly having forgotten all about it. "They said no."

So I went back to Mrs. Hughes.

"If you're going to fight to get into a stage school," she told me, "it might as well be a good one. That one you're talking about will turn you into a performing monkey."

She researched better stage schools, one of which offered me a scholarship. Then she called a meeting with my caseworker. Who basically said that I was settled where I was, and any more upheaval wouldn't be in my best interest.

Which was typical, I thought. *You* can move me four

times in three years, but when *I* want something, it's suddenly too traumatic to contemplate.

It took me three years of campaigning, but eventually I got my way. The day I walked into that drama school, it was like I'd finally found my new family.

7

call Marcie and beg for more work. Eventually, she comes up with an audition for a non-union music video.

In a basement casting studio I say my name, height, and agent's name to a video camera on a tripod. Two producers, both male, ignore me, turning to watch my image on a monitor instead.

The casting director, a woman, asks me to state for the camera that I'm comfortable with partial nudity.

"Well, if the part demands it," I joke nervously.

"Honey, the part is called Topless Dancer," she says impatiently.

"Of course." I look at the camera and say brightly, "My name is Claire Wright and I'm comfortable with partial nudity."

Hope someone puts *that* on my gravestone.

"Okay, Claire, when you're ready," the casting director says. She puts on some music.

After about a minute one of the producers says something and the music cuts.

"Thanks, Claire," the casting director says. "Could you send in the next girl on your way out, please?"

As I turn to go the second producer says something I don't catch.

"Wait . . ." the casting director says.

There's a brief murmured conversation, then she adds, "Leave your details at the desk."

That afternoon I get a text asking me to come to the producer's office at eight. I raid Jess's closet for suitable clothes and put on my best face. When I arrive there's no reception-ist, only a security guard. Everyone else has gone home.

I go down the corridor until I see the producer in an of-fice, talking on the phone. He waves me in. I sit on a swivel chair while he continues his call, something about the other person needing to stop being an asshole and order a dolly rig from Panavision.

At last he puts the phone down.

INT. OFFICE SUITE—NIGHT

PRODUCER

Moron! Hey, Claire.

ME

Hi! And thanks for calling me back.

PRODUCER

This isn't strictly a call-back, Claire. I'm cur-rently casting for a range of projects and I

thought it was worth reaching out to see if any
of them could be right for you.

ME

Great! Uh, you know I don't have a green card?

The producer shrugs.

PRODUCER

It's a problem. But it may not be insurmount-
able. As a producer, I have access to the Actors'
Equity exchange program. I may be able to arrange a swap with a colleague in London.

ME

Fantastic! What kind of projects are we talking
about?

PRODUCER

We can discuss specifics later. Right now, I'm
more interested in seeing whether you have the
ambition and the commitment to join the team.

He comes around the front of the desk and puts his hand on
my shoulder. Then he pushes, so the chair swings around to
face him. I'm left staring at his crotch. He gives the top of
my arm a friendly squeeze.

PRODUCER

I guess you know what I mean.

For a long moment I freeze. Then I hurl myself out of the chair, pushing him away with both hands, shouting at him to *Get away from me.* My hand slams into his nose and he staggers back.

ME

Fuck you you fucker—

He cowers, hands protecting his head, his nose bleeding, a tiny red Hitler mustache dabbed under his nostrils.

PRODUCER

Okay! Jesus! Just go, will you?

I back off, giving him space to get up. But then he comes at me, fists clenched.

PRODUCER

Bitch . . . You'll pay for that.

That's when he finds himself staring down the barrel of Jess's gun.

PRODUCER

You're not going to use that.

My hands are shaking, and the gun with them. *Good.* The less I look like I'm in control of myself, the more he'll think I might just be crazy enough to shoot him.

ME

Self-defense? You bet I am.

I nod at my bag.

> ME
>
> There's a camera in there. It's all on tape. Maybe
> you'd like your wife to see it?

> PRODUCER
>
> What the *fuck*?

On the face of it, I have the power now, not him. But inside,
I'm panicking. What if he rushes me? What if he simply
takes the gun from my hand and points it at *me*? What if my
finger slips on the trigger?

> ME
>
> I'm walking out of here now. And you're stay-
> ing right where you are.

I back away, trying to look like I'm confident about this. As
I go he snarls:

> PRODUCER
>
> Good luck working in this industry, bitch.
> You're fucking insane.

I hold it together until I reach the street. Then I collapse,
stumbling away from there, weeping and shaking. Self-
doubts ricochet around my brain—*How could I have been so
stupid? Was it the way I handled it? Did I somehow give the
impression at the audition that I'm the kind of woman who'd do
that?*

Did I even encourage it, somehow?

My name is Claire Wright and I'm comfortable with partial nudity . . . I recall how I smiled as I said those words. Was that my mistake? Did it come across as ironic? Had I sounded *unprofessional*?

Even though another part of me, the rational part, is trying to reassure me that *No, he was the sleazebag. He had no right to even think that. He's the one in the wrong, not you*, I know this debate is going to continue in my head for hours.

And, sleazebag or not, was my reaction disproportionate? Would a simple, dignified refusal have worked just as well, maybe even led to an apology, a productive discussion about jobs?

Good luck working in this industry, bitch . . .

I almost stop dead as I think about the implications of that particular phrase. Is he going to badmouth me to casting agents now? Tell his friends I'm trouble? It would take so little for my British reputation to cross the Atlantic and join up with a few hints and rumors here, and my second chance would be over.

Oh God, should I simply have gone along with what he wanted?

It's about forty blocks back to Jess's. I walk the whole way, lost in misery and self-recrimination. I can't afford the subway and I can't even land a part as topless eye candy without getting myself molested. There's no snow on the streets anymore, but it's still damp and cold. The tears on my cheeks feel first warm, then icy, then warm again as more keep coming.

I'm a hundred yards from the apartment when my phone rings. I check the screen before I answer.

EXT. NEW YORK STREET—NIGHT

HENRY

Hey, Claire. You free this evening?

I look longingly up at the apartment building. All I want to do is crawl into bed and cry. But there's Jess's dad's money to think about.

ME

I guess.

HENRY

I have an assignment. But the client wants to meet with you first.

ME

Why?

HENRY

Who knows? Maybe she wants to make sure you're her husband's type. Which I know you will be.

ME

Well, okay then.

HENRY

How soon can you get here? She's staying at the Lexington. Ask for the Terrace Suite.

8

was already dressed up to meet the producer, so I'm at the Lexington in under twenty minutes. I go to the Ladies' restroom in the lobby, redo my makeup, and do a breathing exercise to center myself. Showtime.

Then it's straight up to the sixth floor in the elevator. I knock at the door of the suite and Henry lets me in. Over by the windows, a woman in her mid-thirties is pacing nervously. Kim Novak in *Vertigo,* I think, studying her: elegant, pearls, beautifully groomed, her shortish blond hair immaculately styled in a way you don't often see these days. Compared to her, I feel like a child who's raided a dressing-up box.

At first I think she's clutching a rosary, but then I realize it's just a keychain that she's twisting around her fingers. She seems distressed, which isn't unusual. A lot of Henry's clients find this part, the part when they're finally going to discover what sort of person their husband really is, the hardest.

INT. LEXINGTON HOTEL, TERRACE SUITE—NIGHT

HENRY

Claire. Thanks for coming. This is Stella Fogler.
                    (to the woman, reassuringly)
I use several girls as decoys, but from what
you've told me of Patrick, Claire is absolutely
the right choice.

STELLA

                    (to me, agitated)
You will be careful, won't you? Promise me
you'll be careful.

I sit down.

ME

Why don't you tell me about your husband,
Mrs. Fogler?

STELLA

He's like no man you've ever met. I mean it.
Don't turn your back on him. Don't *trust* him.
Do you promise?

Trust him? I think. *Not much chance of that. Another married
scumbag is all I need right now.*

HENRY

Claire's very professional. She knows what she's
doing.

ME

Just show me a photograph and tell me where
to find him. I'll do the rest.

HENRY

Well, Mrs. Fogler? Do we proceed?

Stella Fogler stops pacing and stares at me, wild-eyed, still
twisting the keychain in her hands.

STELLA

Yes. All right. But please—be careful.

9

INT. FLAHERTY'S BAR, NEW YORK—NIGHT

An old, wood-paneled bar on the Upper West Side, the tables well spaced and sparsely populated. PATRICK FOGLER sits at one of them, reading a paperback and making notes on a pad. He's in his late thirties, dark-haired, with a long, aquiline face. His eyes have a pale-green hue to them. Good-looking, in a quiet, intellectual way.

Like a younger Dan Day-Lewis, I decide, studying his reflection in the long mirror behind the bar. Who just happens to be one of my all-time favorite actors. But Patrick Fogler is even more tautly wound. Intense-looking.

To be fair, he doesn't look like a cheating scumbag. But sometimes they don't. Sometimes they're likable and charming. Those tend to be the ones who cheat the most, actually.

Why? Because they can, I guess.

Right now, I'm more interested in seeing whether you've got the ambition and the commitment to join the team . . .

I shake my head, focusing, trying to push the memory of that producer out of my brain. Just do the job, I tell myself. Smile, flirt, let Patrick Fogler make a pass at you, get out. One hour, tops. Then you'll be home with four hundred dollars in your hand and you can throw up and cry and get drunk.

And there'll only be another seven hundred dollars to earn.

As if on cue, Patrick Fogler gets up and comes toward me. *Easy.* I turn, a quarter-smile of greeting on my face. Too late, I realize it isn't me he's approaching. He's holding out a twenty-dollar bill to the bartender.

PATRICK
Could I have some change?

His voice is precise, well modulated: a sense of power held in check. As the bartender opens the cash register, Patrick Fogler's eyes meet mine in the mirror. Again I give him the tiniest hint of welcome—the faintest softening and widening of my eyes. He looks puzzled, nothing more. As if he isn't sure whether he should recognize me from somewhere.

When he has his change, he nods his thanks to the bartender and leaves the bar. But he's coming back. He's left his drink on his table, along with the paperback.

I go over and pick it up. It's a book of poetry: a well-thumbed copy of *Les Fleurs du Mal* by Charles Baudelaire.

Translated and edited by Patrick Fogler, I note. So he's some kind of academic.

Quickly I flick through the pages, looking for some-

thing I can use. That's when he returns, catching me at it.
Just as I intended.

ME
(guiltily)
Oh, I'm sorry! This yours?

PATRICK
Yes.

He sounds amused. He looks around the almost-empty bar,
as if to say, *Who else's would it be?*

ME
I hope you don't mind . . . I never read any
Baudelaire before.

He glances down at the page I'm on.

PATRICK
Well, don't start with that one.

Taking the book from me, he flicks forward a few pages,
finds a place, and reads aloud:

PATRICK
*I have more memories than if I had lived a thousand
years.
An old desk full of dead ideas
Is not more full of secrets than my aching head . . .*

His voice is rich with conviction, the rhythm quiet and in-sistent as a pulse. He hands the book back, still open. I look down and take in the next verse at a glance, then speak it back to him, holding his eyes, continuing the beat, milking the language:

ME

It's a necropolis; a grave in which the dead—
Those bodies I once loved—are tumbled willy-nilly,
Prodded and nudged incessantly
By morbid reveries, like worms.

And now he continues in turn, his eyes fixed on mine, speak-ing from memory, something dark and weird I can't follow about becoming the opposite of flesh.

PATRICK

. . . Like some old statue of a half-forgotten god,
Abandoned in the desert, starved of blood . . .

I join in the last lines, matching his rhythm, fitting my voice to his.

ME / PATRICK

. . . Whose enigmatic, weather-beaten frown
Lights up, for a moment, as the sun goes down.

There's a silence that, for a second or two, neither of us breaks.

PATRICK

You read it well.

ME

Thank you . . . What's it about?

PATRICK

His love life, you could say.

ME

He must have had a pretty complicated love
life.

Patrick smiles.

PATRICK

When he wrote that, Baudelaire was involved
with two women. One was a famous beauty, the
toast of nineteenth-century Paris. He called her
Vénus Blanche, his White Venus. The other was
a mixed-race cabaret dancer who sold her body
on the streets. He called her his *Vénus Noire.*
Black Venus.

ME

Interesting . . . A love triangle.

PATRICK

If you like.

ME

How did it pan out?

PATRICK

He started writing poems that he sent anonymously to the White Venus. The things he
wanted to do to her; the things he did to the
Black Venus. Poems that touch on every kind of
depravity. He said other poets had written
enough about the flowery realms of beauty. He
wanted to be the first to write about the beauty
that comes from evil.

ME

Les Fleurs du Mal . . . The Flowers of Evil.

Time to make my move.

ME

I guess he understood that some women are attracted by the forbidden.

Patrick Fogler shakes his head. As if I've somehow disappointed him.

PATRICK

I have to go.

What?

ME

Really? I was enjoying—I'd love to hear some
more—

I try to hand him the book. Which he waves away.

PATRICK

Keep it. A memento of an interesting encounter. I liked hearing you read.

ME

Look, I . . . I don't usually do this, but I just had a really shitty evening and I could do with some company. Would you stay and let me buy you a drink?

He smiles again, creasing the lines at the corners of his eyes.

PATRICK

I'd love to. But I'm married.

ME

Oh, I didn't mean—

He's already walking away. He calls over his shoulder:

PATRICK

I know. But I did. And unlike Baudelaire, I prefer my Venuses one at a time . . . It was nice meeting you.

And then, almost as if he's speaking to himself, I hear him say something in French.

PATRICK

Ô toi que j'eusse aimée, ô toi qui le savais . . .

ME

What's that mean? Hey, maybe we could—

Nothing, dammit. I'm left staring after him, the book of poetry still in my hand. And realizing that, for the first time since I started working for Henry, I've just been given the brush-off.

10

"So I guess it's good news," I say flatly. "Congratulations, Mrs. Fogler. Your husband's faithful."

Good news for *you,* anyway. I'm still smarting.

We're back in Stella Fogler's suite. Weirdly, she seems to get even more agitated at this news.

"Faithful!" she wails, wringing her hands. "I should have known it wouldn't work. Oh God! God!"

"What do you mean?" I say, puzzled.

It comes out in a rush.

"I thought maybe I could get something on him. Something to stop him coming after me," she says wildly.

What? I look at Henry, confused, but he doesn't meet my eyes.

"He figured out it was a trick." Stella turns to Henry. "She was wrong for it. It should have been a dark-skinned girl. They're the ones—" She stops.

"Black Venus," I say slowly. "He talked about that."

"He *never* talks about that," she says sharply. Again she appeals to Henry. "I knew this was a mistake."

I'm getting pissed off now. And not only because she's

acting like this is somehow all my fault. But because I'm just realizing that this whole attempted pickup was the exact opposite of what I thought it was.

"Look, most of the neurotic bitches I do this for would be counting themselves lucky," I say angrily. "Your husband didn't hit on me. And believe me, that's a first. If you were using me to try to blackmail him, you should have told me." I stand up. "I'd like my money, please. Four hundred dollars."

Stella pulls an overnight bag from under the bed and unzips it. Taking out a fat roll of bills, she peels off four. Her hands are shaking.

"I don't mean to sound ungrateful. I'm sure you did your best. And I wasn't intending to blackmail him, not exactly. I just wanted some . . . insurance."

I take the money. "Thanks," I say coldly.

"I'll walk you out, Claire," Henry murmurs.

The door of the suite is barely closed behind us before he's spinning me around, his hand on my shoulder. "Hey! What was that about? *Neurotic bitches,* Claire?"

"She *is* neurotic."

"And a *client,*" he insists.

"Henry . . . Don't you think that's fucked up? She *wanted* him to make a pass at me. What happened to *the innocent should have nothing to fear*?"

He shrugs. "You needed more work, didn't you?"

"You *knew,*" I realize. "You knew that's what she was after. *Jesus.* I mean, doing this to scumbags who already cheat on their wives is one thing. But when it's the *wife . . .*" I shake my head in disbelief. "I'm *out.*"

As I stride away he calls after me, "Don't be such a diva, Claire. You love this stuff. You know you do. You just didn't

like it that this one didn't go for you. Call me tomorrow,
when you've gotten over yourself."

INT. LEXINGTON HOTEL—FOYER—NIGHT

As I leave the hotel I remember something. I pull the copy
of *Les Fleurs du Mal* Patrick gave me from my bag, then turn
back the way I came.

INT. LEXINGTON HOTEL—CORRIDOR—
CONTINUOUS

I knock on the door of Stella's suite again.

> ME
>
> Mrs. Fogler? Stella? I have something of Pat-
> rick's. I guess you should have it.

There's no reply.

> ME
>
> Hello?

Nothing. I shrug, turn away.

11

There's a brilliant exercise, created by the legendary acting coach Sanford Meisner, in which two actors simply repeat each other's words. It's designed to show that words mean pretty much whatever you want them to. That the script isn't a bible, it's a starting point. Text and subtext.

It's three days later. Scott and I are circling each other in the rehearsal space while the other students look on.

"You're smiling," I tell Scott eagerly, like he must have good news to share with me.

"You're smiling," he says back. Only he says it like we're in the middle of an argument, and this is the proof I'm not taking it seriously.

"You're . . . *smiling*?" I say incredulously, like he can't even be bothered to hide the fact he just behaved like a shit.

"You're smiling," he calls out triumphantly, like I've been trying not to and he's made me.

"You're smiling," I whisper, like it's the first time I've seen him happy in a year.

"You're smiling," he says, with the unspoken implication, *But I'm not.*

"Good. Now run with it," Paul says.

"You're smiling," Scott says accusingly.

"I was not!"

"So what are you thinking about?"

"I was thinking about that time we rolled in the snow together."

"That was the last time, wasn't it? The last time we were happy."

"Excellent," Paul says, stopping us. The other students clap briefly.

"Just remember," Paul tells the group, "it's all about using what the other actor gives you. An ounce of behavior is worth a pound of words."

There's a knock at the classroom's open door. One of the admins is standing there with a uniformed policewoman.

"I'm looking for Claire Wright," she says.

Shit.

"That's me," I say with a smile. "How can I help?"

12

The policewoman takes me to One Police Plaza, where I wait in a small, stale room on the eighth floor. I've asked her what it's about but she won't tell me, just says she's been told to collect me and everything will become clear soon. Or "momentarily," as she puts it.

It must be that producer, I'm thinking nervously. He must have filed a complaint. Whatever happens now can't be good. I know gun laws are a lot less strict over here but I don't think you can just wave them at people.

Eventually a burly man in plainclothes comes in and introduces himself as Detective Frank Durban. I jump up eagerly and shake his hand, trying to make a good impression. Detective Durban looks a little surprised, but indicates the younger, shaven-headed man holding a pile of papers who comes into the room behind him. "And this is Detective Davies."

"Do I need a lawyer?" I say anxiously.

"That depends. What have you done?" Durban says. I laugh, because he said it kindly, like a joke, but I notice he gives me time to answer before he adds, "You haven't been arrested or charged, Claire. We just want to ask you some questions. About Stella Fogler."

"Who?" Then I remember. Not the producer after all.

"I understand you do some occasional work for a law firm called Kerr Adler," Durban adds as we sit down. "That correct?"

"Yes, it is."

"Tell me about that."

For a moment I consider lying—the job may be non-union, but I'm pretty sure it's breaking my visa conditions—but since they clearly know quite a lot already, I do as Detective Durban says and tell them everything: Marcie, the decoy work, the hidden camera in my bag. After a while Davies pushes his papers to one side and starts taking notes.

"And was there anything unusual about the assignment for Mrs. Fogler?" Durban asks. "Anything out of the ordinary?"

"Well, I was asked to meet her beforehand. That doesn't always happen."

"Why was that?"

I shrug. "Henry said she wanted to take a look at me. See if she thought I was suitable."

"And how did she seem on that occasion?"

I think back, remembering the way Stella Fogler had paced up and down by the windows. "Well . . . nervous."

"Can you be more specific?"

I say slowly, "It was like she was frightened of something."

The two men don't look at each other, but I feel them go rigid with attention. "Is Mrs. Fogler all right?" I add.

"Just tell us what happened, Claire," Detective Durban says. "In what way, frightened?"

I tell them about Stella, then how I approached her husband in the bar. When I get to the point where Patrick gave me the book of poetry and walked away, Detective Durban stops me. "Think he'd guessed what was going on?"

"I don't see how."

"Okay. And Mrs. Fogler? How did she react when you told her how it went? Was she pleased? Reassured?"

"Not exactly." I repeat what she'd said about getting something on her husband. Somehow it sounds more ominous now. The way these two are grilling me so intently feels like it can't be good.

"Are Patrick and Stella okay? Did something happen?" I ask, and again they don't answer my question.

"When she paid you, did you see any other money? In her bag, maybe?" Durban asks.

I shake my head. "But there must have been at least a thousand in the roll she got out. She paid me in hundreds."

"So you took *four* bills." Durban puts a lot of emphasis on the word *four.*

"Yes," I say, puzzled. "Like I told you. That was what she owed me."

"What happened to the rest?"

"What *rest?*"

"We didn't find any money on her person," he says flatly. "And she'd made a large cash withdrawal that morning. Substantially more than a thousand dollars."

I stare at him. "*On her person . . .* You mean—she's dead?"

"That's correct." He's watching my reaction.

"Oh my God," I say, appalled. "How? What happened?"

"We're treating it as a homicide. That's all I can tell you at present." He continues looking at me steadily. His expression, which had seemed friendly, even avuncular, has hardened. "I *can* say that she died in her suite, sometime before dawn. The same night you were with her."

"Oh no," I whisper. "That's terrible. You can't think . . ."

"If you'd just finish answering our questions, Claire."

He takes me over it again, and then a third time. Davies keeps scribbling notes.

"What happened to the video?" Durban says at last. "The one from the hidden camera. Who has it now?"

I think back. "I gave it to Stella. Mrs. Fogler. That's standard. She'd paid for it, after all."

"And the book of poems?"

"Still in my bag. I don't usually read poetry but these are really interesting, in a weird—"

"We'll need it," he interrupts.

He gets an evidence bag, turns it inside out and uses it as a glove to take the book from me. "You ever find out what that French stuff meant? The thing he quoted at you as he left?"

"Yes—I'm pretty sure it's from a poem called *A Une Passante*, 'To a Passer-by.' It's about seeing someone in the street, exchanging a glance, but still going your separate ways . . . The literal translation is, 'O you who I had loved. O you, who felt it too.'"

Durban snorts. "That's nice. I should try to remember that. So you leave the hotel . . . Then what?"

"I went out with some friends."

"To a bar?"

I nod. "The Harley Bar. There were plenty of people who can confirm I was there by nine thirty."

"And you got home when?"

"About seven A.M. I . . . met someone."

"His name?"

"Er—Tom."

"Last name?"

"I—I'm pretty sure I have his phone number some-where." I rummage in my bag and find a scrap of paper. "Yes. This is it."

Detective Durban scrutinizes it as he takes it. "Looks like an *i* to me. Tim, not Tom. We'll contact him."

"What did you do with the money, Claire?" Detective Davies says. It's the first time he's spoken.

"The four hundred dollars? I gave it to my roommate. I owe her a lot of back rent, so—"

"Not the four hundred," he interrupts. "The twenty thousand dollars you stole from Stella Fogler's hotel room."

I stare at him, my head swimming. "What? No—you can't think—"

"Just answer the question," Durban says.

"There never was any money—not that amount. At least, I never saw it. Am I a *suspect*?"

"A suspect?" Davies snorts. "You've already confessed to recording without consent, working as an unlicensed inves-tigator, soliciting, and conspiracy to blackmail. We just need to wrap up theft and murder and we're done here."

"Murder?"

"According to Henry North, you had an argument with Mrs. Fogler that night."

"I told you—*she* was the one acting weird—"

"So you went away, brooded on her rudeness . . . And then you went back to her room," Davies says. "Where she just happened to have a large quantity of cash. Henry North told us about your financial problems. It must have been galling, to see a woman like that with so much wealth."

I shake my head, mystified. "I told you, I only went

back to return the book. And look, Henry told me everything I did for that firm was legal. So long as you record
them in a public place, he said. And you're not soliciting if
they make the first move." A thought strikes me. "Have you
questioned *him*?"

"Of course. And we'll check his account very thor-
oughly. Just as we'll check yours. With this Tim."

"Did you kill Stella Fogler, Claire?" Detective Durban
asks, as matter-of-factly as if he's asking whether I take sugar
in my coffee.

I look him straight in the eye, ignoring the thudding in
my chest. "No. I did not."

There's a tense silence. "Detective, shall we confer outside?" Durban says.

They step out. I hear the murmur of voices through the
door. Then Durban comes back alone.

"I'll need the details of at least three people who can
confirm you were at the bar by nine thirty," he says. "After
that, you can go."

I stare at him, light-headed with relief. "So you *don't*
think I did it?"

"We'll double-check everything you've told us. If you've
been telling the truth, we should be able to eliminate you
from the investigation pretty fast. But don't leave the city
without checking in with us first. And my strong advice is
not to undertake any more work for that law firm. This is
a murder investigation, Ms. Wright, not an immigration
check, but if we find out you've broken the terms of your
visa again, I won't hesitate to pass along that information to
the relevant authorities."

And with that he starts scooping up the paperwork,
sorting it into piles. It was all a performance, I realize: the

classic good-cop, bad-cop grilling, designed to put the fear of God into me.

And it worked too. I'm still shaking. If I *had* done anything wrong, I'd have confessed to these two in a heartbeat. The mixture of confidence, friendliness, and aggression reduced me to a cowering wreck within moments.

But even now, in the midst of my relief, I find myself thinking, *What can I use from that?*

13

When I get home Jess is channel-hopping, her head turbaned in a towel, simultaneously checking Facebook and painting her toenails pale blue.

"Good day?" she asks, not looking up.

"Not exactly." I tell her about the police, the murdered client. Pretty soon she's staring at me, openmouthed. "I feel awful," I conclude. "Apart from the hotel staff, it looks like Henry and I were just about the last people to see Stella Fogler alive."

"The police say how she died?"

I shake my head. "They were pretty vague. But the way they were quizzing me, it sounded like some kind of robbery. I'll probably have to go and give evidence in court."

Just for an instant, unbidden, the scene starts to unfold in my head:

INT. NEW YORK COURTROOM—DAY

CLAIRE WRIGHT takes the stand, dressed like Vera Miles in *The Wrong Man*—cool, aloof, but visibly nervous.

PROSECUTOR

Ms. Wright, thank you for coming today. Your
evidence will be crucial to the outcome of this
trial—

"Did you say Fogler?" Jesse interrupts.

"Yes. Why?"

"There was something on the news—" She thumbs the
remote, uses it to point at the TV. "There."

On the screen Patrick Fogler, his handsome features
dark with fatigue, is standing outside an apartment building, speaking to a battery of microphones. Flashes strobe his
face.

"That's him," I say. "Turn it up."

As the volume increases we hear him say: *". . . grateful
for any assistance, any assistance at all, that can be given to the
NYPD."* He stops, and the barrage of flashes redoubles.
Someone from the back shouts, "How was your relationship
with your wife?"

"Press ambush," Jess says significantly. "You know what
that means, don't you?"

"That he's talking to the press?"

"No, dumb-ass. The police think he did it." She sighs at
my incomprehension. "When the police know who did it,
but a lawyer's stopping them from asking any really tough
questions, they tip off the papers so the journalists can ask
the questions for them. Next time you see him, he'll be in
handcuffs."

I flash back to the meeting with Stella, those odd things
she'd said.

STELLA

You will be careful, won't you? Promise me
you'll be careful.

ME

Why don't you tell me about your husband,
Mrs. Fogler?

STELLA

He's like no man you've ever met. I mean it.
Don't turn your back on him. Don't *trust* him.
Do you promise?

I thought she'd meant her husband was a groper. That was
before I'd met him, of course—no one could be less gropey
than Patrick Fogler. But had she really meant something
totally different?

Was it *him* she'd been frightened of? Or at any rate, was
that how Detective Durban had read the scene, when I'd
described it to him?

I look at the TV again, at Patrick Fogler—so calm, so
intelligent, so *likable*—and think how impossible that is.

"Not him," I say, shaking my head. "I don't believe it.
He was the one who *didn't* hit on me, remember. A genuinely nice, attractive, faithful guy."

"Don't give me that crap," Jess says lightly, toweling
her hair. "There's no such thing—that's what you always say,
isn't it?"

14

The murder makes the front pages. From there it gets picked up by bloggers and commentators, each with a different theory about what happened. The first angle they pursue is that it was a robbery gone wrong. A few years back, an armed gang targeted upmarket suites in Midtown hotels, holding guests up at gunpoint. But the members of that gang are all serving prison sentences, and there haven't been any hotel holdups in Manhattan since. Even so, there's a whole thing on social media about what this might mean for tourism. Visitors are being advised to open their hotel room doors on chains.

Pretty soon the attention switches to Stella herself. What was a woman who lived across town, in Morningside Heights, doing in a hotel only a short distance away? There are two theories: one, that she'd quarreled with her husband, and two, that she was waiting for a lover. There are also rumors that a large amount of cash was stolen from her suite, which the police refuse to confirm or deny.

The maid who found the body, Consuela Alvarez, told a reporter the room looked like there'd been some kind of struggle. Stella's body had been left on the bed, a sheet pulled over it, she said. Weeping, Consuela described the head as "smashed in—terrible—so much blood."

The hotel's CCTV showed nothing of any use, apparently.

Gradually, the two theories start to merge together. Stella *was* waiting for a lover, and she was estranged from her husband too. That was why he'd killed her, was the implication.

Of course, I know that can't be right. Stella was only staying in that hotel so I could make my move on Patrick. And whatever problems the two of them were having, he wasn't prepared to be unfaithful, which suggested that he, at least, believed they could be resolved. But the police know that too. I keep waiting for them to close the speculation down by telling the journalists about *me*, but for some reason they don't. Nor do they come back to ask me more questions.

I tell a few friends I was with Stella Fogler that night, but only a few. The last thing I want is for my freelance activities to be splashed across some blog. In any case, I can't satisfy my friends' appetite for the grisly details, because I don't know any. I'm as much in the dark as anyone.

When I haven't heard anything from the police after two weeks, I call Henry.

"Claire," he answers. A statement rather than a question. As if he's surprised to hear from me.

"Can we meet? There's something I want to ask you about."

A pause, then, "Okay. But not at the office." He names a hotel where we did a couple of assignments.

When I get there he's already sitting at the bar, down at the end where the bartender won't overhear us. I go and join him.

"I thought you might have heard something," I say. "About the investigation, I mean."

"All I'm hearing is, they're getting nowhere." He shrugs. "But they no longer think robbery was the real motive. Apparently there are details that point to the husband."

"What kind of details?" I say, surprised at this confirmation that Jess might have been right.

"They're not saying. That's pretty standard. So they can spring them suddenly if they need to, in an interview. But the word *frenzied* has been used." He looks at me sideways. "They give you a hard time?"

I nod. "You?"

"Nothing I haven't done to others. Just doing their job."

"Henry . . . Is there any chance I can do some more work for you? My situation's getting pretty desperate."

"No way," he says. "The firm was lucky not to get slammed with a fine for using an undocumented worker. If I wasn't an ex-cop, I don't think they'd have cut us the slack they did." He hesitates. "Fact is, Claire, we were about to ditch you anyway."

"Because I didn't have the right papers?"

He shakes his head. "We'd had a complaint. A lawyer. Guy called Rick. Remember him?"

I remember him. *For that you get quite a lot in Seattle.*

When I'd shown the tape to his wife, her eyes had blazed with anger through her tears.

"He dropped an affidavit on us a couple of days after the assignment," Henry's saying. "Claimed that after you met him in the bar, you'd gone up to his hotel room, had sex, took the thousand dollars you'd negotiated as your fee, and only *then* shopped him to his wife. Which, of course, would make you guilty of a criminal offense, and us accomplices. It would also make the video inadmissible in his wife's divorce suit."

"He's lying," I say furiously. "Just look at the tape."

Henry says steadily, "We did. The video ends with you telling him to go ahead, you'll meet him in his room. Then you turned the camera off. Rick provided a full timeline, Claire, as well as bar receipts and room key information. You were in that hotel for what—two hours? Plenty of time for his story to stack up."

"The video ends because I had what I needed," I insist. "And the reason it took two hours was because I waited an hour for him to leave his table. *Jesus,* Henry, what is this? You know that was how I worked."

"I knew you liked to get into your part. I never asked too many questions about that. So long as we got what we needed."

"I never did that," I say flatly. "He was a creep, for Christ's sake. A scumbag. And a *lawyer.* He knew exactly what lies to tell to get that video excluded from his wife's deposition."

"I'm not saying you did what he said, Claire. I'm just saying we'd have had a hard time disproving it. And anything you did for us after that was going to be tainted, from an evidence point of view. So I'd been told by management to find someone else. If you hadn't called saying you needed rent money, I'd never have let you do Stella Fogler. It was one last gig for old times' sake."

I could almost cry at the unfairness of it all. "Okay. So I can't work for your firm. There must be some other way—"

Henry shakes his head. "Don't even go there. Listen, you're a great girl and I've enjoyed working with you. I really hope our paths cross again. But this particular show is over." He waves at the bartender. "I'll get the tab, okay?"

15

Time passes. Three months, maybe more.

For a while the Lexington Hotel murder remains a sensation, pontificated on by bloggers, speculated about in bars and offices. Then a soap star is photographed in a swingers' club, the Lincoln Tunnel is closed for repairs, and the president sends more American troops to the Middle East.

People move on.

Jess's dad gives me a little leeway on the rent. But without the law firm's work, I still end up having to do some of the things I told myself I'd never do. Things I don't like to think about and no one else knows about.

Anything to keep acting.

PART TWO

16

The room is filled with sunshine. We're lying on the floor, staring up at the ceiling. Eight of us, in a starfish pattern, our heads almost touching.

"This is a very old improv game," Paul's voice says, off to my left. "It's called The Story Tells Itself. We're going to beat a rhythm on the floor. And each time we make a beat, we're going to take turns adding one word to the story."

"What's the story about?" someone asks.

"I don't know. That's the point. Nobody knows. The story's there already. All we have to do is let it out."

The exercises have been getting harder lately. Paul's had us spend whole days calling things by the wrong name, just to see how it feels. He's had us improvise ever-crazier characters—a salesman with a suitcase full of sweaters knitted from giraffe wool, a soldier armed with an invisible machine gun—then sent us out, in character, to accost passersby on the street. To my surprise, the passersby have usually been happy to listen. Either I'm getting better at this, or New York's getting nuttier as the heat kicks in.

And with every exercise, he reminds us of the one and

only rule. *Acting isn't pretending. The clue is in the word. Acting is* doing. *Being. Becoming.*

"Let's go," he says now, slapping his palms on the floor. A slow, loping rhythm. Gradually we all pick it up.

"Once," he says.

A fraction off the beat, the student to his left says, "Upon."

"A"

"Time"

"There"

"Was"

"A"

Suddenly, it's my turn. *Don't think, act.* Though in truth there's no time to do either, the driving rhythm forcing me to say the very first thing that comes into my head. "Princess."

And the story passes on, gathering momentum as it goes around and around. A fairy tale, something about a prince who falls in love with a statue in his garden.

The next time, Paul makes it harder. If you hesitate, you drop out. And the rhythm will get faster each time it goes around. It's all about learning to react instinctively in the moment, he explains.

This time he doesn't start with anything so obvious as "Once."

It's a strange, glittering story that emerges, a dark fantasy about a little girl who lives in a graveyard among ravens and crows.

One by one the students falter, get to their feet.

All except me.

And in the end it's just the two of us, me and Paul, lying at right angles on the floor like two hands of a clock, our hands slapping the boards in triple time, the words flowing so thick and fast it's as if we've memorized them.

I feel possessed, exhilarated, captured. As if I'm just the mouthpiece of another personality. A host to some voodoo spirit. The real me obliterated, annihilated, by a force stronger than any orgasm.

I get it now. *Don't think.*

At last he stops, and I lie there for a few seconds, coming back to my senses, savoring the moment.

The group stands silently, watching. Usually at the end of a good exercise they applaud. I raise my head and look.

That cop is standing with them. Detective Durban.

"Ms. Wright," he says. "Claire. Can we talk?"

I take him to the cafeteria. Around us, students sit in groups of two or three, chatting or working on their laptops.

It's too hot for coffee. He gets us Diet Cokes from the machine.

"America," I murmur in a funny Yankee voice as he hands me mine. "Land of the calorie-free."

He doesn't smile. I notice how tired he looks.

"I'd like you to do something to help us, Claire," he says brusquely.

"Of course. Anything. If I can. What?"

"We're backtracking over some old ground on the Fogler murder. Rechecking statements, seeing if there's anything we missed first time around."

"You haven't made an arrest, have you? I've been checking online."

Durban frowns. "We've eliminated a great many people from our investigation. Including all one hundred and twenty-six guests who were staying at the Lexington Hotel that night. We haven't been sitting on our hands."

"Sorry. I didn't mean—"

"Though most of our work has centered on one individual," he adds.

"The husband," I say. "Patrick."

He doesn't respond to that. "Can you still recall the details of your conversation with Mr. Fogler?"

"Of course."

"We have someone new looking at the case for us. A psychological profiler. I'd like you to meet with her."

"Sure, if you think it'll be useful . . . When?"

"Now would be good."

I glance in the direction of the rehearsal room. "I'm in the middle of class."

"This is important, Claire." His tone has hardened.

"It's just—I don't see how I can be of much help. Patrick Fogler and I only spoke for a few minutes. He wasn't interested in me."

Durban nods. "Maybe. But why did he leave?"

"What do you mean?"

"Fogler. When you tried to pick him up, you said he seemed eager to get away. That's what I keep wondering about. Since he was only going home, and he believed his wife was out of town, why the rush? Why break off a conversation with a friendly young woman who's prepared to discuss French poetry like she actually gives a shit?"

"Perhaps I bored him."

"That's one possibility."

"Is there another?"

He doesn't answer me directly. The flow of information is always one-way with this man, I realize. "Either way, I'd

like you to speak to this profiler." He leans across the table.
"Look, I never did get around to reporting you to my friends
in Immigration. But it's not too late."

"Seems I don't have much choice, then," I say with a
tight smile.

"No," he agrees. "You really don't."

We take a yellow cab. Durban gives an address in Union
City. The driver's turned the air-conditioning off, to save
fuel. It's the first really hot day of May and we sweat on the
vinyl seats. My skirt rides up my bare legs and once or twice
I see Detective Durban glancing at them before he turns his
head and looks out the window instead.

17

We pull up outside an ugly, nondescript office, in a block full of ugly offices and empty parking lots. The windows haven't been cleaned in decades and the paintwork is peeling.

The security guard at the reception desk makes me sign in. After that, I don't see a single other person as we go down a long, airless corridor. At last Detective Durban knocks on a door. The nameplate says SUITE #508. DR. KATHRYN LATHAM ABFP, FORENSIC PSYCHOLOGIST.

"Enter," a female voice answers.

Inside, a woman is sitting behind a cheap wooden desk, working on a laptop. I put her age at sixty, maybe more. Her hair is so gray it's almost blond, cut short, and she's dressed more stylishly than I was expecting from the surroundings.

Her eyes, when she looks up, are blue and shrewd. "Claire Wright, yes?"

"Claire, Dr. Latham," Durban says, introducing us.

"Call me Kathryn. And take a seat. You don't mind being recorded, I hope?"

She nods at one of the walls, which I now see is made of

dark reflective glass. Some kind of two-way mirror. Behind it I can just make out the red dot of a camera in filming mode. Automatically I pull my shoulders back, as if I'm at a casting, before realizing how stupid that is.

"Now then," Dr. Latham says. "Tell me about your encounter with Patrick Fogler."

I tell her everything I can remember, emphasizing that Patrick behaved properly throughout. It doesn't take long. Dr. Latham listens, her head tilted, blue eyes on me, saying nothing. When I'm done, she nods. "Thank you, Claire. You've been very helpful."

"That's it?" I say, surprised.

"Sure. You can go now."

"Kathryn . . ." Detective Durban protests, as if that wasn't what he was hoping to hear.

"She isn't right for it, Frank," Kathryn Latham says firmly.

I frown. "Right for what?"

"Claire, could you give us a moment?" Durban says. "Just wait out in the corridor."

I step out and he closes the door behind me. I can hear the rumble of their voices but even when I press my ear to the wood I can't make out what they're saying.

The next door along must lead to the room behind the two-way mirror. I open it carefully, in case there's someone in there, ready to say I was just looking for the bathroom, but it's empty except for a monitor and a small camera on a tripod. The sound is turned on and I can hear them perfectly.

DETECTIVE DURBAN'S VOICE
. . . her class. She's good. She can *act*.

KATHRYN LATHAM'S VOICE

They all *act*, Frank. MAWs, they're called. Model, Actress, Whatever. It doesn't mean she could do something like this.

DETECTIVE DURBAN'S VOICE

This is at Pace—the Actors Studio course. I'm told they're pretty selective. And she's . . . attractive.

KATHRYN LATHAM'S VOICE
(pointedly)

Is she, Frank?

DETECTIVE DURBAN'S VOICE

Sure, we have female cops who'd do it. No disrespect to my colleagues, but have you *seen* them? I think Claire would stand a better chance of getting under his defenses.

KATHRYN LATHAM'S VOICE

Didn't work last time.

DETECTIVE DURBAN'S VOICE

He gave her the book. You said yourself—for him, that's intimacy.

There's a pause while Kathryn Latham thinks about this. Next time she speaks, she sounds fractionally less emphatic.

KATHRYN LATHAM'S VOICE

Even so, you can't get around the fact she's a
civilian. It's a safeguarding issue.

DETECTIVE DURBAN'S VOICE

We'd be right there if anything happened. And
the great thing about her is, she has no records.
No bank account, no Social Security number for
him to check out. She can be whoever we need
her to be.

I've heard enough. I go back into the corridor and walk
straight into Dr. Latham's office without knocking.

"I'll do it," I say. "Whatever it is. But you need to pay
me."

It's quite the entrance, but Kathryn Latham looks un-
perturbed. "Do you have *any* idea what we're talking about?"

I shrug. "I caught some of it."

"It can't do any harm to tell her, at least," Detective
Durban says quietly.

Dr. Latham studies me for a moment, unblinking. "Very
well. We have a suspect in the murder of Stella Fogler—"

"Her husband."

"Please, don't interrupt. We have a suspect. This individual is highly intelligent, highly disciplined. He can't be
provoked or tricked into revealing himself. There's been a
suggestion that an undercover operation might succeed
where other methods have failed."

"You mean—*entrap* him?"

"Not *your* sort of entrapment." Dr. Latham says it witheringly. "This would be a highly sophisticated, psychologi-
cally based operation. The suspect would be encouraged to

reveal various aspects of his personality, which could then be compared with my profile of Stella Fogler's killer. If the two match . . . Well, it would strongly indicate that suspect and killer are one and the same."

"Would it be dangerous?"

"Of course."

"You'd be wearing a wire," Durban says reassuringly. "We'd have people standing by, ready to pull you out."

"If I did it, how much would I get paid?"

"Whoever acts as decoy will have the satisfaction of knowing she's doing her civic duty," Dr. Latham says frostily. "A woman *died*, Claire."

"We could probably pay something as well," Durban adds.

"I want a green card," I say slowly. "Full pay, and a green card."

He shakes his head. "Not possible."

"You said yourself, you have friends at Immigration—"

"There's not going to be any green card," Dr. Latham interrupts. "Because there's not going to be any operation. You're not doing this."

We both stare at her.

"At least, not unless *I* decide you are," she adds.

18

sign some forms, then Dr. Latham runs a battery of psychological tests on me. The Wechsler. The Minnesota Multiphasic Personality Inventory. The Hare Psychopathy Checklist. She makes me hold electrodes in each hand while she flashes images onto a screen. Dogs, babies, clouds, and then, abruptly, a knife, pornography, more clouds.

But mostly, we talk.

"Why New York City, Claire?"

I shrug. "Why not?"

Dr. Latham looks at me shrewdly. "You were a foster child, I understand?"

"Correct," I say, wondering how the hell she knows that.

"And you got on well with your foster family?"

"Foster *families*. Plural. They didn't like us to get too settled. And no. Not really."

She waits for me to continue.

"Take the one I spent longest with," I say at last. "Julie and Gary. Julie was a manager in the Health Service. Gary worked in marketing. From the outside, it was Happy Families . . . at least, when the social workers were around. I suppose I was about eleven when I realized the two of them didn't actually like each other very much. But they were stuck. If they got divorced, they'd lose the side business they had going—which was being foster parents. Ten thousand pounds per kid per year, tax free. So they struggled on, trying to pretend everything was fine."

I pause. "Go on," Dr. Latham says quietly.

"It was a year or so later when I first noticed Gary starting to look at me a different way. If I bumped into him coming out of the bathroom, he'd smile like we shared some kind of secret. One time I cut my leg, and I remember he ran his hands up and down it to see how bad it was. And then sometimes he'd rub my back . . . I liked it at first. I mean, it was better than being ignored, right? I finally had something that made him pay attention to me—something his wife didn't. It was a while before I realized what that something was.

"He never actually *did* anything. Nothing serious, anyway. Just groped me a few times when I made the mistake of being alone with him. It didn't surprise me when Julie eventually kicked him out and he ran off with some woman he worked with."

Dr. Latham nods. "And the decoy work you were doing for that law firm?"

"What about it?"

"How did it make you *feel*?" she asks, and I sense this is an important question for her.

I shrug. "It was a shitty job that paid the rent."

"Was that all it was, Claire?"

"Look," I say, annoyed by her persistence, "those women thought that if their husbands let someone like me pick them up, they weren't worth being married to. But the truth is, almost any man will try it on in that situation. That's just the way men are."

"That's taking a pretty cynical view. Maybe those women wanted to be able to trust their partners."

"Then they should try trusting them. Not testing the relationship to destruction." I shake my head. "Men think with their dicks. Get over it."

"All men, Claire?" Dr. Latham asks quietly. "Or just men like your foster father?"

I stare at her. I've finally realized where she's going with this.

> ME
>
> The decoy work . . . I'm acting out the story of my childhood, aren't I?

I feel the tears spring to my eyes.

> ME
>
> Breaking up other people's families, just like *my* family was broken. Punishing those men because no one was there for me when I was a kid. No father to love *me*. Just some slimy pervert looking for a feel.

A tear spills onto my cheek. I swipe it away.

Kathryn Latham lifts her hands and, to my surprise, applauds, slowly and sardonically.

"Very good, Claire. It's Freudian bullshit, of course. But I am impressed with the way you took my suggestion and ran with it. And the tears are a nice touch."

She tosses me a box of tissues and ticks something on her pad.

"Right. Let's move on to your sex life. This may take some time, I imagine."

And then at last we're back in a room with Detective Durban and he's looking at her expectantly.

"Well," Dr. Latham says matter-of-factly, "she's insecure, impulsive, fragile, emotionally incontinent, can't handle rejection, and although she tries extremely hard to hide it, she craves approval like a junkie craving a fix. What can I say, Frank? She's an actress. On the other hand, she's also quick, observant, talented, and brave. Somewhat against my better judgment, I think this might actually be worth a try."

19

She takes me to a conference room in the same building, still littered with disconnected cables from some previous occupant.

"Twelve years ago, Patrick Fogler was questioned in connection with the disappearance of Constance Jones, a prostitute." Dr. Latham brings up a photograph of a young black woman on an audiovisual screen. The woman stares at the camera defiantly. It's a police mugshot, I realize. "She'd been seen getting into a car similar to Fogler's. But the witness didn't get the license plate and there was no forensic evidence. Constance was never found. Patrick protested his innocence and no charges were ever pressed."

She changes the picture. Another mugshot.

"Four years later, the body of another prostitute was found in an empty property not far from the university in Massachusetts where Fogler was then teaching. She'd been decapitated. The head and the body had been posed separately from each other. Again, there was nothing specific to link him to the crime."

"But if there was no link . . ." I say.

Dr. Latham holds up a finger. "Except for one thing. Something so tenuous and circumstantial, it could never be used in court."

She hands me a book. I recognize it instantly as the one Patrick gave me. *Les Fleurs du Mal, translated by Patrick Fogler.*

"Page fifty-six," she says. "Read it aloud, would you?"

Mystified, I do as she asks.

ME

The girl lies naked, sensuously sprawled,
Her limbs spread wide to curious eyes;
Her secret places shamelessly exposed,
A glimpse of pink between her amber thighs.

Only a crimson swathe of blood,
Encircling the severed head,
Reveals that she is perfect now,
As all are perfect who are dead.

I stop short. I understand now why she asked me to read this particular poem. *Encircling the severed head . . .* I hear a click and look up. Dr. Latham is flashing more images onto the screen—horrible, horrible images, so grotesque I have to look away. But not before one in particular has seared itself into my brain. A woman's head, severed, posed among thick church candles. She's still wearing her big hoop earrings. Her eyes are partially closed: You can see her green eye shadow. The expression on her face is glassy and resigned.

"Please, go on," Dr. Latham says calmly.

Reluctantly, I lift the book and continue.

ME

Tell me, cold beauty, did your intimate in death—
Whose lusts you could not, living, sate—
On your inert, voluptuous corpse
His monstrous passions consummate?

No matter where that man goes now,
He cannot hope to hide or flee,
For he has tasted death's sweet fruit,
And loves for all eternity.

I stop, my throat dry. "It doesn't prove it was *him*, though, does it? It doesn't prove it was Patrick."

"Exactly," Dr. Latham agrees blandly. "It proves nothing."

"And Stella? Was she . . . Was her death like this?"

"We'll come to that. But shortly *before* she died, Patrick met someone in a bar—a young woman. When she picked up his book, she turned down the page to mark his place. Do you remember?"

I nod.

"Would you find the place now, please?"

I do. The poem Patrick Fogler was staring at so intently that night was called "The Murderer's Wine."

My wife is dead. I am free.
Now I can slake my heart's desire.

"When you go back into Patrick's past," Dr. Latham's saying, "you discover that, wherever he's living, young prostitutes disappear. Not many; just one or two a year. Not enough to make the headlines—because who cares about a few crack whores, right? But enough to make a pattern. The bodies are rarely found. But when they are, they've been mutilated, in ways that reflect different poems from *Les Fleurs du Mal.*" She flashes more pictures up. Awful, haunting pictures. "Shanice Williams. She'd been stabbed seven times in the heart. That corresponds to a poem called 'To a Madonna,' in which Baudelaire says, *'I will take seven knives, one for each deadly sin, and plunge them in your panting, sobbing heart.'* Jada Floyd. Her breasts had been sliced open. That corresponds to a poem in which Baudelaire describes how *'some men like to bite and kiss the sucked-out breasts of anorexic whores, extracting every drop of bliss, as if they sucked an orange of its juice . . .'* Stop me if you've heard enough."

"I've heard enough."

But Dr. Latham doesn't stop. Another photo, then another. "Jasmine Dixon, whose stomach was slashed open in a way reminiscent of the poem 'A Carcass.' Imani Anderson, whose head had been brutally shaved, like a poem in which Baudelaire compares his mistress's locks to *'the black ocean of burning Africa.'* Precious Coleman, stabbed through the spleen. Annie Washington, ditto—Baudelaire wrote several poems with the title, 'Spleen.' And these are just the victims we *found,* remember." She clicks her remote, and the screen goes mercifully dark. "Then, after Patrick's marriage to Stella four years ago, the murders stop."

"Why would that be?" I ask, as much to distract myself from what I've just seen as anything else.

"Perhaps he was trying to be good. Perhaps he was in *love.* Or perhaps he just got better at hiding the corpses. Either way, the *absence* of killings, coinciding with a major event in Fogler's life, is one more slender thread tying him to the series." She leans forward, her eyes bright with fervor.

"This is about much more than catching Stella Fogler's killer, Claire. This is about nailing a *sociopath*. That's why I say it's dangerous."

"What will I have to do, exactly?"

"I don't know—not exactly. I can only tell you who you have to *be*."

"An improvisation." I feel my pulse quicken.

"Yes—except that in *this* play, the dead bodies won't get up and take a bow when it's over. Please understand, Claire: You're going to have to trust me more than you've trusted any director or acting coach you've ever worked with. Frankly, I still have serious reservations about going ahead."

"But this might still all be coincidence. Patrick *might* be innocent." I'm still struggling to reconcile Dr. Latham's terrible pictures with the amused, intelligent academic I met in that bar.

"Yes. In fact, we have to approach the operation at all times as if he is. It's the only way we'll stay objective." She looks at me steadily. "But let me tell you this. I've been working on these killings for over six years—long before Stella's murder. And for most of that time I've been convinced that Patrick Fogler is by far the most credible suspect."

20

After a sleepless night of terrors and doubts, I'm back in Dr. Latham's office. I sit at her desk, working through more papers. She stands over me, watching.

Consent forms. Dozens of them.

Personal injury disclaimers. Surveillance permissions. Confidentiality agreements. Privacy waivers. And forms about the forms. Forms that say I understood what I was doing when I signed those other forms. Forms that say I gave my agreement freely and in the almost certain knowledge that working undercover could screw up my life, my career, and my mental health.

I sign them quickly, barely reading them, initialing each page and dating where requested.

"Welcome to boot camp, soldier. Now your ass is mine," Dr. Latham growls.

It's the worst Denzel Washington impression I've ever heard, but effective. I don't manage a smile.

. . .

Training continues in another conference room, deep in the bowels of the building.

"Let's take a look at some monsters," Dr. Latham says calmly. She clicks a button on a remote and the house lights dim.

She paces back and forth as she speaks, obscuring the face now on the screen.

"This is Peter Kürten. Otherwise known as the Beast of Düsseldorf. His wife told the police psychologist their sex life had been completely normal. Kürten, on the other hand, told the shrink he'd fantasized about strangling his wife every single time they made love. She'd never had any idea what he was really thinking. These next slides are some of Kürten's victims, just as he left them."

When I can bear to look again, there's a different face up there.

"Béla Kiss, who preserved his victims in empty gas drums . . . Hans van Zon—like many serial killers, he was superficially charming, good-looking, and extremely charismatic. Among other victims, he killed his own girlfriend and had sex with her corpse. Again, she'd apparently never had any idea what was really going on inside his head."

On and on it goes, a sickening roll call of evil.

"I'm not telling you all this just to spook you, Claire," Dr. Latham says mildly. "As a result of studying these people, we know a lot about how a sociopath's mind works. We can look at the way he leaves a murder scene, for example, and make deductions about his personality, his intelligence, his relationships, even what kind of car he drives." She holds up a bulging folder. "This is everything we know about the man who murdered those prostitutes. I warn you, it doesn't make easy reading. But you need to study it carefully. Your life may depend on it."

"This is what they call a psychological profile?" I ask as I take it from her.

"That's part of it, yes. And there are more photographs, case histories, excerpts from textbooks . . . Our job is a bit like bomb disposal. Before you start pulling at the wires, you'd damn well better know which one leads to the explosive."

"*If* he's guilty."

She looks at me steadily. "We haven't told you how Stella Fogler died yet, have we?"

I shake my head. "But I remember the housekeeper who found her saying it was brutal."

"The police have been keeping the full details from the media, to weed out false confessions." Dr. Latham pauses. "And, frankly, because they didn't want to cause alarm."

She reaches for the copy of *Les Fleurs du Mal* and hands it to me. "Page eighty-two."

The poem on that page is titled "To One Who Is Too Cheerful."

"Aloud, if you don't mind. Just the last three verses."

Even though there's no need, I try to read it properly, doing justice to the rhythm. But as the meaning of what I'm reading sinks in, I can't keep it up. By the time I get to the end, my voice is dry and flat.

ME

How I should like, one quiet night,
When the hour for pleasure nears,
To creep like a thief
Toward the treasures of your flesh.

To strike and whip your joyous limbs
And bruise your yielding breasts;
To slice, quick and sudden, down your flank
A gaping, bloody wound,

And—dizzying sweetness!—
Through those new lips,
So bright and glistening,
Infuse my venom, oh my sister!

"It was a blow from a lamp that killed Stella," Dr. Latham says matter-of-factly. She flashes up more photographs. I recognize Stella's hotel suite. On the bed is a body. Bruises blossom up the bare legs. Then, abruptly, one of the photographs zooms in and there's Stella's face, surrounded by a dark halo of blood, soaking the sheet underneath. Instinctively, I recoil.

"The debris on the floor is consistent with some kind of struggle," Dr. Latham's saying. "That, along with the missing money, was enough to make the NYPD treat it as a robbery gone wrong, initially. But right from the start, there were certain details that didn't quite fit. The body was left covered by a sheet, for one thing. Robbers who have just killed someone don't do that—they get the hell out of there, as quickly as possible."

"Who does?" I say. "Do that, I mean? And why?"

Dr. Latham shrugs. "It could be a gesture of reverence. Respect, even. A final goodbye. Or it could just be someone who didn't like seeing Stella's lifeless eyes staring up at them reproachfully." She clicks the remote and the image changes to a close-up of Stella's leg, a bloody gash several inches long. "More significantly still, there was a deep cut on her right thigh, probably inflicted postmortem with a broken wineglass—just like the wound described in the poem, although of course the cops weren't aware of that at the time."

She clicks again. "In any case, it seemed unusual enough that they ordered swabs. It was fortunate they did, as it gave us the most important piece of evidence so far. Analysis revealed that the interior of the wound bore traces of nonoxynol-9, a lubricant found on common brands of condom." She pauses. "There was a condom machine in the men's bathroom at the bar where you met Patrick. You've told us, and your video confirmed, that Patrick asked the barman for change, just before you tried to pick him up."

Her words pour over me—macabre, horrific, sickening. I stare at the book in my hand. The poem, its poisonous words laid out as innocuously as the verse in some sappy greeting card. And then the photographs on the screen, the horrible implication in Dr. Latham's explanation. The terrible desecration Stella's killer perpetrated on her corpse.

It wasn't him. It couldn't have been. He wasn't like that, a voice inside my head insists. *I liked him. He was* nice, *for chrissake.*

Actors are trained to trust our instincts. Often, they're all we have. But then I realize the point of Dr. Latham's little lesson just now. *Like many serial killers, he was superficially charming . . .* With people like this, she's telling me, instincts may be wrong.

"But—why?" I manage to say. "Stella wasn't a prostitute like the others. Why kill her at all?"

"We don't know. Perhaps she'd found out about the other women. Perhaps he realized she was leaving him and he wasn't prepared to let that happen. Or perhaps he just couldn't contain himself any longer."

I think again of the words Stella spoke to me.

STELLA

I thought maybe I could get something on him.
Something to stop him coming after me . . .

If she suspected her husband was a killer, no wonder she'd been terrified. Had she even expected him to be violent with *me*? Was she half hoping that was what my hidden camera would capture? I thought I'd simply been testing her husband's fidelity, but was it a darker, more desperate game Stella Fogler was playing that night?

"The fact that Stella's death breaks the pattern makes her particularly interesting," Dr. Latham's saying. "Where the other killings bear the hallmarks of careful planning, this one seems hurried—spontaneous, even. That could be a sign of overconfidence. Or it could be an indication he was under pressure in some way." She clicks her remote, and the screen goes blank. "Either way, it's good news. It means he's starting to make mistakes."

21

Patrick Fogler knocks on the door of the Terrace Suite.

"Who is it?" Stella Fogler calls cautiously.

"Room service."

"I didn't order anything."

There's no reply. Impatiently, Stella goes to the door and pulls it open. "You have the wrong—"

But Patrick has already pushed his way in. "Hello, darling. Waiting for someone?"

"Patrick, please. This isn't what it seems—"

Fogler throws a bag onto the floor. It makes an ominous, heavy noise. He looks over at Dr. Latham. "Do I hit her now?"

"Probably. You'd want to establish control of the situation."

Frank Durban nods. Back in character, he empties the bag onto the floor. A tangled snake-coil of metal chains, handcuffs, and strips of cloth for gags tumbles out.

"I'd scream," I object.

"Not necessarily. However much people tell themselves they'd resist in these situations, the reality is that victims are often paralyzed by a combination of indecision and disbelief. Plus, if Patrick has hit you, you'll be in shock. He'll use that interval to get the restraints in place."

Frank mimes hitting me across the face, then twists me around and snaps a cuff onto my wrist. His hand on my arm is heavy, implacable. I feel the masculine strength of him and yelp.

"Sorry," he says, easing up.

"No cuffs," Dr. Latham says. "They'd have shown up on the autopsy. Let's run the scene again. Without the cuffs, this time."

At a nearby restaurant, we discuss sex murders over the dish of the day.

"Get this straight, Claire. Our killer isn't a sadomasochist in the modern sense of the word. But it's likely he chooses to hide among practitioners of BDSM, because he shares certain of their interests. Where they use bondage as a shortcut to sexual pleasure, he uses it as a shortcut to the things *he's* interested in: humiliation, degradation, control. The power of life and death over another human being."

The waiter comes over to top up our water. He smiles at me. Dr. Latham, oblivious, goes on talking.

"BDSM is very interesting, actually. Why is it suddenly becoming so mainstream? It used to be thought a fetish for being caned was a result of corporal punishment in childhood—*le vice anglais.* But strangely enough, it's the Spock generation, the ones who were never smacked as kids, who've grown up wanting to experiment with bondage and domination."

The waiter, fascinated, can't tear himself away.

"One possibility is that deviance is simply the flip side

of libertarianism. Once you get people thinking they have a right to pursue their own happiness at the expense of social norms, you end up with a small but growing number at the margins who don't see why they shouldn't indulge their darkest, most predatory instincts too. Our killer may actually see himself as some kind of romantic antihero. Rather than as a sick, twisted individual who needs to be stopped."

Afternoon session. Dr. Latham, Frank Durban, and I each stand in front of a whiteboard.

"Okay," Dr. Latham says. "I'm the killer. Frank, you take Fogler." She tosses a marker to Frank, who writes FO-GLER on his board, just as she's written KILLER on hers.

"What do I do?" I ask.

"Nothing, yet. But if we both write the same word—in other words, if there's an overlap—then you put it on your board too."

"First up," Frank says, "he's smart." He's writing HIGH IQ on his board.

"Same here," Dr. Latham says. "Claire, that's your first overlap."

"And interested in all that decadent crap."

Dr. Latham nods. "Here too."

Obediently, I write down HIGH IQ and BAUDELAIRE. Soon my board is covered in words, and Dr. Latham comes over to circle the ones that matter most.

"So this is the essence of your character," she's saying. "The weaknesses he'll be drawn to. NAÏVE, to appeal to his need for control. DAMAGED, to appeal to his predatory instincts. SECRETIVE, to arouse his curiosity . . ." Her pen squeaks across the shiny plastic.

"If he's such a controller, why would he risk getting involved with Claire?" Frank objects.

"Because he's lonely. He'll be all too aware he's crossed a threshold that separates him from other men. If I'm right, he'll welcome the opportunity to connect with someone who seems to share his predilections."

"As a playmate? Or a potential victim?"

"I'm not sure he sees a distinction," Dr. Latham says.

"I think he does," I say slowly.

They both look at me.

"That night in the bar, Patrick talked about how Baudelaire divided women into two types—the *Vénus Blanche* and the *Vénus Noire*," I say. "Apparently Baudelaire liked to tell the White Venus about the things he did with the Black Venus—almost as if he wanted her approval. And you said it's prostitutes our killer usually targets. Maybe what he really wants is someone to share all this with—all these terrible things he's done to other women. Someone he can be honest with."

Dr. Latham points the end of her marker at me.

"That's good," she says. "That's very good, Claire."

On my board, with a flourish, she writes down SOUL-MATE.

22

Welcome to Necropolis.com.

This is a members-only adult website for those whose fantasies include power exchange and domination. It contains material offensive to the vast majority. We do not apologize for what we are, but we do warn you not to enter if such content is not for you.

sign up, wait while the computer submits my form. Minutes later, there's a ping. My membership activation.

Earlier, Dr. Latham handed me a slip of paper. "Today's assignment is this website. Find out everything you can about the people who visit these places. Talk to them, Claire. See if you can figure out what makes them tick."

"Won't they want to talk back?"

"Of course. You'll have to start thinking about your own backstory." Dr. Latham glanced at her watch. "I'll come by later, see how you're getting on."

I type my password into a login screen, and I'm in. The site's divided into different sections: "Photos," "Fantasies," "Forums." A message appears:

Since you're new, why not create a profile? Read what some other new members have said, or go directly to the forums and say hello.

What to put? I find myself wishing Dr. Latham were there to help. Then I realize the psychologist is deliberately letting me do this alone. Taking my first baby steps into the character we're creating.

>>Hi. My name is Claire. I'm twenty-five years old, British, and I live in NYC.

I take a deep breath.

>>I don't know if I would ever have the courage to explore my fantasies for real. But I would love to share experiences, dreams, and thoughts with other members.

Within moments I have three replies.

>>Hi Claire. Like the photo?

I watch, wincing, as a picture downloads. It's gross. But in truth it's so obviously fake that it's barely more threatening than a cartoon.

>>Not really.

The second reply is more detailed. The writer—who calls himself The Beast—wants me to know that he would like to strangle me. He wants to hear me beg for mercy. He wants to hear me beg for more. I type:

>>I seem to do a lot of talking for someone who's choking to death.

I type. The third reply says:

>>Leave her alone, you idiots. Claire, why don't you tell us what brought you to the site?

An hour later, I've made new friends: Victor, who sent that third reply, Carrie, The Brat, Beethoven, and The Marquis.

>>In BDSM, elegance is everything. There's no satisfaction in trussing up a submissive like a steer and booting them in the stomach. To the accomplished top, half the pleasure lies in selecting a posture or activity in which the slightest movement will produce exquisite suffering.

That's Beethoven. Carrie adds:

>>Absolutely. One of my favorite toys is a simple plank of wood, turned edge-on and raised just a couple of inches too high to comfortably stand astride. My bottom has to get on the very tips of her toes to straddle it.

I type:

>>"My bottom"? I'm sorry, I don't understand.

Victor responds:

>>She doesn't mean part of her anatomy, Claire.
  She's talking about her submissive partner.

This is a world as jargon-ridden as acting, I'm discovering. The acronyms alone are making my head spin. CP, CBT, YMMV. I've plucked up the courage to ask about some, though discovering that *YMMV* means "Your Mileage May Vary" hasn't actually clarified matters.

As for the conversations about neck snaps, Wartenberg wheels, top space, and pony play, I'm floundering.

Carrie says:

>>Your innocence is delicious, Claire. Sure you
  wouldn't like to meet up IRL?

Victor intervenes.

>>Leave her be, Carrie. Claire is with us this evening
  purely as a curious observer.

I find myself quite liking Victor. He seems to have appointed himself my guide to this strange new underworld.

>>Sort of, try before you buy?

That's Carrie, sneering at me. I type back:

>>More like, look before you leap. And actually, I'm
not entirely new to this. Someone I knew and
loved was into it in a big way—but I was very
young. Too young, I guess.

Even as I type it, I know this is good; that the "Claire"
Patrick will meet should have such a past.

>>Where'd he go, Claire?

>>Unfortunately, he died before he could show me
much.

A tragic past. Which makes me both attracted to this
world, but also on some level repelled by it.

Dr. Latham was right. Slowly, this is bringing who I
need to be into greater focus. No longer just a list of attri-
butes on a whiteboard, but a living, breathing person.

It's past midnight when I log off. My eyes are gritty and my
wrists ache from typing.

Going past Dr. Latham's open door, I hear her call my
name. She's at her desk, surrounded by paperwork.

"You're working late, Claire."

"You too."

"I have something for you." She holds up an envelope.
"We don't pay overtime. But we do pay. Your first week's
salary."

"Is it a check? Only I don't have a U.S. bank account—"

"We know. Don't worry, it's cash."

As I take the envelope I glance down at her screen. She quickly minimizes the document she's working on, but not before I've glimpsed its title.

Claire Wright. Psychological Profile.

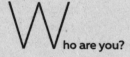

23

Who are you?

My name is Claire Wright.

Where do you come from?

I was born in Ferry Springs, near Boise. My father died in a car crash that killed four people when I was ten. He'd been driving. My mother never re-married. I guess I've always had a thing for older men, for interesting authority figures who can teach me about the world.

Go on.

I had the usual high school boyfriends, lost my vir-ginity when I was fifteen ... After that, sex came easily. I hung out with some pretty wild-seeming guys. But they were never really all that wild, un-

derneath. Then, at college, I had an affair with one of my teachers. He was married.

What was his name?

Mr. Fairbank.

You didn't use your lover's first name?

Sorry. Eliot. Eliot Fairbank. That was when I discovered I had a darker side, a part of me that wanted to be pushed to go further than I'd ever been before. We couldn't be together as much as we'd have liked, so he used to write me stuff . . . fantasies. He'd send them by email, usually, or leave them in my mailbox.

Good, Claire. What happened to him?

His wife found one of the emails on his computer. She took it straight to the dean.

And how did you feel about that?

Elated. I thought once he'd been fired and had left his wife, there'd be nothing to stop us getting together. But he couldn't handle it—knowing that everyone knew about him and me. He . . . He killed himself. But not before he'd sent me one last email.

Which said what?

He wanted me to join him. To do it together. A suicide pact.

But you didn't.

I was tempted. But I never really felt the shame he felt. I'd thought he was the strong one, the one who'd help me break out of those small-town boundaries ... Turns out it was me leading him astray, not the other way around.

And then?

I traveled. With hindsight, I suppose I was running away from a situation that had spun out of control.

You were running? Or you were searching?

A bit of both, I guess. No—probably more searching.

And what were you searching for?

I don't know. But I'm still curious ... I guess I need a guide.

Don't say that. That's too overt. He'll see your potential for himself. Now, one more time: Who are you?

24

"Today," Kathryn Latham says, "we're going to analyze a scene. A *crime* scene, that is." She flashes yet more images onto a screen. "I'm going to walk you through one of the murders in detail."

"Why?" I ask.

"Why?" she echoes, surprised. "So you understand exactly what this man is capable of, of course."

"I don't want to know."

"It's called background briefing, Claire. It's called giving the agent the tools to do her job—"

I sigh. "I know my job. And it's called *acting*. That's *my* area of expertise. You need to stop thinking of me as an undercover agent and start thinking of me as a *character*. Don't you get this? How can it possibly help me to go on a date with this man if I'm constantly thinking how he might have stabbed some poor woman through the heart or whatever? My *character* needs to believe I'm out with a nice guy— someone I'm intrigued by, who I find attractive, who I could imagine having a relationship with."

Dr. Latham thinks. "*Do* you find Patrick attractive, Claire?"

"Yes," I say after a brief pause. "I do."

"Well, then. I would say no great acting skill is required." Dr. Latham returns to her grisly photographs. "This first image was—"

"I have to see the gray."

She turns back to me, an inquiring expression on her face.

"That's what Henry—the ex-cop I worked with—used to call it," I explain. "He told me, when you're undercover, you have to believe in whatever the people you're infiltrating believe in. Otherwise, they can sense it."

"Henry the ex-cop isn't running this operation. I am. And believe me, I *want* you jumpy. Because jumpy means *safe.*"

"Then it won't work." I hesitate, then say in a rush, "Look, for all you say you're objective about this, you're clearly already convinced Patrick's a killer. How is that even *ethical*? You're like some director who announces on the first day of rehearsal that such-and-such is the real villain, or the play is actually all about totalitarianism. It's bad practice—it makes everything one-dimensional. I can't work that way. I need to believe in who *I* am, and to do that I need to believe in who *he* is. And if that means telling you to shut up sometimes . . . Well, too bad."

I stop, partly because I've said my piece and partly because I have a strange sensation that, all through this little outburst, Dr. Latham wasn't really listening to me. She was *studying* me. Like a casting director, giving me marks out of ten.

"Okay." She nods. "We'll do this your way. See the gray,

Claire, if you think it helps. No more murder stuff." Her voice hardens. "But in every other respect, I'm in charge. Got that?"

She clicks the remote and the screen goes black.

"Thank you," I say, a little surprised.

I can't help remembering that other thing Henry the ex-cop used to say. *Some guys, the gray takes hold of them, and they can't make it let go.*

25

Along with everything else, I'm learning about Baudelaire.

The *Vénus Blanche* and *Vénus Noire* have names now: Apollonie Sabatier and Jeanne Duval. The one pale-skinned, graceful, and so regal her admirers nicknamed her "La Presidente"; the other a half-Creole dancer who prostituted herself when the poet was too poor to provide for the two of them. Apollonie's salon was at the center of nineteenth-century Parisian intellectual life: She numbered Balzac, Flaubert, and Victor Hugo among her admirers. But it was Jeanne to whom Baudelaire returned, year after year. He infected her with syphilis. She got him addicted to opium. Two damaged characters, yoked together by poverty and obsession.

"Baudelaire sent the poems to Apollonie Sabatier over a number of years, anonymously," Dr. Latham says. "When *Les Fleurs du Mal* was finally published, under his own name, Apollonie obviously discovered who had written them. But there was a twist. The book was seized by the authorities. Thirteen of the poems, including six he had written about

her, were censored, and Baudelaire was put on trial for obscenity. Baudelaire went to Apollonie and asked if she'd use
her connections to help him. If she did, she was unsuccessful—
most of the banned poems remained banned—but in the
aftermath of the trial Baudelaire finally got to sleep with his
White Venus. No one knows exactly what happened that
night. The only clue is a letter of rejection *he* sent *her* a few
days later, saying he had a horror of passion, because he
knew all too well the abominations into which it could
tempt him."

"You think Patrick might be the same? That he'll be
suspicious of intimacy, because it might lead him to reveal
himself?"

"I'm sure of it. You need to show him you're not put off
by the darkness you sense in him. That, on the contrary,
you're intrigued by it. That you can match him, horror for
horror."

"How do I do that?"

She hesitates, then indicates the book where it lies between us.

"The poems. Patrick clearly responded to something in
them, speaking to him across the centuries. So now they
speak to you too. The poems are your way in, Claire."

She's had my hospital records sent over from the UK.

"You weren't trying particularly hard," she says dismissively, glancing through the faxed pages. "Three relatively
shallow lateral incisions in the left cubital fossa. It probably
looked dramatic. But it would have taken you hours to bleed
out. A classic cry for help by a confused hormonal teenager."

"It felt rather more than that at the time."

"I'm sure it did." She looks up at me, her eyes shrewd. "Use that, Claire. Not the self-harm, of course, but the intensity that led to it. He has to sense the instability behind the pretty face. The darkness. He has to know you're an outsider. Just as he is."

Frank comes to the apartment building to pick me up, as he does most mornings now. I go down to meet him, but he stops me at the lobby.

"You need to pack a bag, Claire. You won't be coming back here after today."

"Where am I going?"

"Kathryn wants you somewhere more consistent with your backstory. We've had a decorator work on something."

"A decorator? I'm going up in the world."

I wake Jess, raiding her closet for emergency supplies. Frank's drummed into me the need for absolute secrecy, so all she knows is that I'm doing something for the police. I've given her the money from Kathryn and told her not to try to contact me, or to approach me if she sees me in the street.

"Look after yourself," she says anxiously. "Don't let these people freak you out."

"I won't." Flicking through her underwear, I see her gun, gleaming amid the lace and cotton. Just for a moment, I'm tempted to ask if I can take it.

But of course I can't. And anyway, I'll have Frank and his team. They'll always be close to me, listening in.

"Break a leg," Jess says, jumping out of bed and enfolding me in a hug. I hug her back, suddenly unwilling to let go.

. . .

Frank insists on carrying my bag to the car. We go north, to East Harlem. Cheap enough that someone like me could afford to live there, but only a short distance from Patrick's workplace, Columbia University.

We pull up in front of a crumbling 1960s development. Parts of this area have been gentrified recently, Frank tells me.

Not this part.

Inside, the apartment is a shithole. Black candles line the walls, beneath mounted animal skulls and ripped heavy-metal posters. A battered bass guitar leans in one corner. The room stinks of stale cannabis smoke.

"For Christ's sake," I say, looking around. *"Really?"*

"It cost a lot of money to make the place look this bad," Frank says mildly. He picks up a skull on which a candle has been mounted. "Perhaps she did go a little over the top."

I've just spotted a glass tank in one corner. Something silver-gray slithers against the glass. "Is that a *snake?*"

Frank nods. "Apparently, that is the kind of thing the kind of person you are would have."

I sigh, reach for my bag.

"And just so you know, Claire. The whole place is wired for video. We'll only turn the system on when we have to. But we'll be testing it sometimes. You'll have privacy in the bathroom. Everywhere else, bear in mind you could be on camera."

"Where will *you* be?"

"In the apartment directly below."

"Won't Mrs. Durban mind that you aren't at home?"

"There's no Mrs. Durban," he says gruffly. "Leastways, there is, but she's living with some guy who makes artisanal wedding cakes now."

"I'm sorry to hear that, Frank. Was it—"

"And this is your wire," he continues, talking over me as he hands me an ugly necklace with a large perforated pendant. "Wear it whenever you're not in the apartment. It's a geolocator, too, so we can track you."

"Help me, will you?" I say meekly, turning around for him to fasten it.

I can hear his breathing, the hoarseness of a big man's lungs, as his fingers struggle with the tiny clasp. When it's done he steps back. "And you should choose a safe word. Something you wouldn't ordinarily say."

"How about . . . Constantinople?"

"Why that?"

I shrug. "It was somewhere I always dreamed of running away to as a kid. I thought it sounded exotic."

He nods. "Constantinople . . . Okay. But don't use it unless you're certain. The moment you say that word, we bust in and take him down. There's no going back after that."

The necklace feels heavy against my chest. Suddenly I feel scared. *I'm just an actress. I wanted to stand on a stage and have people applaud. How did I get into this?*

But then I think of the green card waiting for me at the end of it. *It's only a job. A job with different rules to what you usually do, sure. But the same skills, the same process.*

"Try not to worry." Frank says it quietly, as if he's read my mind. "And try not to think about the bad stuff too much. Remember, we'll be close by. Our number one priority is that you're safe."

·   ·   ·

And lastly, the finishing touch.

"This will really help?" Frank asks as the stylist's scissors flash in front of my eyes. "Making her look more like his wife?"

"I don't know, Frank," Kathryn says. "No one does. Hardly anyone's done an operation like this."

"Whether it helps Patrick isn't the point," I say as the clumps of hair tumble around me. "This is what we do, Frank. This is how we prepare."

I stare at the woman in the mirror. And I feel excitement gripping my guts, the terror and euphoria of a performance that's about to begin.

Tomorrow. I'm approaching Patrick tomorrow. Kathryn's decided I'm ready.

Showtime.

26

INT. THE APARTMENT KITCHEN—NIGHT

t's past midnight. I sit at the kitchen counter, drinking.
Half the bottle is already gone. I'm wearing a loose top,
my legs bare.

I run my fingers through my new, shorter haircut. It
feels different, like I'm already someone else. But maybe
that's the alcohol.

A little unsteadily, I go and kneel in front of one of the
tiny cameras.

ME

I didn't take your advice, Frank. I started to
think about it. And now I'm getting scared.

INT. APARTMENT BELOW—CONTINUOUS

Frank's watching me on a monitor. I know he is.

                                ME

          But all I have to do is say my magic word and
          you'll come running. That's right, isn't it? De-
          tective Frank to the rescue.

I get up. My head's out of shot now. Only my bare legs remain in the frame.

                                ME

          I know you're there, Frank. Watching me.
          Thanks for the *Only when I have to* speech but . . .
          I know what men are like, remember?

My top drops onto the floor.

                                ME

          I'm going to bed now, Frank. You can watch
          over me if you want. My knight in shining
          armor. I'd quite like that, actually.

Turning my back to the camera, I walk away. Downstairs,
Frank exhales slowly.

27

INT. COLUMBIA UNIVERSITY LECTURE ROOM—
DAY

PATRICK FOGLER

We cannot hope to understand Baudelaire if we try to judge his attitudes, and particularly his attitudes to women, by the standards of the present. *"Moi, je dis: la volupté unique et suprême de l'amour gît dans la certitude de faire le mal"*—"For me, the unique and supreme pleasure of sex lies in the possibility of doing *evil.*" For Baudelaire, women are not simply individuals. They are idealized representatives of their gender; symbols, of both perfection made flesh, and the impossibility, in this corrupt world, of perfection proving to be anything more than a momentary illusion.

We debated a bunch of different ways to approach him. But in the end Kathryn decided to keep it simple. His weekly lectures. The NYPD has a whole department dedicated to setting up fake identities. The ID card they've given me has my name and photo on, but now I'm a student at Columbia.

I sit at the back, not taking notes, my whole body craned forward. Spellbound.

PATRICK

This conflict was apparent in Baudelaire's life, as well as his poetry. You may remember the famous letter of rejection he sent to the *Vénus Blanche,* in which he said—

For the first time since he began speaking, twenty minutes ago, he consults his notes.

PATRICK

"You see, my dear, a few days ago you were a goddess: so noble, so inviolable. And now you are a woman . . . I have a horror of passion, because I know too well the abominations into which it can tempt me."

I'm not the only person who's enthralled, I realize. Every student in the room is riveted.

PATRICK

For Baudelaire, sex is not a physical itch. It's a metaphysical yearning. Not some mindless aerobic exercise, but a connection, however fleeting, with the terrible dark mysteries of the universe. Like all mystics, he is of course doomed to disappointment. The achievement— the heroism—lies in the attempt. Questions?

A student near the front raises her hand, and he nods at
her.

PATRICK

Megan.

MEGAN

You're saying he treats women as sexual objects,
to be manipulated and despised. By putting
him on the syllabus, aren't you giving this guy
a platform for misogyny?

He deals with her point courteously and methodically—
that it is not only those we approve of we should study, but
those we disagree with too; that for all his personal faults,
Baudelaire was an innovator who brought a new dimension
to the arts. T. S. Eliot, for example, cited him as one of his
greatest influences, and even incorporated fragments of *Les
Fleurs du Mal* into *The Waste Land.*

PATRICK

Without *Les Fleurs du Mal* there would have
been no Decadence, without Decadence, no
Modernism, and without Modernism, no us.
We study Baudelaire not because of his morals,
but because of his genius. Are there any more
questions?

There aren't. The students close their laptops and clatter
out, joking with one another. Patrick sorts his notes together.

    Hesitantly, one of the students approaches him.

ME

Professor Fogler?

I'm using the same midwestern accent I used last time we met. I hope.

If he recognizes me, he doesn't show it. His expression is one of professional politeness. But again I'm startled by the amusement deep in his mint-green eyes.

PATRICK

Yes?

ME

I just wanted to say, thank you so much.

I show him his copy of *Les Fleurs du Mal*.

ME

You won't remember, but you loaned me this.
I started reading it . . . and I got so intrigued,
I decided to take your class.

PATRICK

Intrigued about Baudelaire?

He pronounces the name with the faintest hint of an accent.
Bod'lair.

ME

Partly . . . and partly about our conversation.
What you said.

"Be direct," Kathryn had told me. "He'll appreciate that. He's not looking for an ordinary woman. You have to stand out."

PATRICK

I do recall you, as it happens. But not everything we talked about. I was a little distracted around that time.

"So we tackle the issue of Stella's death up front. You saw it on the news. It doesn't bother you. Maybe it even excites you a little."

ME

I know. It was in all the papers. And I saw you on TV.

PATRICK

Celebrity of a kind, I suppose.

ME

I keep thinking about what you told me—how Baudelaire would send those poems to his White Venus. I wonder if he thought they'd shock her. Or whether he guessed that at some level she'd welcome the intimacy he was offering—being allowed, little by little, into his darkest fantasies.

"He'll be bored and irritated by sympathizers and grief junkies. If he did kill Stella, he wants a different adventure now. Something to celebrate his newfound freedom."

> PATRICK
>
> "What the White Venus knew." That would be an interesting subject for a dissertation, actually. One that probably couldn't be written by a man, though.

> ME
>
> Perhaps *I* should write it.

> PATRICK
>
> Why not? Anyway, it was nice talking to you.

Inside, I'm shaking. The whole operation depends on the next few seconds. And a proposal that, last time I tried it, led to me getting rebuffed.

But he had a wife then. And I am someone else.

> ME
>
> Could we talk about it some more? Over a coffee, maybe?

He hesitates, glances at the door. Then—

> PATRICK
>
> All right. But not here. Before it was the Maison Française this building was an asylum for wealthy lunatics, and sometimes I think it still is. Let's go somewhere off-campus.

INT. NEARBY SURVEILLANCE VAN—DAY

Frank and Kathryn are listening through headphones.

FRANK

It's going to work. It's really going to work.

KATHRYN LATHAM

We'll see.

INT. NEW YORK BASEMENT BAR—DAY

It's a warm, sunny evening, but he takes me to a dimly lit basement bar on Amsterdam Avenue. Candles in glass jars flicker on the tables. We're the only people down here. Does he not want to be seen with me, perhaps? Is he covering his tracks, trying to make sure no one connects the two of us, later?

I push the thought out of my head. I'm my character now; that other, more confident, more impulsive Claire, not the terrified acting student who sat through Kathryn's grisly presentations.

We sit in a quiet corner, talking.

ME

. . . that desire to push the limits, to go beyond the everyday hypocrisy and complacency of the average bourgeois. Sure, people pretend to be shocked by what he wrote. But really, they're just scared—scared by their own conventionality.

"Naïve, to appeal to his sense of control. Damaged, to appeal to his predatory instincts . . ." But something else as well, something all my own: a passionate, intellectual fervor, an almost adolescent excitement with ideas that says: *I fall in love with brains, not bodies.* Your *brain? Why not?*

PATRICK

A lot of people say things like that. They don't
really mean them.

ME

I'm not most people.

INT. NEARBY SURVEILLANCE VAN—CONTINUOUS

Kathryn nods. Not bad.

INT. BASEMENT BAR—LATER

PATRICK

. . . People think Baudelaire wrote about decadence. Really, he wrote about *trust*.

ME

How so?

PATRICK

Trusting another human being with the very
worst things inside your head—there's no leap
in the dark more terrifying.

ME

I like being terrified.

Patrick smiles, as if at a child's presumption. Undeterred, I
hold his gaze. And something gives—

PATRICK

Let's see. Give me your hand.

"Some things we can predict, even plan for. But mostly it will just be you and him, playing whatever games he chooses to play."

Taking my hand, Patrick places it on the glass jar with the candle in, so my palm is directly over the flame.

PATRICK

One of my students showed me this game. Whatever happens, you mustn't take your hand away.

ME

It'll burn me.

Already I can feel the flame gnawing at my skin.

PATRICK

No—the flame will die from lack of oxygen before it can cause any damage. I promise.

He puts his hand over mine, pressing down lightly—not forcing me, just feeling the trembling of my own hand as I try to leave it in position, even though every instinct and nerve ending is screaming at me to pull away.

PATRICK

It's not easy, trusting someone, is it?

I have played trust games many, many times before—they're a staple of actors' warm-ups. But none like this. I stare at the flame. It's a long, jagged fingernail, a talon jabbing at my hand. The pain turns from mere discomfort into something that makes me want to throw my head back and howl, a circle of needles burrowing deep into my skin, a mounting crescendo of agony. My eyes water. I can feel my flesh liquefying, bubbling, like crackling on a roast—

Abruptly, the flame gutters. An instant later, it goes out.

PATRICK
(surprised)
You trusted me. Thank you.

I snatch my hand back. There's a red disk, like a hickey, across my palm. But no blisters.

I put it to my mouth and suck the sting away. The pain was mostly in my head, I realize.

ME
I hardly know you.

PATRICK
That's what makes it interesting, isn't it? Where do you live?

ME
East Harlem.

PATRICK
Shall we go there?

                 ME

What for?

               PATRICK

To fuck, of course. Isn't that what this is about?

                 ME

If you like.

INT. NEARBY SURVEILLANCE VAN—CONTINUOUS

Frank turns to Kathryn, alarmed.

                FRANK

We haven't planned for this. What if it gets physical?

            KATHRYN LATHAM
                 (calmly)

It's already physical.

                FRANK

Jesus!

He fiddles with the controls.

INT. BASEMENT BAR—CONTINUOUS

                 ME

We could have—what did you call it earlier?— mindless aerobic sex, and then forget we ever met each other. Or . . .

                    PATRICK

    Or?

                    ME

We could keep talking.

Patrick smiles.

                    PATRICK

    Very well. Let's talk.

    INT. NEARBY SURVEILLANCE VAN—CONTINUOUS

Frank sighs with relief. Kathryn just shrugs and turns her
attention back to her notepad.

        INT. BASEMENT BAR—LATER

Patrick brings over two more glasses of wine.

                    PATRICK

    Do you always pick up your professors?

                    ME

    No. Well, one time, I guess. But that ended
    badly.

                    PATRICK

    Oh?

                    ME

The whole relationship was pretty extreme.

PATRICK

Define *extreme.*

ME

You know. The usual stuff.

PATRICK

I really don't . . . Tell me.

ME

The usual stuff people mean when they use the word *kinky.*

PATRICK

You? Kinky?

ME

Why not?

PATRICK

You don't seem the type.

ME

Maybe I'm not a type.

PATRICK

Now I'm intrigued.

"He'll be on the lookout for someone like you, and his eagerness may make him take risks. In fact, the risk might even be part of the thrill for him. This is something you'll appreciate, Claire—at some level, he's a performer. All sex killers are. That's why they create *elaborate rituals around their murders, or pose the bodies for those who'll find them. What they really crave is an audience."*

INT. BASEMENT BAR—LATER

ME
. . . He didn't really want to hurt me, I think. He just wanted to see how far I was prepared to—

PATRICK
Trust him?

ME
You keep using that word.

PATRICK
Some people think I murdered my wife, Claire. Anyone who gets close to me is going to have to live in the shadow of that. So yes, trust is very important to me.

ME
Did you murder her?

INT. NEARBY SURVEILLANCE VAN—CONTINUOUS

Frank cranes forward intently. Kathryn barely looks up— she knows it won't be this easy.

INT. BASEMENT BAR—CONTINUOUS

PATRICK

Of course not.

ME

Did you *love* her?

PATRICK

Very much. But, unfortunately, not in a way she
always recognized as love. And, after a time, the
fact that I loved her so unconditionally became
part of the problem. It can be hard to be adored.

ME

She was your *Vénus Blanche*.

PATRICK

I suppose she was.

For a moment I think he's going to say more. Then:

PATRICK

We should probably call it a night.

EXT. AMSTERDAM AVE, NY—DUSK

PATRICK

Thank you. I enjoyed this evening.

ME

You sound like you didn't expect to.

PATRICK

There are very few people whose company I expect to enjoy. And even fewer I actually do.

As he walks away I call after him.

ME

I *will* see you again, won't I?

PATRICK

You've still got the book, haven't you? Good night, Claire.

Back at the apartment, Kathryn's jubilant.

"It's a good start. He's opened the door to you—only a crack, but frankly it's more than I'd dared hope for." She paces up and down, full of nervous energy. She must have been more tense about this evening than I'd realized.

For my part, I slump in a chair, exhausted. I was too focused to be frightened at the time, but now that the adrenaline's wearing off I'm wrung out. I feel like I've just played round after round of mental tennis.

And there's something else, too: a realization that Patrick Fogler is going to be a far more challenging proposition than any of the men I flirted with in hotel bars.

Frank comes and squats next to me, examining my hand.

"It'll be all right tomorrow. Maybe just a mark. Jesus." He gives my fingers a gentle squeeze as he stands up. "Well done," he says quietly.

"If he contacts you now, don't reply," Kathryn's saying. "We need to think very carefully about how we play him. We'll probably go quiet for a while, keep him guessing—"

"Play mind games, you mean?" I say. "Is that really a good idea?"

She gives me a distracted look, as if she's only just remembered I'm here. "It's going well, Claire. You should be proud of yourself."

"Proud!"

"Yes. Why not?"

I shrug. "A young professor, recently widowed, makes a halfhearted attempt to screw a student who's made it clear she has a crush on him. If that's a crime, I bet every man on the teaching faculty would be in jail. Really, I got nowhere."

"Nothing he said or did tonight is incompatible with my profile of the killer," Kathryn says sharply. "Frank, show her the AV."

Frank clicks the remote at my TV screen, then navigates through some options. A grainy image appears. Patrick and me, sitting in the shadows of the basement bar.

"We managed to get a camera on you from the stairwell," he says. "Nineteen oh five, you went to the bathroom. See what Fogler does next."

I watch as, in the film, I exit the frame. Patrick waits a moment, then reaches across the table for my bag and searches it, taking out my things item by item. He scrutinizes my ID and examines the bag's lining with his fingers. Finally, his expression unchanged, he puts everything back. As he replaces my perfume, he pauses and sniffs the nozzle.

"He probably wanted to be sure I wasn't a reporter," I say. "He told me he had quite a few approaching him, trying to get stories, after Stella died."

"Possibly," Kathryn says. "Either way, it's good we went

to the lengths we did." My student ID is watermarked with Columbia's crown logo and a real card number.

"Right now, he's like a predator circling a lone antelope before deciding whether or not it's worth the chase," she adds. "Don't let your guard down, Claire. Not even for a second."

29

A nd then . . . nothing.

For two weeks we wait. And for two weeks, Patrick Fogler doesn't get in touch.

"He figured out it's a trap," Frank worries.

"He didn't figure it out," I say. "I'd have known."

"So why haven't we heard from him?"

"Maybe he had second thoughts. Or maybe he just wasn't that into me."

Frank looks at Kathryn. "Should we change the plan? Have Claire approach him again?"

She shakes her head. "We wait. Let's see what happens."

"It can't hurt for me to go back to his class, though," I argue. "After all, I'm fascinated by Baudelaire."

"Absolutely not. You're playing hard to get, remember? Stick to what we agreed."

She does let me continue with my acting classes. It'll keep me occupied, she concedes.

At the next session, Paul introduces us to mask work.

The masks are Japanese, their painted features saved from caricature by a hint of cruelty. I get the Waif: an innocent, a lost child with a smile that, though it never changes, seems somehow both eager and coquettish in turn.

Paul talks about them as if the masks, not us actors, are the real people. When one of the students, having put on the mask of an old man, comes up behind another student and pokes her with a stick, Paul says: "He's always doing that, the old rogue."

Rather than act a scene together—there are no eyeholes, and we'd have been bumping into one another—he has us stand in a line, facing him. The story is about a landlord who comes to the rice fields and rapes a woman whose family can't pay the rent. The Rich Man knocks at an imaginary door: Farther down the line, the Waif opens it. When the Rich Man attacks me, he has to mime his aggression, and me the Waif's fear, six feet apart, without either of us being able to see what the other's doing.

Suddenly I realize that, underneath the mask, I'm crying. I don't know why—it's as quick and inexplicable as a nosebleed. For me, used to being able to turn my tears on and off at will, the lack of control is as unsettling as the crying itself.

When the scene's over I sit down and pull the mask off, gasping. Paul comes over, squatting so his eyes are at my level. "You okay, Claire?"

I nod, not trusting myself to speak.

"It's like that sometimes," he says quietly. "Sometimes, when you wear a mask too long, you find it sticks to the skin."

He says it so seriously that I just nod again, unable to

tell him that the real mask, the real stage, is somewhere a long way from this room.

By Thursday, I can't stand the waiting any longer.

I take the subway uptown, to the 116th Street station. I love this part of New York—a world away from the hustle and razzmatazz of Times Square. The green spaces and classical buildings remind me of England. Not to mention a dozen great movies, from *Ghostbusters* to *Still Alice.*

I walk with the other students up the steps of the Low Library, then veer right to Buell Hall. Once inside, I scan the noticeboard. *Professor Patrick J. Fogler: The Aesthetics of Decadence from De Sade to Baudelaire* is on the schedule for noon. Next to it is a handwritten note. *Today this class will be taught by Dr. Anne Ramane.*

"Excuse me," I ask a woman who looks like she works here. "Do you know why Professor Fogler isn't teaching today?"

"Sure. He's attending a conference in Europe," the woman says.

"Oh. Thanks."

So Patrick's away. No big deal.

But how come, I think, Detective Durban and Dr. Latham didn't know that?

"An oversight," Kathryn says dismissively. "We'd have tracked him down soon enough. The bigger question, Claire, is why you went against my explicit instructions not to attend the lecture."

"It's a good thing *someone's* being proactive around here," I point out.

"We have to be able to trust you—"

"Strange how right now you sound exactly like him," I interrupt. "Like your *sociopath*. And trust has to work both ways. *I* have to know I can rely on you not to screw up."

Kathryn frowns at my tone.

"Claire does have a point," Frank says. "After all, we're asking her to use her initiative in her interactions with Patrick."

"Someone has to be in charge here," Kathryn says coldly. "And it certainly can't be Claire. She seems to have forgotten how dangerous this is."

Or perhaps I'm just less obsessive than you are, I think. *Less of a control freak.*

Because I'm already starting to wonder: If Kathryn could make a mistake about something as simple as Patrick Fogler's schedule, what else might she be wrong about?

30

Patrick's absence is actually an opportunity, Kathryn decides.

"While he's at a distance from you, he might be induced to reveal what he fantasizes about."

"Why would he do that?"

"First, because if he *is* our killer, fantasies will be extremely important to him—they're all he has to sustain him between killings. Second, because he'll enjoy the process of sounding you out—playing games with you, teasing you, choosing what he reveals and when. As you gradually become more intimate, the detail of his fantasies will—if I'm right—increasingly come to resemble the actual details of the murders. Which is to say, the imagery of Baudelaire's poems. We'll drop him an email. Or rather, you will. Nothing too eager, mind."

To: Patrick.Fogler@columbia.edu
From: strangegirl667@gmail.com
Our meeting

Hey Patrick,
Just to say, I missed you in class yesterday. Dr. Ramane was great but no substitute ... Plus she
didn't take me out for drinks afterward.
    Sorry if I overshared that evening. I think it was
just the adrenaline high from your trust game. So
look, it was nice to meet you, and maybe our paths
will cross again one day.
Best wishes,
Claire

"He won't reply," Frank predicts.

"He will if he's the killer," Kathryn says calmly. "If he's
the killer, he'll be drawn to her vulnerability the way a
shark's drawn to the scent of blood."

To: strangegirl667@gmail.com
From: Patrick.Fogler@columbia.edu
Re: Our meeting

Claire,
Nice to hear from you. Perhaps we can meet up
again sometime, when I'm back.
Patrick Fogler

To: Patrick.Fogler@columbia.edu
From: strangegirl667@gmail.com
Re: Our meeting

Really?
    To be honest I got the impression you weren't
that into me.
Claire x

To: strangegirl667@gmail.com
From: Patrick.Fogler@columbia.edu
Re: Our meeting

I don't know what gave you that idea. I'd have been
in touch sooner, but there didn't seem much point
with me being away.

To: Patrick.Fogler@columbia.edu
From: strangegirl667@gmail.com
Re: Our meeting

That's very conventional of you ... How would
Baudelaire have played it?
    I love to imagine myself as his Venus, receiving
all those extraordinary poems. I wonder whether he
knew she'd be turned on by the things he'd dared
to conjure up.
    I say imagine ... but in fact I was once in a sim-
ilar position myself, and I know what it's like, being
allowed inside someone's mind. An amazing feeling.
    I guess some people would call what that man

wrote for me pornography. But to me they were as
beautiful, and as honest, as any poems.
x

A long wait, three days passing with no reply. Until,
without warning:

To: strangegirl667@gmail.com
From: Patrick.Fogler@columbia.edu
Re: Our meeting

In that case, perhaps the enclosed will keep you
amused in my absence.
     <<forclaire.doc>>

31

"It's all there." Excitement flickers on Frank's normally impassive face as he re-reads Fogler's fantasy for the third time. "Sweet Jesus, it's all there."

Dr. Latham doesn't answer. The only sound is her pen, tapping against her lips.

"It's just as you expected, isn't it," I say to her. "Everything you said he'd write about. Violence, pain, control . . ."

Frank reads aloud: "*The musky smell of your arousal fills the room like the sickly perfume of a rare flower, an orchid that releases its heavenly odors only as it starts to wither and decay . . .* This is some weird shit, Kathryn."

The tapping stops.

"He could have gone down to the bookstore and copied that out from any one of a dozen books in the adult fiction section," Kathryn says reluctantly. "It's mildly deviant, certainly. But I couldn't put my hand on my heart and say only a killer could have written it."

"He hasn't eliminated himself, though."

She shakes her head. "No."

"So what do we do now?"

Dr. Latham turns to me. "He's holding back. You need to show him you're more into this than he thinks. Write back. Give him something in the same vein, but stronger."

"You want *me* to write it? Couldn't you—?"

"Why do you think I got you to spend time on those websites? This needs to be in your voice."

Sitting at my laptop, I have to remind myself that I've done harder things than this, that I once went out into the New York streets and sold sweaters made of giraffe wool to commuters.

To: Patrick.Fogler@columbia.edu
From: strangegirl667@gmail.com
Re: Our meeting

Dear Patrick,
Thank you for the fantasy—I enjoyed it. But believe me, the things you describe are fairly tame for me. The things I like, sometimes I scare myself with how extreme they are—God, why am I telling a total stranger this? Sometimes I look at the things that turn me on—things that make me feel powerless and vulnerable and afraid—and wonder if there must be something wrong with me.

I'm telling you this because I think you might actually understand . . . but now I'm almost nervous of you writing anything else in case you get it

wrong. Perhaps it would be better to say goodbye
now, before this takes us any further.

I wrote something myself. Tell me if you like it.

Claire xx

<<forPatrick.doc>>

To: strangegirl667@gmail.com
From: Patrick.Fogler@columbia.edu
Re: Our meeting

What a remarkable person you are turning out to
be, Claire.

I enjoyed what you wrote for me, and I look forward to meeting up when I'm back. In the mean-
time, you may find the attached more to your taste.

<<forclaire2.doc>>

In his second fantasy, Patrick describes how he would
blindfold me and beat me with a belt.

In his third fantasy, which arrives just a few hours later,
he describes me lying on a bed of freshly laundered sheets
surrounded by candles, like a body laid out on an altar. "I
pick up two candles, one in each hand. They're fat and heavy,
like the candles in a church. The flames are spear-points,
white-hot, tipped with black smoke, the wicks surrounded
by brimming disks of clear, molten wax. I hold the first one
above you and tilt my hand. You flinch, but don't cry out.
The wax hardens on your skin, turning milky as it cools, like
a scar."

In his fourth fantasy, he describes me being surprised in
a hotel room by a cold, mysterious stranger, who ties me to
the bed before throttling me.

. . .

"This is good," Dr. Latham says, reading Patrick's latest over my shoulder. "We're getting a lot of material here."

"Like what, specifically?" Frank's frowning.

"The candles, the restraints . . . And setting it in a hotel room—that's a very significant overlap with Stella's killing."

"But nothing only the killer would know," Frank objects. "No knife, for that matter. And a lawyer would say maybe he chose a hotel room because that's where he was when he wrote it."

"Give him time, Frank. On the strength of this, I can already say that Patrick Fogler has a sexual predilection shared by only a small section of the population. Let the net close slowly. It'll be all the tighter when it does."

To: Patrick.Fogler@columbia.edu
From: strangegirl667@gmail.com
Re: Our meeting

Very nice, Patrick. But—I wonder—how much further can you go?

As for meeting again—well, let's see. I've been let down so many times before. And once . . . Once, as I told you, I wasn't let down, and that was even worse in the end.

Keep writing me, Patrick. Please.

Claire X

32

"Today," Kathryn says, "we're going to learn how to listen."

"What?"

"I said, today—" She stops. "Oh. Ha ha. Funny."

It's been ten days since Patrick went to Europe; five since his last email. We know he's back in Manhattan, but since asking him to keep writing, I've heard nothing. Kathryn's trying to keep me busy, but I sense her heart's not really in it, any more than mine is. We're all of us marking time, waiting for Patrick to get back in touch.

"What I'm going to show you now," Kathryn continues, "are some basic neurolinguistic techniques."

She puts up a chart. It's divided into two columns, WRONG and RIGHT.

"First, judgments. Try to refrain from making any. Saying *That's disgusting* or even *That's great* is less useful than a neutral response such as *I see,* or *Go on.* And remember that the most effective interrogator of all is silence." She stops. "You're fidgeting, Claire. Is something wrong?"

I groan. "We covered all this in week one of my acting class. Except we called it blocking and accepting."

She frowns at me. "Claire, my training lasted seven years. I hardly think a few extra days—"

"I hardly think a few extra days—" I mimic, so exactly that Kathryn flushes.

"That reminds me," she says frostily. "You must tell me when your periods are due. We may have to structure the operation around your less moody times."

Wow. Even by Kathryn's standards, that's bitchy. Not to mention clinical. I stare at her, incredulous.

"All right," she says, throwing up her hands. "Email Patrick. Ask him to meet you. We certainly can't go on like this."

33

My friend hasn't showed.

That's what you'd think if you saw me here, in this quiet West Village bar, trying to make my Virgin Mary last all evening. Just another student waiting on her date. A little more dressy than some of the other women here, maybe.

"Hello, Claire."

He startles me, approaching from the shadows, and I have to stifle the instinct to flinch. He bends down to kiss my cheek, and just for a moment, as his pale-green eyes brush mine, I'm certain he can see everything, knows everything: that he can sense the wires taped to my skin and the betrayal in my heart.

"What are you drinking?" he asks as he drops casually into the next seat. He signals to the bartender.

"Actually, we're not staying. We're going someplace else. Another bar."

He frowns. "So why didn't we meet there?"

"It's not the kind of place you can arrange to meet people. Shall we go?"

I don't explain any more until we're almost there. One of the last of its kind from the old days, Kathryn's told me, when places like Mineshaft and The Vault made New York City a byword for sexual exploration.

Eventually I stop. "This is it."

There's no sign, just a buzzer. We go down some steps to a small lobby that contains only a greeter, a lectern, and a curtained door. The greeter looks down her studded nose at me. Since I'm wearing a brand-new Prada jacket, bought with my second month's pay, that's faintly irritating.

When we've completed the membership formalities, signed a copy of the rules, and stepped through the door, I understand why she wasn't impressed. Prada doesn't count for much, in here.

In fact, anything made of fabric doesn't count for much in here. In here, the favored materials are leather, PVC, rubber, and Saran wrap. Oh, and skin. They like skin a lot. Particularly if it's pierced, written on, or tattooed.

My first thought, irrationally, is *How the hell do they ever get home, looking like that?*

A man walks past us. He's wearing leather trousers, nothing else, and holding a chain. The chain leads to a ring embedded in the nipple of a breathtakingly pretty girl. The word SLAVE is written across her breasts in marker pen.

Looking around, I see leather masks, harnesses, strange golf-ball gags. Another man is wearing a hood that covers his entire face, with just a tube to breathe through. Music pulses through the crowd, so deep and low I feel it in my solar plexus.

On a raised podium, two men are taking turns to paddle a woman who's strapped into a frame. A small knot of people have gathered to watch. The wall behind the frame is

covered with implements, neatly hung on pegs as in a join-
er's workshop: coils of ropes and leather restraints, handcuffs
and clamps, elaborate cat-o'-nine-tails and Charlie Chaplin
canes.

Patrick and I watch for a while. Eventually, at some pre-
arranged signal, the men stop. One of them makes the
woman kiss the paddle while the other unties her. People
drift away, some into the darkened side rooms.

"What do you want to do next?" I say to Patrick. I have
to yell over the music.

"Find somewhere that serves alcohol," he says. "Preferably a good Burgundy. And preferably somewhere we can
hear each other talk."

"So what did you think? Honestly?"

"Honestly?" Patrick studies me over the rim of his glass.
"I suppose I was a little surprised to find myself there. Then
intrigued. And finally, I had to stop myself from laughing."

"Laughing?" I repeat, puzzled.

He shrugs, smiling. "It's all so very *earnest,* isn't it? And,
at the same time, absurd. All those ridiculous rules about
permissions and safe words. The fact is, it's about as dangerous as a ride at Disney World."

"Oh."

"But I do appreciate the honesty with which you've
shared your desires with me, Claire," he adds. "Even if games
of submission and control aren't to my own taste, I can appreciate why others might like them."

"What do you mean, not to your own taste?" I say. "You
wrote those fantasies—"

He shakes his head. "I'm a translator of other people's

work—a copyist. I can slip into the style of Baudelaire, or
the style of Proust, or the style of drugstore porn for that
matter. It's all the same to me. In fact, half the pleasure is
assuming a new identity—getting inside the mind of another person. It doesn't mean that's who I really am."

"So you don't . . ." I frown. "You don't get off on S
and M?"

"Only in as much as it gives my partner pleasure. I have
no particular interest in it myself."

"Then why agree to write that stuff in the first place?"

He smiles. "Because *you* asked me to. And I very much
wanted to give you a gift you'd appreciate. Besides, I like to
know what makes people tick. I put it down to being an
orphan."

I stare at him. "You're an *orphan*?"

"Yes." He looks surprised by my reaction. "But I was
one of the lucky ones—I got on well with the family I
was placed with. Why?"

"I'm . . ." This is frying my brain. My character has a
dead parent, I recall, but only one. So I can't tell Patrick I
was fostered too.

"I lost my dad when I was ten," I mutter. "And I'm not
close to my mom. But I know it's not the same thing at all."

He nods. "Perhaps not. But I thought I could sense
something about you . . . a kind of toughness, mixed with
fragility. A detachment . . . It's hard to explain. But when
you feel it yourself, you learn to recognize it in others. People who are looking to love and be loved unconditionally,
but who find it hard to accept when we find it. Outsiders
trying to be insiders, searching for a substitute family . . .
And sometimes we think we've found it in a club or a
group. Maybe that's what drew you to the fetish scene,

Claire. Maybe you were simply looking for a different set of outcasts to belong to."

"Maybe," I say, but in my head I'm running that paragraph again. Replacing the words *fetish scene* with *actors*.

You got me, Patrick.

"There's a feeling you become used to, when you're orphaned," he adds. "It's like when you're swimming in the ocean at night, and you suddenly start to wonder what's underneath you. And you realize that if you don't keep moving, you'll drown . . . because there's nothing holding you up. Just darkness and deep water. You're alone, utterly alone. It's all of them, but just one of you."

I know. Patrick, I know.

We go on talking for what seems like hours. Which itself is pretty weird. Usually when I talk to men, they're hitting on me, or vice versa. Either way, conversation's wrapped up in thirty minutes, tops. Just chatting about stuff—poetry, New York, his trips to Europe—is something new for me.

And, despite all my attempts to keep a professional distance, I like him. He's clever and well-read, and though he clearly knows far more about literature and art than me, he's never patronizing. He seems genuinely interested in my opinions.

It takes an effort of will to remember to drop some of Kathryn's verbal lures into the conversation, the oblique references to my dark backstory that are supposedly going to draw him out.

They don't, of course. He doesn't respond to any of them and fairly soon I give up on them altogether.

.   .   .

When we leave the bar, he insists on sharing a cab and dropping me off outside my apartment. East Harlem's a rough area, he says.

He walks me to the door, and that's when he pulls me toward him and kisses me for the first time. I knew he was going to. And of course I have to kiss him back.

It's only a stage kiss, I tell myself. Just like you've done a hundred times before. It doesn't mean a thing. Your character enjoys the feel of his arms, the hard heft of his chest, the press of his lips, the knowledge that you're finally breaking through this man's layers of reserve and discovering that he likes you, just as you like him. Your character.

Not you.

34

"We're going to have to be more subtle," Kathryn says.

They arrived a few minutes after I got in. But the euphoria is noticeably absent this time.

"He's clearly going to be ultra-cautious," she adds. "Secrecy has become a way of life for him."

"Not so long ago, you said his loneliness would lead him to take risks," I object.

"This isn't an exact science, Claire."

"It doesn't seem to be much of a science at all," I mutter.

"We make a hypothesis, then we test the hypothesis," Kathryn says crisply. "If it doesn't stack up, we move on."

"But he still hasn't incriminated himself." For the first time I detect a note of frustration in Frank's voice.

"I always said he might *hide* among the BDSM community, but he was unlikely to be *part* of it. In a sense, that's been borne out by this latest development—"

"We can't go to a judge for a warrant on the basis that our suspect appears to be a regular guy," Frank says tersely. "We've got nothing."

"No," Kathryn admits. "So far, there's nothing."

That's because there's nothing to find.

The realization falls into my brain like a thunderbolt.

Patrick's innocent.

I don't say it out loud. Partly because I know Kathryn will tell me it isn't my place to make judgments like that. But also because while I keep it to myself, it's my secret, something I can hug like a comforter.

The way I'd like to hug Patrick.

I wonder what it will take to make Kathryn and Frank understand he's not their man. And what they'll do when that moment finally comes. Will they just disappear from his life and expect me to do the same?

I don't want that day to come, I realize. Not yet, anyway.

Or is there a chance that won't be how this plays out? Is there a possibility that one day Patrick and I could have . . . I hardly dare put the thought into words.

Could he and I have something together?

It seems almost impossible. But then, nothing about this crazy situation is following any normal logic.

Frank and Kathryn leave, still bickering. But I can't relax. The apartment feels claustrophobic. Staring around at the grunge and filth, I realize how tacky it is, how one-dimensional. Like the set of some terrible student production, the kind of over-the-top one-woman show that involves shouting at the audience.

This isn't me. And it isn't Patrick, either.

The snake, which seems to be nocturnal, writhes in a complicated knot-pattern against the wall of its tank. I have no idea if it's male or female, but lately I've found myself calling it Kathryn.

I need some air.

Seeing as how I'm dressed up anyway, I go to a club, just for the sheer physical release of stepping onto the dance floor and feeling my body taken over by music. There's a dealer by the fire exit who lets me have two pills for the price of one, since it's a weeknight.

By three, my body's tired but my brain's still buzzing. That's when I think of the Harley Bar, the one with the motorbikes hanging from the ceiling. And Brian, the Australian barman with the dishcloth tucked into his jeans, who gets off at three.

Sure enough, when I get there he's just closing up. It doesn't take much flirting before he asks me back to his place.

But for some reason, tonight the whole sex-with-a-new-person thing doesn't work its usual magic. Instead of making me feel dangerous and bold, tonight it just seems a bit pointless.

Because however much Brian tells me I'm beautiful or amazing or scary or crazy, the person I really want to hear those things from isn't there.

get back to the apartment just before noon. My eyes are gritty and my mouth feels like the stuff florists arrange flowers in. I walk in and stop dead, not sure what I'm seeing.

Overnight, the place has been transformed. The walls are a delicate cream. The animal skulls and thrift-shop props have vanished. Now there's Swedish furniture, West Elm sofas, bright Turkish kilims. The guitar and amplifier are gone; high-end Sonos speakers whisper classical music instead. In place of rock posters, prints in bleached wood frames line the walls. A glass coffee table bears a stack of art books about Georgia O'Keeffe and Toulouse-Lautrec.

And as if by some wave of a magician's wand, the snake has turned into a tortoiseshell cat, regarding me lazily from the sofa.

"She's called Augusta," Kathryn says, coming in from the other room to find me stroking its ears.

"Really?"

"What—you think the cat needs a cover name? Of course she's called Augusta. Where have you been?"

"I needed some downtime." I indicate the new décor. "What prompted all this?"

She looks at me, lips pursed. For a moment I think she's about to bawl me out, but she just says, "In the future, make sure you take the necklace, will you? We need to be able to check that you're all right."

"The microphone wouldn't have been appropriate last night, believe me. Not unless you wanted Detective Durban to have a heart attack."

She ignores that. "In answer to your question, I was thinking over something you said. About the *Vénus Noire* and the *Vénus Blanche*. Maybe you need to be more of a White Venus—the pure, elegant beauty he can fantasize about desecrating."

"Whoa," I say. "That's quite a character shift. I need to think that through—"

"Well, don't think too long. Patrick's got two tickets for the Booth tonight."

"For *Hedda Gabler?*" I say, surprised. It's a production I've been dying to see. Tickets are like hen's teeth.

She nods. "He's picking you up at seven—there's a message on the voicemail. Until then, try to get some rest. Frankly, Claire, you look terrible."

36

He likes my apartment, he says. It's just the sort of place he'd imagined me living in. Unpretentious, but with impeccable taste.

I excuse the faint odor of paint by saying I've just redecorated.

We get a cab to the theater, where we walk past the SOLD OUT signs and a queue for returns and I wonder how on earth he managed to get these tickets. But of course, he's wealthy. Stella came from old money. And since they weren't divorced when she died, Patrick inherited every cent.

It was one of the first things that made the police suspicious, Frank told me. Which is illogical when you think about it. It's hardly Patrick's fault his wife was rich. And what Kathryn suspects Patrick of has absolutely nothing to do with money.

Once again I can't help reflecting on Kathryn's obsession with Patrick. If this was a play, bringing him down would be her through line—Stanislavski's term for a character's overwhelming inner need, the thing that drives them to make tragic errors.

I just have to hope that, in this case, she realizes her error before it's too late.

Stay professional, I tell myself. *It's just acting. Just a part.*

But even as I think that, I realize it isn't true anymore. If it ever was.

Patrick loves the theater. That much is obvious even before we settle ourselves in our seats. He seems to come alive, drinking in our surroundings, the other theatergoers, the buzz of anticipation.

He's always been drawn to illusion, he says, the idea that one thing can represent another.

"My dream is that one day I'll write my own play about Baudelaire and the two Venuses," he tells me as we wait for the play to start. "It seems tailor-made for theater. Not a theater like this, of course—it would have to be somewhere experimental, somewhere prepared to deal with really provocative material."

"How would you do it?"

He thinks. "I'd probably structure it around Baudelaire's trial—when *Les Fleurs du Mal* was banned for obscenity. I love a good courtroom drama."

"Me too."

"Really?" He glances sideways at me. "Best courtroom movie?"

"Easy. And it's not *12 Angry Men,* even though it's directed by Sidney Lumet. It's—"

"The Verdict," he finishes approvingly. "Written by David Mamet."

I nod. "But my very favorite genre is film noir. Particu-

larly New York noir. There's one called *Laura* with Gene
Tierney in the title role—"

"I must have seen it a hundred times. Do you remember
the bit where—"

Waiting for the house lights to dim, talking about movies and plays we both love, it occurs to me that this evening
probably qualifies as one of my better dates. So long as I
don't think about the microphone and the listeners, of
course.

And I don't. Or at least, my character doesn't. My character's having the time of her life.

The first half of the play is even better than I'd hoped. I can
relate to Hedda, a woman who does all sorts of apparently
crazy shit just because she's bored with everyday life, gradually getting herself in deeper and deeper until she's spiraling
out of control. The performances are so good that, at the
interval, I don't even want to talk. I want to stay inside the
bubble of Ibsen's world until it's time for the second half.

Picking up on my mood, Patrick says quietly, "I'll get
us drinks. We don't need to chat."

Waiting for him to return, I hear a voice behind me say
poisonously, "Of course, all that overacting always goes
down well with *audiences*. They don't know any better, the
sweethearts. Oh, *hello*, Claire."

I try to slip away, but it's too late. An actor—Raoul
something. A friend of a friend of Jess's.

"Darling. Isn't it *dreadful*?" He offers his cheek for me to
kiss.

"I'm enjoying it," I say faintly. At that moment, Patrick
returns with two plastic containers of wine. He puts them

down and looks quizzically at Raoul and his friends, waiting to be introduced.

"Yes? Perhaps when you haven't actually worked for a while it gets harder to judge," Raoul sneers.

"This is Raoul," I say reluctantly to Patrick. "He recently played a singing rat in a musical."

"A singing squirrel, actually," Raoul says. His eyes narrow. "Really, Claire, what is that *extraordinary* accent? Have you gone native in the hope of getting work?"

"I've heard the second half is better," I say, to distract him.

But Raoul, once started, isn't going to give up. "Talking of accents, I saw that delicious piece of rough from the Harley Bar earlier. I gather congratulations are in order . . . ? *Jeez, what a time I had with Claire last night. If we'd fucked any harder I'd have ended up circumcised.*"

He gets Brian's Australian twang note-perfect. His friends laugh sycophantically. Patrick chuckles too.

He steps forward and clasps Raoul by both shoulders, as if he's congratulating him on the wittiness of his joke. Then, abruptly, he brings his head down on Raoul's nose. Raoul crumples like a marionette and falls to the floor. Behind us, a woman gasps in shock.

Raoul, on his knees, salaams gently to the carpet. Blood and mucus drip from his nose.

"Do you want to see the second half?" Patrick says calmly to me. "Or would you rather leave?"

37

"Not a pleasant fellow," he remarks when we're outside. There's a light summer drizzle, but Patrick seems not to notice.

"Actors can be so bitchy," I agree shakily.

We start walking west. "What did he mean, by the way?" Patrick asks, as he glances around to scour the traffic for a cab.

"Which bit?"

"About you not working."

"Oh—" I shrug. "I had this dumb idea I might try to become an actor. Raoul and his friends soon made me realize what a stupid ambition that was."

"I think it's an excellent idea. You need something to give your life direction. And you'd be good at it. You should check out the Theatre Program at Columbia. They do private coaching." A cab appears and Patrick stops it with a gesture. "East Harlem," he says to the driver, holding the door open for me.

"I can't afford coaching," I say once we're seated and the driver's pulling out into the traffic again.

"I'll lend you the money."

"Patrick, don't be ridiculous."

"What's ridiculous? I can afford it. And then I'll write my play, and you can star in it."

"You don't know anything about me," I say. I'm getting angry now. "You don't know anything about *us*. I could just disappear with your money—I could be a con artist. It happens."

"You, a con artist?" He sounds amused. "I think I know everything I need to know about you, Claire. Trust, remember?"

"I'll see about classes," I mutter. "But I can't take your money."

We drive uptown in silence.

"What he said about that Australian guy—" I begin.

"You don't owe me any explanations, Claire. Until you decide you want to be with me, who you sleep with is your own business."

"Patrick, I *want* to explain."

And I do, I really do. I have this almost irresistible urge to tell him everything.

Because I'm certain that when he finds out this is all some stupid sting, he's going to feel utterly betrayed. That he'll hate me. And it's important to me that Patrick doesn't hate me.

I open my mouth to say something that will stop that happening. Some hint or warning or promise—

Then I think of Frank and Kathryn, following us in an unmarked van. Listening. Relying on me.

Reluctantly, I drag myself back to the script.

"I think I told you I lost someone close to me."

"Yes. Your teacher. Fairbank."

"I've never really told you how he died."

He nods. "I was waiting until you were ready to talk about it."

"As well as being my teacher, he was married." I stare out of the cab window at the wet blur of passing streets. "When it all came out about him and me, he was fired. His wife left him, and of course there wasn't a prayer of him getting another job in teaching. He ended up . . ." I take a deep breath. "It was supposed to be a suicide pact. But I didn't have the courage to go through with my side of it. And I haven't managed to find the courage since."

The tears are coming now, trickling down my cheeks. Not entirely fake tears. They're tears of shame at the lies I'm telling. At the tawdriness of this stupid story.

The driver brakes suddenly, leaning on his horn, and swerves to change lanes. Patrick puts his arm around my shoulder to stop me falling off the seat. It feels good.

I could love this man, I realize. *Instead, I'm lying to him.*

"That's why I dropped out of college and came to New York," I say. "Ever since, I've felt like someone standing on the edge of a high diving board. Too scared to jump, too embarrassed to go back."

Patrick, I could love you.

"The bastard," Patrick says softly. "The despicable, cowardly, self-serving *bastard.* Seducing you—that's bad enough. Making you go along with his pathetic sexual fantasies—that makes my blood boil, although you say you enjoyed it. But to lay the burden of his guilt on you as well—that's just *spineless.*"

I look at him, astonished. "Is it?"

"Who could do a thing like that? If he wasn't already dead, I'd kill him myself."

He smiles and strokes my cheek. But I remember Raoul, crumpling to the carpet, and I don't doubt he means it.

At my apartment building he gets out. For a moment I think he's going to send the cab away and my heart leaps into my mouth. But then he stoops and says to the driver, "Just a minute."

"So you're not asking yourself up," I observe shyly as he walks me to my door.

He studies me for a moment. Rain glints in his hair. "Did I ever tell you how the relationship between Baudelaire and his White Venus ended?"

I shake my head. "I know they slept together. And that it didn't work out."

Patrick nods. "He told her he preferred to remember her as a goddess, not a woman."

I laugh. "I'll tell you now, I'm hardly a goddess. Maybe a bit the opposite."

"My point is, sex can be a test for any relationship. As Baudelaire's friend Flaubert said, we should be wary of touching our idols, lest the gilt come off in our hands." He reaches up and tucks a stray strand of hair back behind my ear. "So if I don't ask myself up, Claire, it's not because I don't want to. Just that I'll wait to be invited." He leaves a pause. When I don't say anything, he smiles. "For now, then, I'll content myself with this." He leans in and kisses me.

If we were in a movie, I think, this would be the climactic moment, the moment when the camera would pull up and away and the credits would start to roll. The lovers, embracing, in the New York night. The rain making everything shiny and new and cinematic: the city lights, the waiting yellow cab, the sappy music coming from the cab's radio. The woman fitting her body to the man's, kissing him back ever more deeply. *I want you.*

38

"Look, when I was working for Henry I could get any man to do or say anything I wanted within about five minutes," I argue. "Yet Patrick still hasn't said *one thing* that incriminates him."

"Claire makes a good point," Frank says quietly.

It's the next morning, and we're debating what to do next. Frank looks tired. The strain of surveillance is taking its toll. Only Kathryn is as full of restless energy as ever, a terrier eager for the kill.

She shrugs. "I never said it would be quick. Or easy."

"But you said we'd get *something*," I point out. "And that if we didn't, we'd stop the operation."

"I didn't mean after just a few meetings. If we end it now, we'll never know if a little more patience would have meant we succeeded." She looks at Frank. "I've been working on these killings for seven years, Frank. The murders of at least eight women. I'm not going to walk away now just because the *actress* has cold feet." The way she says *actress* drips with scorn.

"It's not cold feet," I retort. "I just don't know what

we're trying to prove anymore. Or where else we can go
with it."

"I'll think of something."

"I'm going to have to sleep with him, aren't I?" I say.
They both react at the same time.

FRANK DURBAN   KATHRYN LATHAM
No way!   Absolutely not.

ME

That was the clue he gave me—when he was
talking about how Baudelaire slept with his
White Venus. He said it was like a test. I think
he meant, that's when you'll get to see the real
Patrick Fogler.

KATHRYN

That's not how I read it.

FRANK

It's crossing a red line. From psychological entrapment to honey trap.

ME

But then we'd know the *truth*. Whether he's a
killer or—or just a nice guy grieving for his
dead wife.

Kathryn stares at me.

                    KATHRYN

My God—you think he's innocent, don't you?
You actually believe every word he's saying!
Claire, as your handler—

                      ME

My *handler*? I'm not a fucking *dog*.

                    KATHRYN

As your *handler,* the minute I think you're starting to believe your own lines is the minute I put
a stop to this. And as for sleeping with him—
forget it.

For a moment we glare at each other, each daring the other
to blink. Then:

                      ME

Fuck you.

I go into the bedroom, slamming the door. Behind me I hear
Frank's voice.

                     FRANK

Star temperament. Maybe I should talk to her.

                    KATHRYN

She's got *you* wrapped around her little finger,
hasn't she?

            INT. THE APARTMENT—BEDROOM—
                   CONTINUOUS

I'm listening through the closed door.

FRANK'S VOICE
What's that supposed to mean?

KATHRYN'S VOICE
Come on, Frank. She knows exactly how to ma-
nipulate men like you. She's been doing it all
her life.

I go over to the mirror and stare at my reflection. In the
glass, my character stares right back at me, unblinking. She
touches the microphone necklace. I imagine her ripping it
off in one violent, extravagant gesture. Turning and hurling
it at the wall, where it shatters. Screaming that we've gotten
Patrick all wrong. That he's no more a killer than Frank is.
As a scene, it would play beautifully. It would be so satisfying. So *right*. But I don't do it.

39

That night, I walk the streets of New York, thinking.

I remember when I had to do a sex scene for *Tumult*. The director talked us through it, rehearsed it fully clothed, reduced the crew to make us feel as comfortable as possible. The irony was, Laurence and I were already sleeping together by then.

I'd wanted to do it for real in the movie, as a dare, but Laurence wouldn't. Even so, it was after filming that scene the rumors about our incredible on-screen chemistry began. That was when he'd started to get nervous. In fact—it occurs to me now—maybe it was no coincidence his wife and kids turned up soon after. Maybe that was just his cowardly way of extricating himself from our relationship. He'd been looking to keep himself amused in a foreign country. Instead, the British teenager he'd picked was turning clingy and intense.

I hadn't minded taking my clothes off in front of the camera, though. Quite the reverse. Compared with Dan Day-Lewis living in a wheelchair to play the part of a paraplegic, it was nothing. But it was proof I was *committed,* that I'd give the role everything I had.

For the same reason, I don't really buy Kathryn's objections to me sleeping with Patrick now. She knew I was attracted to him when we started, and she ruthlessly used that for her operation. She can hardly set things up the way she has and then bleat that it mustn't get sexual.

No, the main reason I'm hesitating is that I have a horrible feeling that if I *do* sleep with him, it'll only deepen his feelings for me. That I'll inadvertently ensnare him even further in Dr. Latham's web.

That, and a sense that our first night together really shouldn't be shared with Frank, Kathryn, and a dozen tiny cameras.

But there are many voices in my head, and they don't all agree.

KATHRYN LATHAM

This is what you do, Claire. You lose sight of the difference between the script and reality. That's why you need *me* to tell you what to do.

MARCIE

You did one unprofessional thing and it screwed up your career. And now here you are again, making the same stupid mistake—falling in love with your costar. I'm done representing you.

FRANK DURBAN

Remember what Kathryn said, Claire? This is like bomb disposal. Touch the wrong wire and— *boom.*

But even bomb disposal teams, I think, when they find a suspect package, don't always bother fiddling about with wires. Sometimes they just jump right in and blow the whole thing up. The best solutions are often the bluntest.

One thing Kathryn definitely is right about, though: I'm too involved, and in a way I never anticipated. Looking back, I can't even tell when my allegiances got so muddled.

But if I pull out, I'll lose Patrick, and that's something I don't want to do.

40

INT. BASEMENT BAR—NIGHT

Patrick and I are back in the same candlelit bar we went to that first evening. We're on our second bottle of wine.

ME

Stella too?

PATRICK

I loved her. We were married for four years, after all. But now . . . I'm not sad she's dead. That's not a nice thing to say, is it? But it's true. Because, if she hadn't died, I wouldn't be here with you.

ME

Don't you ever wonder who killed her?

PATRICK

All the time. But the police are so incompetent,
I doubt we'll ever know.

He pulls out a package—a thin, square box—and places it
on the table.

PATRICK

Open it.

I do as he says. Inside is a necklace—a gorgeous, intricate
torque made of silver.

ME

It's beautiful.

Something occurs to me.

ME

Was it hers?

PATRICK

She wore it, sometimes. But now it's yours. Put
it on.

ME

But—my God, Patrick. It must be worth a fortune.

PATRICK

That's why I want you to have it. You won't
mind taking off that one you always wear?

ME

This?

I touch Frank's faux-gilt monstrosity.

ME

I honestly won't mind if I never see this again.

But then I hesitate. Does taking off the microphone mean
they won't be able to hear us? Or will it be sensitive enough
to pick up what we're saying from my bag?
    Patrick mistakes my hesitation for something else.

PATRICK

I want you to have it, Claire.

I make a decision.

ME

Help me, would you?

I lean my head forward, baring my neck for him. As he's
swapping the necklaces over, I make another decision too.

ME

Can we go to *your* apartment? Tonight, I mean?

PATRICK

Why? Yours is hardly far away.

INT. SURVEILLANCE VAN—NIGHT

Grimacing, Frank twiddles knobs to get sound from the microphone, muffled now that it's in my bag.

> MY VOICE (FAINTLY)
> I don't feel comfortable in mine.

> FRANK DURBAN
> (under his breath)
> Shit!

I can picture the scene all too easily. And I find I really don't care.

> INT. PATRICK'S APARTMENT—NIGHT
> Patrick lives in a beautiful modern apartment overlooking the cathedral in Morningside Heights, filled with Turkish rugs, books, and European art. I wander around, looking at everything, while he fixes us drinks.
> I know I should really talk this through some more with Frank and Kathryn. But I don't want to. I want to do it now, right away: to commit, to leap before I've looked.
> *Don't think. Act.*
> Patrick turns around—and sees I've undone my shirt. I've taken off my bra.

> PATRICK
> I thought you weren't ready for that.

> ME
> So did I.

I step toward him.

                              ME
                        (whispering)
        Do whatever you want with me, Patrick.

                            PATRICK
                         (considering)
        Oh, I will.

He slips his hand inside my shirt, sliding it up to cup my
breast, then tugs gently on my nipple, making me gasp. He
pulls harder, so I'm forced to walk with him as he steps
backward into the bedroom.

            INT. PATRICK'S APARTMENT, BEDROOM—
                         CONTINUOUS

                            PATRICK
        This is what I want, Claire.

He kisses me gently.

        INT. PATRICK'S APARTMENT, BEDROOM—A LITTLE
                            LATER

We're making love on the bed. Passionately, fiercely—but
tenderly, without any hint of violence.

41

"That was unbelievably stupid. Not to mention risky," Kathryn rages before I've even gotten the door to the apartment all the way open.

Frank's face is gray with fatigue. They've clearly waited up for me all night.

"Good morning," I reply politely. "How did you sleep, Claire? *Very* well, thank you. Anyway, it was fine, wasn't it? Which is yet more proof you've read this situation all wrong."

"What—you think a sociopath can't fake vanilla sex? Haven't you been listening to a single thing I've been telling you?"

"Sociopath? *Really?* Because nothing he did or said last night—"

"He's hardly going to confess with your pussy rammed into his mouth," she snaps.

I'm not letting her get away with that. "Is that a note of jealousy I detect, Dr. Latham?"

"Ladies," Frank says desperately. "Please."

Kathryn takes a deep breath. "Right. This has happened

now. The question is, how do we salvage something from the situation?"

"What do you suggest?" he asks.

She thinks for a moment. "Next time, you need to persuade him to hurt you," she says to me. "Tell him how much *you* want it. *That* should test his self-control."

"Oh, for God's sake—"

"And then I *would* be jealous. Frankly, I'd enjoy beating the hell out of you myself."

"When did you get to be so paranoid about people?" I ask her, my voice rising. "So *untrusting?*"

She sighs ostentatiously. "Oh, Claire. Grow up. You're not that adolescent fighting with your foster parents anymore. This is *real.*"

"He isn't a killer," I insist. "Don't you see—*you're* the one with the obsession. *You're* the one who can't see further than your own nose. *You're* the one who's trying to twist the facts to fit your stupid pet theory, over and over. All that stuff about the murders being based on poems—it's so tenuous, it's laughable. And as for the bullshit about so-called sexual deviance, it's like you're living in another century. People experiment sometimes—get over it. Patrick is actually one of the gentlest, most considerate men I've ever slept with."

"Well, I may not have your extensive experience," she flings back. "But I *do* happen to have studied serial killers. They have a lifetime's experience of pretending to be normal. They excel at faking it—it's what they do, day in, day out. Most of the ones I've met are better actors than you'll ever be."

"Fuck *you,*" I say furiously, lunging at her.

Effortlessly, Frank raises an arm, blocking my way. "That may have been too much, Kathryn," he mutters.

She ignores him, her blue eyes boring into mine, daring me to come at her again.

"I'm going to take a shower now," I say coldly. "I'd like you both to leave." I turn and walk into the bathroom without a backward glance.

42

But the next night, when I'm with Patrick again and we're undressing each other, I find myself pulling the belt from his trousers and offering it to him.

"You can whip me if you want," I say tentatively.

He takes the belt, flexing it between his hands, testing its suppleness. "And if I *don't* want? Is that acceptable too?"

"Of course."

"Then that's what I choose." He tosses the belt to one side.

"Patrick . . ." I say.

"Yes?"

"Suppose I told you I was never really into all that stuff I talked about? That I was just trying to . . . I don't know, shock you or something?"

He smiles. "I'd say, thank you for being honest with me now. *Were* you trying to shock me?"

"Something like that," I mumble. "Impress you, maybe."

"Claire Wright, you're adorable, did you know that?"

"Do you believe in fate, Patrick?"

"What sort of fate?"

"The sort that says, whatever either of us has done to get to this point doesn't matter. It was just something that had to happen. We're here now. And that's all that counts. Because it was always meant to be."

He shakes his head, still smiling. "I don't believe in that kind of fate, no. Only coincidence. Which of course I will be eternally grateful to, for bringing us together."

Later, we lie entangled on the floor, sharing wine amid the debris of our clothes.

"Claire . . . There's something I have to say to you," he says softly. "Something important . . . You know the other day, we were talking about Stella?"

Involuntarily, I freeze. Then all those relaxation and centering exercises come into play.

"Yes?" I say, as casually as I can.

He touches my nipple curiously, squeezing it gently, turning it this way and that, as if it were a radio he has to tune to the precise, elusive wavelength he requires. "If Stella's death has taught me anything, it's a horror of secrets."

Oh no.

"Do you have a secret, Patrick?"

I say it to him, but also to the microphone in my bag, just a few feet away.

"Yes," he says. "Just one. Something I need to confess."

The way he says it, so solemn and hesitant, tells me this is something big, something that really matters. He even seems nervous. And Patrick is never nervous.

Was Kathryn right after all? Have I got this all wrong?

I wait, as I've been taught. *Silence is the best interrogator.* My heart is thudding in my rib cage. He must be able to feel it through the tips of his fingers.

"I think I'm falling in love with you," he says.

43

"Today we're going to work on two of the most important tools in the actor's repertoire, sense memory and affective memory. Over the years, affective memory in particular has acquired a certain mystique in our profession. But really it just means reaching into your past, remembering some emotion or event, and making it come alive for you so you can bring its truthfulness to the role you're playing now. Let me give you an example of why we need to do that."

Paul chooses Leon, a tall, lanky midwesterner, and asks him to act losing his wallet. We all watch as Leon—who isn't one of the most talented students in the group—mimes patting his pockets, then looks worried, then becomes more and more frantic until he's almost pulling out his hair.

"Okay," Paul says at last. "Now let's try something else. Leon, when you hung your jacket up earlier, I actually took your wallet out and hid it somewhere in this room. And I'm not going to give it back. You have to find it."

Leon blinks. "My MetroCard's in that wallet."

"I know," Paul says. "And about eighty dollars. And a

picture of your girlfriend. And your credit cards. Better start looking."

"Shit," Leon says disbelievingly.

Visibly annoyed, he goes to the tables at the side of the room and starts to rummage through our bags, tipping the contents onto the floor before moving on to the next bag. His neck is a deep, angry red.

Gradually, as he realizes it isn't going to be anywhere obvious, his searching becomes more methodical. Occasionally he turns and shoots Paul a hostile stare.

"Okay," Paul says. "That's enough." He reaches into his pocket and pulls out Leon's wallet. "Here."

"What the fuck—" Leon begins.

Paul ignores him. "I don't need to tell you which of those two performances was more real," he says to us. "But why? First, of course, it's because only when the imagination truly believes the situation is genuine that the truth of it gets conveyed to the audience. But it's more than that. We all sensed, the second time, that Leon had an *objective,* a concrete purpose, and therefore an emotion that was attached to it. He knew if he didn't find his wallet, he'd have to walk home. And you could all sense his anger at being manipulated by me, just to make a point in class."

A few people laugh. "Screw you," Leon snarls.

There's a dangerous silence. Paul turns to him. "What did you say?"

Leon's face is now also very red. "Screw you. And screw your fucking *mind* games. It's all just a power trip to you. You have your favorites and you tell them they're wonderful. Like *her.*" He stabs a finger at me. "The rest of us might as well not be here."

"I'd praise you too, if you put an iota of effort in," Paul

says calmly. "But you don't. It's just another class to you, isn't it? Another grade to count toward your degree."

"I'll get a better job than yours, anyway," Leon jeers. "If you're so hot, how come you aren't famous? It's like they say. Those that can't do, teach." He grabs his jacket. "Fuck you. I'm out."

When he's gone, Paul says: "Good. A class like this doesn't need deadwood. Josh, why don't you show us searching for your keys?"

Later, Paul explains how we have to relax, then remember a situation with a strong sensory input.

He starts us with some easy ones. A situation where we ate something really delicious. And a situation where something made us sick.

I close my eyes and remember a breakfast I ate a couple of months back. I'd been out all night, I hadn't eaten for a whole day, and although I couldn't really afford it, the smell of frying bacon had drawn me in to a neighborhood diner. I picture myself sitting at the booth, the leather warm under my legs, a thick white mug of steaming coffee in my hand, as the waitress puts down a plate of poached, runny eggs, still damp from the pan, and crisp, brittle bacon . . .

My mouth's watering. That's the goal, Paul's told us. When your body tells you it's real, it is.

And then I think about the time I bought some scallops that were being sold off cheap at the end of the day, and forgot to put them in the fridge. How I ate them next day anyway, and knew within seconds I shouldn't have. Involuntarily, I start to gag.

"Okay," Paul says at last. "Now let's add in an emotion. We'll start with happiness."

That's an easy one, of course. I only have to think of last night and a big smile spreads over my face.

Patrick, me too. I feel the same about you.

This is what I've been searching for ever since I was a child, I realize. Unconditional love. Complete acceptance.

In a relationship that can't possibly have any sort of a future. But I'm not going to think about that. I'm not.

Focus on the happiness.

"Good, Claire," Paul says as he passes me. "That's very good."

After class is over, Paul pulls me aside.

"What Leon said earlier," he begins. "There may be some truth to it. I *do* see talent in you, Claire."

I start to stammer my thanks, but he holds up his hand.

"But I also see something I've seen before in certain students—a tendency to *rely* on that talent. The really good actors know when to let go of technique. There's a reason we talk about getting in touch with your feelings—the best actors have something still and calm at their center. A kind of *integrity.* Not a hollow, shapeshifting core. Do you understand what I'm saying?"

I nod.

"Affective memory can help with that, if you let it," he adds. "If you let it take you to where your feelings really are. For some, those are pretty dark places, Claire. But you still have to go there."

The look he gives me is almost sympathetic.

44

"We need to reset this," Kathryn Latham says.

We're all three of us getting sick to death of one another, of being forced to spend so many long hours in one another's company. Like a play that's gone on too long, given too many matinees; one of those hackneyed murder mysteries that just keeps on selling out, year after year. I've come to like Frank, but I wish he'd stand up to Kathryn more. Kathryn I just don't get at all. Her desire to catch Patrick out is so overwhelming, so focused, it blots out every other aspect of her personality.

"We need to be clear what we want to happen, and how we intend to control events to achieve that outcome," she's saying. "I'd half-hoped for a pillow-talk confession, but it seems that moment has passed."

"What do you suggest, Kathryn?" Frank asks.

I tune them out and watch sunlight diffracting through a bottle of Evian on the table. A disk of light on the ceiling becomes an ellipse, then a figure-eight, then fattens once again into a disk.

He loves me he loves me he loves me he loves me . . .

"Claire? Do you agree with what Kathryn's saying?"

I drag my attention back to them. "Agree with what?"

Kathryn sighs. "As you know, I had my doubts about the path we've gone down. Now that we're here, though, we have to consider how best to use this clearly intense relationship that's developing."

"In what way?"

"I think we should change the narrative. If Patrick's a killer, in part it's because he feels he's been betrayed by women. I suggest we have you betray him."

"You mean—let him catch me with somebody else?" I say incredulously.

"Why not? If he's as hooked on you as he appears to be, he'll be angry. For an ordinary man, that anger might be expressed verbally. If he's a killer, perhaps he'll become violent."

"Jesus, Kathryn. It's a high-risk strategy," Frank says.

She shrugs. "Do you have a better suggestion?"

"I'm not doing it," I say without hesitation.

"You're the *actress*," Kathryn says. "You don't get to write the script."

"If we do that to Patrick," I begin, then stop. *He'll hate me,* I want to say. *He'll never trust me again.*

But of course, that's exactly why Kathryn's proposing it.

I've finally found a man I don't want to mess with. And here I am, about to do just that.

I hear Paul's voice in my head. *There's a reason we talk about getting in touch with your feelings—the best actors have something still and calm at their center. A kind of integrity . . .*

I set down my glass of water and stand up. "I'm out," I say quietly.

"You're what?" Frank frowns.

"I'm not doing this anymore."

"Oh, for pity's sake," Kathryn says. "Claire, stop show-ing off and sit down."

"I mean it. It's over. Sorry."

Kathryn looks at Frank. "Detective?" she says. In that instant I realize they've discussed this contingency, planned for it; that Frank's now supposed to say or do something to stop me.

But he doesn't. He says heavily, "Well, Claire, I guess that's your choice."

"Tell her, Frank," Kathryn insists. "Or I will."

"Tell me what?"

"If you pull out, you'll be put on a plane back to the UK."

I stare at her.

"You signed the contract," she adds.

"I didn't *read* the contract. You didn't give me time."

Kathryn shrugs.

"We couldn't take the risk of you giving up partway through," Frank says apologetically.

"We still can't," Kathryn adds. "This isn't over until I say it's over." The look she gives me has no more concern or compassion than if I were a lab rat. "Now, shall we get back to work?"

45

"You're quiet tonight, Claire."

Patrick climbs back onto the bed with a bottle of wine and two glasses. "Is everything all right?" he adds.

"Of course." I sit up and force a smile. "Just a little . . . thoughtful, that's all."

He smiles back. "So tell me what you're thinking about."

I sigh. "If only I could."

In my head, I was replaying the blazing argument I'd had with Kathryn and Frank after I'd found out what would happen if I pulled out of the operation. I'd shouted, pleaded, even wept; all to no avail.

I'm trapped. Just a puppet, a zombie. Parroting their lines, performing their moves.

How did it ever come to this?

Kathryn isn't going to stop until she's got something she can use as evidence against Patrick, I've realized. However tenuous it is, however ambiguous, she'll pounce on something he eventually says or does and then use it to get him locked up.

Even if it's just an orphan's understandable rage at being betrayed by the woman he loves. The woman he thought loved him unconditionally in return.

"I thought we were going to trust each other with the very worst things inside our heads," Patrick says gently. "Believe me, Claire, there's nothing you could tell me now that would change how I feel about you."

Wait till you discover what Kathryn's got planned for you, I think.

But then I think: *What if I did tell him?*

The idea is so crazy, and at the same time so brilliantly simple, that I almost gasp out loud.

What if I break character? What if I tell Patrick everything?

If he and I are to have any chance of a future, he has to know the truth about me sometime. But once he knows, the sting's over. I'll be deported.

Unless—and now my mind is racing—I tell him without Frank and Kathryn knowing. If I let Patrick in on the secret. And together, we go on fooling Frank and Kathryn until they lose interest in him.

Instead of entrapping him, I could be the one to save him.

"Why are you smiling, Claire?" he asks.

"Hold that thought," I say, jumping up. "Hold that thought and don't go away. There's something I need to tell you—something really shocking. Something . . ." I stop, aware of the enormity of what I'm about to do. "Something that'll probably blow your mind. I'm going to take a quick shower. Then we'll talk."

"I can't wait," Patrick says. He sounds amused.

.   .   .

Pausing only to grab a robe, I go to the bathroom. I take the microphone necklace from where it was hidden in the pocket of my jeans and ram it deep into Patrick's laundry basket, piling towels over it.

Sorry, Kathryn. But you shouldn't have tried to force my hand.

I take a breath, focusing, centering myself, quickly running through the scene ahead in my mind. How I should stand, what I should say. And my tone. Serious? Excited? Apologetic? Tearful? No: calm, I decide. After all, it'll be a lot for him to take in. And I'll only get one shot at it. No second goes, no retakes.

Just for a moment, it crosses my mind that Patrick might be angry with me. I remember his flash of temper in the theater, Raoul's bleeding face.

But this will be different. *Believe me, Claire, there's nothing you could tell me now that would change how I feel about you.* I have to trust in that.

I'm scared—terrified—but also happy. I know there's a chance this will backfire. But there's also a possibility, however slim, that he'll understand the pressure I was under and forgive me. And that slim chance is all I need to make me feel giddy with joy.

Finally, we might be able to love each other without all this deception.

I turn on the shower and reach for the shower gel. The bottle slips through my wet fingers and rolls behind the washbasin. I crouch down to pick it up.

And that's when I see it—a wire, as thin as a strand of vermicelli, clinging to the back of the porcelain.

I touch it. It's sticky. Getting one nail underneath it, I gently pry it away. It leads up around the taps and through a tiny hole. I follow it to where it disappears behind the mirror.

For a moment I stare at my own reflection, not believing.

Then I pull the mirror off the wall and turn it over. Stuck to the underside, where a tiny aperture has been scratched in the silver, is an electronic chip. A miniature surveillance camera.

I know that's what it is because it's the exact same type as the ones they installed in my apartment too.

What does it mean? I can't get my head around this. Frank always told me the reason I had to wear the necklace at all times was because they couldn't risk bugging Patrick's apartment. So how did this get here?

Breathless now, I follow the wire the other way, down to the floor, pulling it away from the wall. The strand of wire lifts itself from a gap between the tiles, like a mooring rope on a beach lifting out of the sand.

I follow it to a cupboard. Where it goes into a junction box. Nestling there like a big black spider, its legs the multitude of wires that spread in different directions.

Not just one camera. Dozens of them, all over the apartment. And wires everywhere. So many, there's no way Patrick can't be aware of them.

I rip the junction box from its hiding place.

Believe me, Claire, there's nothing you could tell me now that would change how I feel about you . . .

"Oh, you fucker," I say out loud. I say it in my real, British accent. Because I've just realized what this means. Why there's no point in pretending anymore.

Patrick knows these wires are here.

He's not the suspect.

I am.

series of rewrites and flashbacks, tumbling through my brain.

FRANK
Detective, shall we confer outside?

INT. POLICE HEADQUARTERS—CORRIDOR—
CONTINUOUS

The two detectives speak in the corridor, their voices low.

DETECTIVE DAVIES
Either she's telling the truth, or she deserves an Oscar.

FRANK
So where does that leave us?

DETECTIVE DAVIES
The husband?

FRANK

Or the possibility that she really is that good.

DETECTIVE DAVIES

Let's dig into Claire Wright a little deeper,
shall we?

Which, presumably, they did. And unfortunately:

DETECTIVE DAVIES

She has a partial alibi, but the man she went
home with that night was drunk and can't remember what time she left his apartment. She
could easily have gone back to Stella's hotel.

The scene now playing out in Detective Durban's head has
changed.

INT. LEXINGTON HOTEL, CORRIDOR—NIGHT

I knock on the door of Stella's room.

ME

Mrs. Fogler? Stella? It's Claire . . . I have something of Patrick's.

There's no answer at first. Then Stella opens the door, a glass
in her hand. She's swaying.

STELLA

Oh, it's you. The girl who couldn't pick up my
husband. What do you want?

ME

We shouldn't do this out here.

And then, a series of unfortunate coincidences.

INT. POLICE INTERVIEW ROOM—DAY

HENRY

So according to this lawyer, Rick, Claire got
into her part a little too deep. A thousand dollars' worth of deep, to be exact.

Followed by coincidence number two:

INT. POLICE HEADQUARTERS OFFICE—DAY

DETECTIVE DAVIES

The producer is claiming she assaulted him,
pulled a gun . . . then demanded money not to
send the video to his wife. And this was the
same night she went on to work for Stella. She
could have had the gun on her the whole time,
used it to threaten Stella . . . then something
went wrong and a fight broke out.

FRANK

Jesus . . . Any proof he's telling the truth?

DETECTIVE DAVIES

Just the security tape of her leaving his office.
She signs herself out like she doesn't have a frig-

gin' care in the world. But you can see the gun sticking out of her bag.

INT. POLICE HEADQUARTERS OFFICE—DAY

FRANK

But if Claire was involved in Stella Fogler's death, why the postmortem wounds to Stella's body?

DETECTIVE DAVIES

She had the book of poems. Maybe that's where she got the idea. She realized rigging the murder scene like that would divert attention from the robbery.

FRANK

Right down to the condom residue?

DETECTIVE DAVIES

Girls who have a lot of casual sex often carry their own rubbers. She could have pushed one into the wound on Stella's thigh, hoping our forensic guys would pick up on it and we'd jump to the conclusion our perpetrator was a male. As, in fact, we did.

FRANK

Only a sociopath could think that coolly when they've just bludgeoned someone to death.

DETECTIVE DAVIES

Or someone who's used to performing under
pressure. On stage, for example.

FRANK

Okay. She's a suspect.

And then, many weeks later:

INT. KATHRYN LATHAM'S OFFICE—DAY

FRANK

So we have almost nothing . . . except this actress, Claire Wright.

KATHYRN

Interesting. I'm wondering . . . What if we let
her think she's been eliminated, as a pretext for
getting her in and running some psychological
tests on her?

FRANK

Is that legal?

KATHYRN

It is if we get her to sign the right consent
forms. We can tell her she's helping me build a
profile of the killer. She'll like that, I think—
the idea she's managed to insinuate herself into
the investigation.

FRANK

At what point do we tell her she's a suspect?

KATHYRN

If she doesn't eliminate herself, maybe never.
We'll cook up some melodramatic story about
Patrick and the poems—something that'll ap-
peal to her sense of theater.

*The Wechsler. The Minnesota Multiphasic Personality Inventory.
The Hare Psychopathy Checklist . . .*

Even at the time, I'd thought it odd they needed to test
me for psychopathy.

Luring me in with the bait they knew I'd go for. First
the video camera, recording me. Putting me on *show.* And
then the appeal to my vanity—

INT. OBSERVATION ROOM—DAY

DETECTIVE DURBAN'S VOICE

Sure, we have female cops who'd do it. No disrespect to my colleagues, but have you *seen* them?
I think Claire would stand a better chance of
getting under his defenses.

KATHRYN LATHAM'S VOICE

Didn't work last time.

DETECTIVE DURBAN'S VOICE

He gave her the book. You said yourself—for
him, that's intimacy.

Waiting to see if I'd burst in and demand a part in their operation. To *insinuate herself into the investigation.*

KATHRYN

Very good, Claire. It's Freudian bullshit, of course. But I am impressed with the way you took my suggestion and ran with it. And the tears are a nice touch.

Meaning: *You might just be our killer, after all.*

run into the bedroom, the junction box still in my hand, and hurl it on the bed. "What's this?" I demand.

Patrick looks startled. "What—"

"You already know most of what I was about to tell you, don't you? You know a hell of a lot, in fact."

He blinks at me.

"What did they fucking tell you?" I yell.

"They told me you might have killed my wife," he says quietly. "They came to me after I got back from Europe and told me you could be her murderer. It seemed to explain so many of the things you'd said, the way you'd behaved . . . And when they told me you'd been in Stella's suite that night, and that you'd had a gun . . ."

"Don't you *get* it?" I say incredulously. "I've *always* trusted you. Not them—*you*. And you—you betraying, evil *fucker*—" I start to pummel him, my fists bouncing uselessly off his hard, lean body. "I fell in love with you," I howl. Even now, in these unimaginably awful circumstances, it feels good to finally say those words out loud. "They told me not to, but I was too damn stupid. Patrick, don't you understand? I love you."

Only when I go for his face does he finally pin my arms to my sides. "Christ, Claire, calm down—"

Then the door crashes open and Frank Durban's pulling me off him. I let myself be pulled. It doesn't matter now, anyway. Nothing matters.

"Claire Wright, I'm arresting you on suspicion of the murder of Stella Fogler—" he begins.

With a yell of rage I shove him away. As he stumbles, I duck under his arm, the stage-fight training finally coming in useful, and run. I've no idea where I'm going. I only know that my whole world, my reality, has just been turned upside down.

"Shit," I hear Frank say as he crashes after me. "Shit." And, into his radio, "Urgent assistance."

48

ventually, I go to Jess's. There's been no further sign
of the cops since I gave Frank the slip and I can't
think of anywhere else.

But Jess isn't there and I don't have my keys. I buy a
bottle of vodka and wait but she doesn't show.

Images whirl through my head on an endless loop, over
and over.

RICK

If you don't mind my saying so, Claire, you
don't seem the type.

ME

Before I realized there are more enjoyable ways
to pay the rent.

PRODUCER

This isn't strictly a callback, Claire. I'm cur-
rently casting for a range of projects.

FRANK

Most of our work has focused on one individual.

KATHRYN

The suspect would be enticed to reveal various aspects of her personality, which could then be compared with my profile of the killer.

ME

"It's a necropolis; a grave in which the dead,
The bodies I once loved, are tumbled willy-nilly . . ."

KATHRYN

Let's see what the Wechsler tells us.

PATRICK

I think I'm falling in love with you.

PATRICK

I think I'm falling in love with you.

PATRICK

I think I'm falling in love with you.

I get through most of the bottle before I realize Jess must be away. And eventually there's nowhere else to go but back to the place Frank and Kathryn put me in, the apartment full of cameras and microphones and lies.

There's no one there either. But I know they'll find me eventually. I wreck the place, ripping the wires from their hiding places, yanking the miniature cameras from behind the mirrors, trashing the West Elm furniture and the Georgia O'Keeffe art books. Deliberately, I raise my foot over the glass coffee table and stamp down, hard. The first time, it clouds with a snowflake of cracks. The second, there's a satisfying explosion of glass.

And then—nothing. Just blank, numb despair. *I'm going to be arrested,* I think. No more Patrick. No more acting classes.

It's like *Tumult* all over again. No, worse. I slump down into the mess, exhausted.

At best, I'll be deported. Back to England. My dream—my second chance—is over.

I pick up a shard of glass.

I'd wanted to show him it hadn't just been acting.

I touch the glass to my wrist. *Hello, old friend.*

The sting is exhilarating. It says: *You were right. Not them,* you. *You were brilliant. You were* real.

I pull it across my wrist, as easy as ripping open a packet of nuts. For a heartbeat, nothing. Then the blood comes eagerly, gushing and pumping. Euphoria and terror crash together in my brain.

Perhaps now they'll realize what they did.

And if they don't, who cares?

Fuck them.

I pull again, dragging the sharp edge across my arm, like a violinist drawing out a note.

My final bow. *Thank you and good night.*

Show's over, folks. It was great while it lasted.

One final slicing motion with the shard. My vision fades, like a tunnel rushing toward me, like a spotlight dimming, and my head slumps down onto my chest.

Cue curtain. Cue applause.

Cue oblivion.

Fade out.

49

INT. CLAIRE'S APARTMENT—NIGHT

The cat picks its way through broken glass, mewing plaintively.

There's a crash as someone outside kicks at the door. It quivers and reverberates under the force of the blows. At the fifth kick, it comes right off its hinges.

Frank Durban rushes in.

FRANK

Jesus!

Claire lies unconscious in a pool of blood. He runs over—

FRANK

Claire! Claire, wake up! Shit!

Pulling out his radio, he frantically thumbs the button.

50

"It wasn't life threatening," Kathryn says dismissively. "She only cut one wrist. A typically melodramatic gesture."

"She'd have died if no one found her," Frank says sharply. "She's still in the emergency department." He turns to Patrick Fogler. "We'll send someone to take down the remaining cameras."

Patrick looks around his apartment. "All of them? You mean—that's it? It's over? Will she be charged?"

Frank shakes his head. "Without a confession, there's nothing that could justify pressing charges. I'm sorry, Patrick."

"But she'll be assessed in a secure psychiatric facility," Kathryn adds. "It's likely they'll be able to keep her there until Immigration and Customs Enforcement arrange to return her to the UK."

Patrick nods. "And what do *you* think? Honestly? *Did* she murder Stella?"

There's a long silence.

"Honestly," Kathryn admits, "I think we'll never know. And I'm not sure we ever would have known, however long we'd watched her. I think that for Claire Wright, reality is whatever she wants it to be."

51

Greenridge. A residential psychiatric center twenty miles upstate. During my ten months in America, I've barely been out of Manhattan. Nothing in my experience of this country has prepared me for the squalor of its public-access health institutions.

The ward I'm on is protected by electronic locks. In theory, we're being kept secure while we're assessed. In practice, we're prisoners. There was some kind of legal hearing, but I was judged unfit to attend and my state-appointed lawyer simply filled in a form saying I was a danger to myself and possibly others. That's par for the course, apparently. One patient, a massive black man the orderlies call Meathead, is cuffed to his bed twenty-four hours a day. The others are mobile, after a fashion, though even they shuffle up and down the polished corridors as if hobbled by invisible leg irons, muttering in an urban patois I don't understand. All seem permanently stunned by whatever meds they're on.

There's a heat wave, and the windows don't open. The male patients go around bare-chested, and even the staff wear nothing under their scrubs. At night, men and women are separated by nothing more than a corridor. My first night, I heard screams as a woman along the hall was attacked. The staff pulled the man off, but two hours later he was back in her cubicle again.

The psychiatrist responsible for me is named Dr. Andrew Banner. He's young, with the bad skin of the chronically overworked. The first time I see him, he spends a long time tapping my reflex points.

"Are you suffering from any physical stress or trauma?" he wants to know.

"I already told you what happened." For some reason my teeth are chattering. "It was a police operation—I was working with the police. They took me to this apartment that was filled with cameras. But they didn't tell me there were cameras everywhere else as well. Because really it was me they were watching." I stop, aware how agitated my voice sounds.

"Nothing like a car crash? Or a mugging?" Banner peers into my eyes with a little flashlight.

"Nothing." I bite down on my teeth to keep them still.

"Any nervous conditions? Epilepsy? Hypoglycemic attacks? Manic episodes? Depression, thoughts of violence?"

"No." I look at my arm, bandaged now. "Apart from this, I mean."

"Ever hear voices you aren't sure are really there?"

"Not really."

He snaps off the flashlight. "Not *really*?"

"Sometimes I imagine I'm in a sort of movie. Watching myself perform."

He makes a note. "Have you taken any nonprescription drugs in the last twelve months?"

"Just Ecstasy. But not very often."

"Ah." Another note.

"Look," I say, for what seems like the fifth time. "It was to do with the Stella Fogler murder, the one that happened back in February. The police used a trick to get me in front of a shrink so she could give me all these tests."

"What tests?"

I try to remember, but the drugs they've given me are clouding my memory. "We talked, mostly. About having foster parents. I think that must have been part of her profile, somehow. The whole Daddy Bear–Mummy Bear–Goldilocks dynamic they set up."

He writes that down too.

"Do you believe me?" I can hear the desperation in my voice.

"Of course."

"Really?" I'm relieved. "*Thank* you. For a moment there it even sounded crazy to me."

Still writing, he says, "I had a patient here recently who thought he had a tree growing in his stomach. He remembered eating an apple core, and he thought the seeds must have germinated inside him. He was suffering from agonizing stomach cramps. Once we'd given him medication, he stopped getting the cramps. He convinced himself the meds were poison, you see, and that the tree had died."

"But he was still insane," I say, not understanding.

"That's not a word we like to use much in here, Claire. We all inhabit our own reality." Dr. Banner's eyes go to his laptop. "A bit like a computer network. Different machines on the network run different software. Sometimes there are little glitches. Compatibility problems, as it were. Then they have to be fixed by tech support. Do you see what I'm saying?"

"Not really."

"Let me put it this way. There are some chemical imbalances in your system that need to be tweaked."

"What do you mean, *tweaked*?"

It turns out he means what he calls attack levels of pimozide, Proverin, and Iclymitol, drugs he assures me have few side effects but which I can feel blunting my thought processes, coating my mind in a gluey syrup of medication. They make me constantly hungry. I spend my days in the television room, waiting lethargically for the orderlies to come around with yet another tray of carb-heavy food. At one consultation I make the mistake of telling Dr. Banner that fear of the other patients is disturbing my sleep, so in addition to all the other drugs I'm given sleeping pills. Like all meds here, once prescribed they're not optional. The orderlies stand over you to make sure you've swallowed. Just like *Girl, Interrupted,* only without Whoopi Goldberg.

It seems ironic Banner's so obsessed with medication, since it's clearly drug abuse that fried most of his patients' brains in the first place. They compare prescriptions with all the savvy of gourmets—"You got meth? Fucking A, all the man gave me were two frickin' tueys and a script for some Susie-Q"—and tell anyone who'll listen about the higher reality they've experienced on angel dust and crack. I don't feel safe lapsing into a drugged coma every night, particularly as I'm sure the sharper-eyed among them know exactly what I've been given. But there's no choice.

After a week or so Dr. Banner produces, with something of a fanfare, my diagnosis. I am suffering from a *paranoid delusional episode.* When I protest that it all really happened, that the police operation was as real as this hospital, Dr. Banner waves my objections away. The facts are not important, he insists. What matters is my response to them. I have been experiencing *dissociation*—an internal separation of different parts of my personality. There is an element of *psychosis,* of not being able to separate perception from reality. He believes these are symptoms linked to an underlying *Histrionic Personality Disorder,* their appearance triggered by *intense stress.*

For all of these, the treatment is the same: increased dosages of the same medications.

Slowly, slowly, whether as a result of the drugs or just the passing of time, my agitation subsides. I no longer jump out of my skin, startled, at every noise, or jolt awake with panic-induced vomit in my mouth. The torrent of fragmented images in my head slows to a trickle. The looping spiral of film slows, then stutters to a halt.

And only rarely do I have glimpses of myself as a performer, striding through the movie of my life.

The ache in my heart, the ache for Patrick Fogler, takes longer to subside. I realize now how stupid it was to let myself fall in love with him. Only the second time in my life I've been in love, and the second time I've fallen for something that wasn't real.

But that doesn't mean what *I* feel isn't real.

It's my precious secret, the one bit of myself I don't confess to Banner or his team of therapists. I'm scared that if I tell them, they'll find a way to make it go away. And it's all I've got to hang on to. The only part of Patrick I have left.

As for Frank and Kathryn, I don't hate them. I don't feel anything for them. Even when I thought she was on the same side as me, I knew I was never more than a chess piece to Kathryn. I never liked or trusted her and now I know those instincts were correct.

> *The days go on forever. Boredom and ennui*
> *Are in themselves a kind of immortality . . .*

At first I wait apprehensively for the police or the Immigration people to come and deal with me. But as the weeks go by, I have to face a different possibility. The system has simply dumped me here and forgotten about me. Until Dr. Banner decides I'm cured, there's no reason why anyone should ever want me to leave.

PART
THREE

52

"I think I'm better now," I say tentatively. "Really, I feel fine."

The look Dr. Banner gives me is almost pitying. "Unfortunately, one of the hallmarks of Cluster B personality disorders is that the sufferer has a distorted self-image. Often, they falsely value exactly those qualities about themselves that cause distress to others and undermine their own personal relationships."

I frown. "You mean, I won't be better until I think I'm ill? That's a bit *One Flew Over the Cuckoo's Nest,* isn't it?"

"I'm saying your own judgments about how well you are might not be as reliable as those of myself and my medical team."

"What about Dr. Latham? What does *she* say?"

"I haven't been able to track down your Dr. Latham, Claire."

Something about that *your* makes me look at him sharply. "You think I made her up?"

"I didn't say that. And in any case the facts—"

"Aren't important. I know. But she *is* a shrink. And she ran all those tests on me. That's data you should have."

"If it exists," Banner replies carefully, "it would certainly be useful. But I can assure you, there's no Kathryn Latham registered with the American Board of Forensic Psychology. I checked."

"I could take you to her office—"

"That won't be possible, Claire."

"Why not? It would only take a couple of hours. And then maybe you'd believe me," I say desperately. I think Banner likes me: I'm just about the only one of his patients he can have a rational conversation with, and I've noticed I get far more consultation time than the brain-fried junkies do. "Maybe I'd believe *myself*. Instead of worrying if all that shit was just inside my own head." To my humiliation, I start to cry.

Banner watches me for a few moments. "All right," he says at last. "If you really feel it would help, Claire. I'll organize a transport."

We go next day in the center's minibus. Dr. Banner, me, and a muscular male orderly named Anton, who's clearly only there in case I make a run for it. When we get to Union City, I start to panic because I can't find the right block. "It's around here somewhere," I say, dashing from side to side of the minibus. "I'm sure of it."

Dr. Banner is noting down everything I say, so after a while I force myself to shut up and sit on my hands to stop from waving them around. Then we turn a corner and, to my relief, there it is—the familiar row of half-empty parking lots and ugly low-rise industrial buildings.

"'That one!" I exclaim, pointing. "See, I told you. Pull up."

We get out. The building looks half derelict. "Don't worry, it always looked like this," I say reassuringly.

I go to the front doors and pull. They won't open. I peer inside. There's no one at the reception desk. Just a sign saying these vacant premises are patrolled by a security company with dogs. And a realtor's sign.

"There's no one here, Claire," Dr. Banner says, stating the obvious.

"Wait," I say desperately. "Let me show you the apartment. The one where they filmed everything. It's just across the river."

Even before we get there, though, I've guessed what we're going to find.

A woman with a South African accent answers the door. She rented the place on Airbnb, she says. It's got great reviews.

Same with the apartment below, the one where Frank Durban was.

Dr. Banner's careful not to meet my eye, but I notice Anton sticks very close.

"Can I use your phone?" I say frantically to Dr. Banner.

"Who do you want to call, Claire?"

"Frank—Detective Durban. He'll be able to tell you where Dr. Latham is."

Banner hesitates. "I'll try him for you. And then we really must get back." Pulling out his phone, he punches in a number and asks for the New York Police Department.

I wait while he gets transferred. He repeats several times that he's trying to reach Detective Frank Durban. Eventually he puts the phone down, his face neutral.

"Well? What did he say?" My heart is in my mouth.

"Detective Durban has been on sick leave for the past three months."

"But that can't be right," I say helplessly. "He was following me around. Watching out for me. I even had a safe word, for chrissake—"

"What was your safe word, Claire?"

"It was Cay . . . Cam . . ." I shake my head in frustration. "I can't remember." I start to cry again.

"Anton," Dr. Banner says gently. "Would you escort Claire to the bus? It's time we got her back to Greenridge."

53

Dr. Banner wants me to do group therapy. It seems a bit pointless—how can talking to a collection of mentally unstable druggies undo any of what happened?—but eventually I agree to give it a try, as much to curry favor with him as anything else.

There are eight of us in the group, which gathers in the canteen at a quiet time between meals. One of the psychiatric nurses, Orla, acts as moderator.

"First today, let's welcome Claire," she says in a low, calm voice. "Hi, Claire, and congratulations on taking this important step." There's a smattering of lethargic applause.

"Okay," Orla says, turning to the young man next to her. "Ethan, why don't you tell us what's been on your mind this week?"

Ethan starts rambling, something about how he feels guilty about stealing money from his sister to pay for drugs. I'm barely listening. I've just realized what this session reminds me of.

People gathered around the teacher in a circle, taking it in turns to perform their piece.

And *applause.*

Following Ethan's lead, the theme of the session becomes Terrible Things We Have Done. One woman stabbed her husband, thinking he was the devil. Someone else tried to throw herself out of a window in front of her children.

At last it's my turn. "Claire," Orla says, turning to me. "Is there anything you're reflecting on that's troubling you?"

"Well," I say, "there was this period when I didn't have any money for rent and the police had stopped me from working. So I went to hotels in Manhattan and pretended to be a prostitute."

"Okay," Orla says after a moment. "Thank you for sharing that. Now, Anna—"

"Whoa," a man named Michael, on my right, says. "Wait up. How did *that* work? You just told some random guy you were a hooker?"

They're all staring at me.

So I tell them.

INT. ROOSEVELT HOTEL BAR, NEW YORK—NIGHT

REBECCA

What's the most you've ever paid for a woman, Alan?

ALAN

Four hundred dollars.

REBECCA

Double it.

ALAN

Are you *serious*?

REBECCA

No, I'm not. I'm having fun—and that's why
I'm worth eight hundred dollars. But if you've
changed your mind . . .

ALAN

No, wait. Eight hundred's . . . fine.

REBECCA

I'll need half in advance.

ALAN
(pulling out his wallet)
You have this all worked out, don't you, Rebecca?

REBECCA

Of course. We'll go up separately—you first.
Don't make eye contact with the concierge.

"I wasn't really planning on having sex with them," I conclude. "But I was used to doing that kind of stuff anyway,
from when I was working as a professional decoy for a law
firm. The only difference was that, instead of the wife paying
me, the husband now paid me direct. And he got to keep
half his cash, and his marriage too. It was pretty much a
win–win situation."

The group is transfixed. I'd done Married Alan's voice as
a New England monotone—he was from N'Hampshah,

where the huntin' was wicked good—while Hooker Rebecca had a trace of the smoky, husky South, where something nice was sumth'n nass.

There's a long silence. Orla seems to shake herself.

"Moving on," she says. "Anna, do you have anything to share?"

54

"I think the group therapy has established you're not yet recovered," Dr. Banner says. "As I suspected it might."

Too late I realize I've walked into another trap. "How long are you going to keep me here?"

"Until you're no longer a danger to others or yourself, Claire."

"When will that be?"

"You're making progress. But while the meds can dampen down the immediate symptoms, they may not be tackling the underlying issues."

"So how will you know when I'm well enough to leave? What do you look for?"

"You mean, what are the behaviors that would tell me you're better?"

I nod.

"If I tell you, I have no doubt you'll mimic them perfectly," he says with a thin smile. "So let me put it this way, Claire: I'll know you're on the road to recovery when you're no longer trying to pretend you are."

55

We aren't allowed on the Internet, but there's an ancient computer in the administrator's office that's connected to the Web. I've seen the orderlies checking Facebook when there are no doctors around.

Patients can request to do small chores, to keep themselves busy. I volunteer to sort the recycling, which gives me access to the office. I hang around, shuffling paper, long enough to watch an orderly type in his password. Then, late at night, I sneak back in and log on.

I do a search for "Histrionic Personality Disorder." A list of links comes up, mostly psychology sites.

Histrionic Personality Disorder is one of the Cluster B psychiatric disorders, I learn. Its characteristics include constant seeking of approval, impulsivity, a persistent need to seduce others, risky sexual behavior, volatility, manipulativeness, thrill seeking, fear of abandonment, reading significance into relationships that isn't really there, and a tendency to distort, dismiss, or misinterpret reality. Eighty percent of those diagnosed with HPD are women. They are disproportionally likely to attempt suicide or self-harm.

I also learn that the word *histrionic* has its origins in the now-discredited term *hysteria,* which in turn comes from the Greek word for "uterus." In the early twentieth century, hysteria was treated with vibrators, since it was noticed that sufferers—who were inevitably female—seemed less agitated after an orgasm. A generation before that, they were simply locked up.

In other words, maybe I'm not crazy. Maybe I'm just the kind of woman who male doctors historically haven't liked very much.

I think back to what Kathryn Latham said, the first time I met her. *Well, she's insecure, impulsive, fragile, emotionally incontinent, can't handle rejection, and although she tries extremely hard to hide it, she craves approval like a junkie craving a fix. What can I say, Frank? She's an actress.*

And I remember how I'd felt when she said that. How *proud.* She'd known exactly how to play me.

But rightly or wrongly, I'm here now, and I need to find a way out. I have to become a model citizen, one without any signs of HPD, the very picture of sanity. Looking at the list again, I realize that, basically, I just need to stop flirting with Andrew Banner and convince him I'm as straight and boring as he is. Then perhaps he'll let me go.

56

"You're making good progress," Banner concedes at my next consultation.

"Does that mean I'll be discharged?"

"I'd be reluctant to change the medications so soon, Claire. And this particular combination of drugs is one that requires close supervision. I'll be recommending to your review hearing that you stay with us a little longer."

Disappointed though I am, my ears prick up. I hadn't even known I was getting a review hearing.

"Well, whatever you think's best, Doc," I say meekly.

That night I go back on the computer and research the civil commitment process. It turns out that, after sixty days, the hospital has to get a court to renew its authorization to keep me here. According to the website I find, *You must be notified when such an application is made, and you have the right to object and to be represented by the Mental Hygiene Legal Service or your own attorney.*

Just for a moment, I have a vision of representing my-

self, of standing up before the judge and making the big
dramatic speech that will change everything. I'm dignified,
polite, but burning with a determined icy fervor. Like Char-
lotte Rampling in *The Verdict*.

> **ME**
> We're here today to defend, not a person, Your
> Honor, but a *principle*. The principle of natural
> justice.

Then I push the thought away. If anything would prove my
underlying condition hasn't improved, it's that.

It's a catch-22. If I seem any better, it must be because
of the drugs, therefore I have to stay here. If I don't seem
better, I need more drugs, therefore I have to stay here. I
want to scream at the unfairness of it all.

Instead, I stare at the screen, desperately trying to think
of some way around this. There must be *someone* who can
vouch for me. Someone who can tell the judge about the
intolerable pressure I was under. Who can swear to the fact
that, while I might have the personality disorder Dr. Banner
has diagnosed—because let's face it, what actor doesn't?—it
wasn't that which pushed me over the edge, but Kathryn
Latham's mind games.

And then it comes to me.

There *is* someone. He won't be expecting to hear from
me. But I have nothing to lose. And his email address is still
lodged in my mind. Just like every other detail about him.

Or is it just how I feel about him that's making me believe he'd be a good person to contact?

Screw it. *Don't think.*

Webmail is blocked here, but I can access the center's

own email server from the computer. I figure most people will open an email that looks like it's from a psychiatric hospital. Just in case, I put *URGENT PATRICK PLS READ THIS—NOT SPAM!* in the subject line.

Dear Patrick,

Please, don't delete this. Not until you've read it, anyway.

I'm stuck in a psychiatric center somewhere north of New York. They won't let me out—my doctor, a guy named Banner, is convinced I'm crazy, partly because I made the mistake of telling him about Dr. Latham and everything, and partly because I made some bad choices after I left your apartment that day.

I can only imagine what they said about me to get you to join in with Kathryn's scheme. (They made up some pretty terrible stuff about you too, by the way, but that's another story.) Please believe that hardly any of it was true.

So why am I writing to you, of all people? Because I'm still convinced that—despite all the lies and the pretending—you and I had a connection, a genuine connection. Dr. Banner would say I only think that because I'm a nutcase with a tendency to distort, dismiss, or misinterpret reality. But the fact is, I'm an actress. And I know there are some things no one can fake.

There's going to be a hearing soon to decide how long I have to be here. The doctor wants me to stay. If he succeeds, I don't think I can stand it much longer. The only other people who could vouch for what really happened, Kathryn Latham and Detective Durban, have vanished. Patrick, if you could write something—anything—to say I'm not quite as insane as they think I am, it would really help. In fact, it might be my only chance.

Your old adversary-slash-lover-slash-soulmate,

Claire

It takes me a long time to write—I haven't done anything requiring this much mental effort since I came here. I put three kisses after my name, then take them off again. I feel exhausted. When I try to read the email back, the words wriggle and dance on the screen.

Well, I think, either it'll work or it won't. I click "Send," then instantly worry I'll come over as needy and plaintive.

As I log off, another fear strikes me. Patrick won't delete the email. Much more likely, he'll send it straight back to the hospital. Dr. Banner, in turn, will use it at the hearing. It'll look like further evidence I'm exactly what he says I am.

Thinking about what I just wrote in that context, I go cold. *I don't think I can stand it much longer.* That's tantamount to saying I might harm myself. My comments about Banner—*The doctor wants me to stay*—could be construed as paranoid. And what I say about Patrick and our supposed connection is classic HPD: reading significance into *relationships that isn't really there.*

A wave of nausea crashes over me as I realize that, far from making things better, I probably just made them a whole lot worse.

57

Patrick doesn't reply. It's between semesters, so maybe he doesn't monitor his university email address.

It's easier to believe that than to think he just looked at it and hit "Delete."

I go back on the computer and research how to fight commitment hearings. The answer is, you don't, not unless you have money. The judge usually sides with the psychiatric hospital's doctors. The only way to rebut their evidence is to hire a private psychiatrist to give a second opinion. But even if I could afford to do that, how would I do it from in here, with my brain clogged up with Dr. Banner's drugs?

On an impulse, I Google Banner's name. The center's own staff page comes up. From it I learn that Andrew Banner MD PhD has "a special interest in Cluster B personality disorders, including Borderline Personality Disorder, Histrionic Personality Disorder, and Narcissistic Personality Disorder, on which he has coauthored several papers."

The bastard, I think. That's why he's so keen to keep me here. He's *studying* me.

Or is that just more paranoia?

I do another search for "Kathryn Latham forensic psychologist." I'm not surprised when nothing appears. She must have been using a false name. For deniability, I guess. Yet another lie she told.

I think for a moment, then type in the URL for Necropolis.com. Of the many things that still puzzle me about Kathryn's operation, one is why she insisted I visit that website in particular. I can only assume she was watching my interactions with the other users somehow. But why? Was she hoping I'd get carried away and reveal some vital bit of information? Or is there some other significance to the site, something I missed?

Necropolis. The city of the dead. An odd name for a BDSM website, when you think about it.

I type in "Necropolis + Baudelaire." A fragment of poetry appears.

> *It's a necropolis; a grave in which the dead—*
> *Those bodies I once loved—are tumbled willy-nilly . . .*

Of course. The poem Patrick and I read aloud together, the very first time we met. It seems a lifetime ago.

Switching back to Necropolis, I enter my old login name, select "Forums," and type:

>>Anyone here interested in Baudelaire?

The silence is deafening. Around me, conversations are going on about different types of whips, illustrated with photographs.

"Claire?"

One of the night staff, a nurse, is staring down at me, astonished. "What are you doing?"

Hastily I try to minimize the window, but I'm too slow. She's seen.

"What is this?" she chides, taking the mouse from me and looking. "What you're doing is against the rules, Claire. And it may be unhelpful for your condition. I'm going to have to inform Dr. Banner."

sit in the TV room reading, or trying to. The only other person here is Meathead, whose restraints have been re moved for a couple of weeks now. He seems friendly enough, though, and I assume that if he's free to roam about he's no more dangerous than any of the other patients.

Since being caught at the orderlies' computer, my meds have been increased. I've given up trying to get myself out of this place. It's all I can do to keep my eyes open.

There's a box of tattered books that I sort through for something my glued-up mind can cope with. They're Westerns and kung fu stories, mostly. And a couple of hospital romances, which in any other circumstance might have struck me as ironic.

Meathead looks up. "Hey, Claire. Whatcha got?"

I glance unenthusiastically at the novel I've pulled out. *"Critical Care.* You?"

He examines the front of his comic and grunts. *"Judge Dredd."*

"Swap when we're done?"

Meathead looks contemptuous. "I don't read no books that don't have no pictures."

I sit down and stare at the first page. The words squirm like maggots. After a while I put it down and gaze at the television. Fifty-eight percent of viewers think the woman should give her straying husband one more chance.

"Claire, you have a visitor."

I must have nodded off. I look up, bleary-eyed, at the sound of the orderly's voice. Next to me, Meathead has abandoned *Judge Dredd* and is gazing dopily at the TV.

In the doorway, staring down at me with a look of horror on his face, is Patrick.

59

We go to one of the visiting rooms. Patrick still seems shocked. I realize what I must look like to him. As well as the weight I've put on, my skin has erupted in pimples, a reaction to the drugs. My hair is greasy and lank.

"Christ," he says. "Christ, Claire, you look terrible."

"You really know how to charm a girl." I thought I'd be overjoyed to see him, but now he's here I'm not sure what I feel.

As I pull out a chair, I stumble. On top of everything else, the meds have affected my balance.

"I'm so sorry . . . Claire, I'm so sorry."

I guess he isn't referring to his remark about my appearance. I want to tell him none of this is exactly his fault, but the words won't come.

"If it's any consolation," he adds, "they lied to me too. Dr. Latham and Detective Durban. I realize that now."

I shake my head. "It's not much consolation, no."

"This might be, though: I'm suing the NYPD. What

they did was grossly irresponsible. That's why I'm here—at least, partly. I want to add your name to the lawsuit."

I can't cope with all this. "Why?"

"You have an even stronger case than I do—if it hadn't been for their sting, you'd never have tried to kill yourself. You'd never have ended up in *here*. I just spoke to your doctor. He's an idiot. You need proper help. I'm going to make sure you get it. And the NYPD will pay. We'll start by appealing against your commitment."

"Patrick . . . Are you . . ." The idea seems so impossible, so wonderfully wrong, and at the same time so perfect, that I laugh out loud. "Are you *rescuing* me?"

"What if I am?" He studies me for a moment. Self-conscious about how I look, I duck my head. Then he says abruptly, "You said in your email we had a connection. But back then, you went a lot further. Do you remember?"

Something flickers through the fog.

ME

> I fell in love with you! They told me not to but I was too damn stupid. Patrick, don't you understand? I love you.

Even through the meds, I can remember how good it felt to finally say those words out loud.

I squeeze my eyes shut. "Yes. I remember."

"Was that real? Or just something they told you to say?"

"I don't know," I confess. "I thought it was real, at the time. So real, it hurt. But that's me, Patrick. Actors do it all the time. Falling in love with your costar. Showmances, they call them. Fool's gold. I seem to do it more than most."

"I see." He glances around at the drab, beige surroundings. "Anyway, the first priority is to get you out of this hellhole. You can stay with me until you decide what to do. After that, you'll be a free agent."

I try to protest, but he interrupts me. "You need looking after. Besides, I have an ulterior motive. I finally wrote my play. I'd like you to read it."

"Patrick . . ." I say helplessly. "I can't even read a comic book."

"Then we need to get your meds changed. I'll speak to the doctors. And to my lawyer, about getting you discharged."

60

Two weeks later I leave Greenridge. Patrick takes it for granted I'll stay with him, and I don't have the energy to resist. He installs me in a spare bedroom, runs baths filled with sweet-smelling Parisian oils, swaddles me in vast soft towels, and cooks me meals made with organic produce from Westside Market and Citarella. His building has a gym room, and I start to exercise, slowly losing the weight I put on in the hospital, all the while avoiding my own reflection in the mirrored walls that reflect a thousand tubby Claire Wrights back at me.

I can't help remembering Kathryn Latham's words. *If he's the killer, he'll be drawn to her vulnerability the way a shark's drawn to the scent of blood.*

But Kathryn was wrong, I think firmly. Not to mention a liar.

Every day a private psychiatrist visits, while Patrick tactfully goes out to leave us alone. The first few sessions Dr. Felix takes blood samples to check for traces of Banner's meds, but mostly we just talk about what happened. When

I describe Kathryn's role in the operation he goes pale with anger. From what he knows of forensic psychology, he says, the sting she constructed was almost certainly illegal. Something similar was attempted in Britain once, with an undercover policewoman as decoy. The policewoman ended up having a breakdown, the judge threw out the evidence as tainted, and the psychologist was charged with professional misconduct.

"Really, you got off lightly, Claire. Anyone would experience identity disturbance under that kind of pressure, let alone an untrained civilian."

Increasingly we also talk about my past, the demons I came to America to escape but which somehow smuggled themselves in with my hand luggage. Dr. Felix suggests coping strategies, areas where I might be able to rescript my thought patterns using a technique called Dialectical Behavior Therapy. We all have life scripts, he tells me, narratives we construct for ourselves as children, which, left unexamined, shape the outcome of our lives. His kind of therapy is all about revealing those narratives and rewriting them.

"There's a theory," he explains, "that Cluster B disorders may result from a mismatch between the emotions a child feels and those her caregiver validates by being receptive to. If your emotional needs were ignored or even thwarted by your foster parents, it could result in the kinds of behaviors Dr. Banner highlighted."

I think of Paul's warning. *For some, those are pretty dark places, Claire. But you still have to go there.*

The night before I left the hospital, Dr. Banner came to see me. I thought he'd be angry I'd found a way to get out from under him, but if so, he hid it well.

"I'm not entirely surprised you're leaving us, Claire," he said. "Most psychiatrists would argue that if a person's functioning okay, they *are* okay. And you're clearly functioning pretty well."

I braced myself for the *but*.

"The reason I think differently is because I've made a specialty of these particular disorders. And I can see what most practitioners can't, which is that you're putting on an act. Pretending to be someone you're not."

I leaned forward and spoke very quietly, so he had to crane forward to hear.

"You're right," I told him. "I'm just as crazy as ever. But so was that guy with the apple tree in his stomach."

A week after I move in, Patrick takes me to Liberty Island on the ferry. I never did the tourist things when I first came to New York, so this is all new to me.

We stand beneath the hollow lady, watching the lights of Manhattan dance on the silver-black water.

"Claire," he says at last, "how much of the person I fell in love with was real?"

"Kathryn was very clever. There was just enough of me in there to make it seem plausible." I glance at him. "I warn you, you may not like the real Claire as much. I'm a lot more actressy than she was, for one thing. Kathryn used the words *desperate for approval* about me. I change my mind in a heartbeat about things I feel passionate about, I like being the center of attention, and I can be strident on occasion. Oh, and I'm rarely meek, not a victim, and never, ever submissive. The Claire *you* got to see had been watered down by Kathryn for male approval."

"You sound fascinating," he murmurs. His eyes are on some fireworks, sparkling in the sky above Battery Park. "I'll take my chances."

I sigh. "And I'm gullible, too. Even when I was certain you hadn't done it, she convinced me I was just believing my own part."

"I didn't kill Stella, Claire."

"I know. I think I always knew." I turn to study his profile. "I didn't kill her either."

He nods.

"I'll take a lie detector test if you want," I add.

Patrick smiles. "That won't be necessary."

We're both silent.

"I knew you didn't do it when we went to the theater," he adds. "After that actor came up to us."

"Raoul," I say. "Raoul the singing rat. The one you headbutted."

"I panicked," he confesses with a thin smile. "I thought he was going to blow the whole thing. But he'd been so vile to you . . . It felt good, what I did. And then, in the cab, when you were upset . . . I told them the next day I was sure you were innocent."

"I was ahead of you there. I'd been saying that about *you* for ages. Poor Kathryn. It's a wonder she didn't call the whole thing off."

Even as I say it, something flickers at the edge of my mind. *Yes, why didn't she? Why still pursue the sting, when she must have known it was doomed?*

Something to do with that website, perhaps?

"Oh, and I'm an orphan, too," I add. "That was one of the hardest things, not being able to tell you that."

Patrick nods slowly as he takes in the implications. "I think I always knew, though. I certainly sensed we were alike, in some way other people aren't."

He reaches for my hand. "I asked you this in the hospital, Claire, and you didn't really give me an answer. But I think you're better now, so I'm asking again. Is there any chance we could start over? Or has there been too much water under the bridge?"

I gaze at the elegant iron tracery of Brooklyn Bridge. And suddenly, wonderfully, everything seems possible.

"Some bridges can span an awful lot of water," I say.

61

That night we make love for the first time since I got out. Or, as we've agreed to think of it, for the first time, period. Him and me, naked for each other in every sense. Without the costume of our deceptions.

He kisses my scars, the three thin red weals across my left forearm. They'll fade in time, the nurse at Greenridge had said. I hope they don't. I'm not ashamed of them.

Then he enters me with infinite gentleness, one hand cupped behind my head so he can see into my eyes.

The thought of being observed so minutely frightens me, and I try to hide myself from him, to force the crisis away. I think about all those times I slept with strangers, pretending to be someone else. Sometimes faking pleasure, sometimes just pretending to myself that I was faking it. But always, always putting on a performance.

This is what I was so scared of, I realize. Being seen for who I really am.

The sense of being so exposed only has the effect of making it stronger. When the climax comes, it breaks over me like a wave, churning and tumbling me in its rip, and I'm lost, a mewling, wailing castaway, incoherent words torn from my throat, my legs spasming, my back arching, all my muscles twitching uncontrollably.

"So that's what you look like when you do it for real," he whispers.

t's several days before I feel well enough to pick up Patrick's play. Even then, the words won't stay still to begin with. But because *he* wrote it, I persevere. Gradually I can read two pages at a time, then three, then whole scenes.

My Heart Laid Bare opens in the summer of 1857, in the run-down apartment Baudelaire shares with his mistress, Jeanne Duval. She's complaining about their poverty. He'd always said the publication of *Les Fleurs du Mal* would make his fortune. Instead, the book has been seized and he's being tried for obscenity. If found guilty, he'll be fined or sent to jail.

Jeanne gives him a choice. Should she sell the jewels he bought her with his advance, or prostitute herself on the street, as she has had to do so many times before?

Baudelaire's torn. He knows it has to be the jewels, but he can't bear for her to sell them until she's worn them for him one last time. Jeanne disappears into their bedroom, and returns naked but for the jewelry. At this point, the dialogue switches to verse:

My darling was naked, and, knowing my desires,
Had kept on only her tinkling jewels . . .

Flicking forward, I see the whole play follows this structure: scenes from life, interspersed with Baudelaire's poems.
A challenge for a director, but an intriguing one.

After they've made love, Jeanne leaves to sell the jewels
and Baudelaire is visited by his friend Flaubert. Flaubert—
who was recently prosecuted for obscenity himself, for *Ma-
dame Bovary,* but acquitted—tells Baudelaire that this time
the authorities are determined to succeed. Baudelaire, he
warns, urgently needs to find influential figures to pull
strings on his behalf.

Baudelaire has come to the same dispiriting conclusion.
There's just one person he can think of: Apollonie Sabatier,
the White Venus: the woman to whom he sent, anonymously, some of the most violent and cruel poems in *Les
Fleurs du Mal.*

The next scene takes place in Apollonie's house. It's the
first time the two of them have spoken since the book's publication; since she discovered that the unknown admirer
who sent her these strange, savage verses was the same pen-
niless writer who frequented her salon. The scene is electri-
fying. She wants to know why. He refuses to explain himself.
When she asks him if this is really what goes on in his
head—whether he genuinely has those violent feelings for
her—he replies that she must interrogate the poems, not him.

She has, she says. And, knowing him as she does, she
chooses to believe that the poems' brutality is just a literary
device, for sensational effect, not glimpses into a truly de-
praved mind.

But her lines are written in such a way that she might be trying to convince herself.

The scene ends with Apollonie saying she'll try to help him, but in return, after the trial, she intends to ask a favor, which Baudelaire must grant, no matter what it is. Baudelaire guesses she'll make him promise never to see or write to her again, but he has no choice. He agrees to pay her price.

At this point I stop to think about what I've just read. The scene with Jeanne Duval was good, but somewhat simplistic. The scene with Apollonie was something else. Her character leaps off the page, complex and torn, both attracted to and repelled by the darkness she senses inside the poet's heart.

Just as I was fascinated by what I sensed inside Patrick's, I think.

The second act of the play is taken up with the trial. In his defense, Baudelaire speaks eloquently of art that has no moral agenda. But, when asked by the prosecutor how he would feel if someone was inspired by one of his verses to commit an act of evil, he falters. He claims the poems may show immorality, but they don't celebrate it. The prosecutor reads out several passages that plainly do just that, and repeats his question. *How would you feel if someone is inspired by one of your verses to commit an act of evil?* Baudelaire insists that we all have vile thoughts: All he has done is given them a voice. But clearly, the idea he might inspire followers doesn't displease him.

The trial lasts less than a day. Six of the most extreme poems remain censored, and Baudelaire is fined the enormous sum of three hundred francs.

He goes back to Apollonie. Too late, he's guessed that, when she interceded on his behalf, she also arranged that the most brutal poems about her should remain banned.

She doesn't deny the accusation. But she reminds him of his promise.

Very well, he says with a heavy heart. What is it that you want?

She tells him she wants to sleep with him.

It's the only way, she's decided, to discover what his feelings for her truly are—whether it's the savagery, or the tenderness, that's the *real* Charles Baudelaire.

Which do you hope for? he asks quietly.

And we can see she's torn; that, at some level, she hopes he really is the devil his poems make him out to be. She's been loved before by sentimental, timid men. She's never been adored by a man who wants to simultaneously worship and desecrate her.

Nevertheless, she insists that she knows him to be a good person at heart.

They go to bed. At the climactic moment, there's a blackout. The next day, he sends her the now-famous letter of rejection.

63

The play is good. Like a true dramatist, Patrick has balanced out the arguments. Far from glorifying decadence, the play reveals it as a kind of narcissism, the self-regard of the artist who pursues originality at any cost.

Most of all, though, it's a story about a man and a woman trying to guess each other's motives. To work out what's really going on inside the other's mind.

It isn't hard to see where Patrick got his inspiration. It's *our* story: the story of the police operation, transposed back to nineteenth-century Paris.

Yet it's also a story that's unresolved. Does Apollonie sleep with Baudelaire for the reasons she gives? Or has she fallen in love with him? Does she even hope that the reality of her naked body will somehow draw the venom of his violent obsession with her? If so, it may have worked. He wrote her no more sadistic poems after that night. He even broke with the *Vénus Noire,* and went to live with his widowed mother in the countryside. The play's final scene shows him picking a fresh flower from her garden, then placing it in his buttonhole.

As for Baudelaire himself, the play never fully answers the question Apollonie first put to him: Is this how you genuinely feel, or are you just trying to shock? *What would I really see, if I could look into your heart?*

All the roles are good. But Apollonie's would be the most interesting to play.

64

"Your play," I tell Patrick when he returns. "I love it. It's provocative, but multifaceted. Nuanced, even."

"So you'll do it?" he says eagerly.

"Do what?"

"Play Apollonie, of course."

My mood crashes to the floor. "Patrick, I can't," I say wistfully. "Didn't Frank and Kathryn tell you? I'm not allowed to work here. That was how they ensnared me in their stupid scheme in the first place."

"Haven't you heard of the Equity exchange program? Swapping a job for a British actor here with one for an American in the UK?"

"Yes, but that's only for producers—"

"I *am* the producer."

"What are you talking about?"

"I'm going to put it on myself. On Broadway."

"Broadway?"

"Twenty-nine Sixty Broadway, to be precise. Sorry it's such a long way from Times Square, but it's the best I could do." When I still look uncomprehending, he adds, "There's a theater at the university. I'm hiring it. I don't kid myself I'll make back my costs, but who cares? It's a small cast, and the reviewers will still come. And there's nothing else I'd rather do with Stella's money."

"Patrick . . ." I protest feebly.

"Just say you'll do it."

"Don't you see?" I'm getting angry now. "You're offering me the one thing I want most. A great role in a new play, premiering in one of the most important cities for live drama in the world. But I can't. Quite apart from anything else, I'm not in shape."

"We'll find a great director," he says simply. "And great costars, of course. My pockets are deep, Claire, and without you there can't be a play."

"I can't accept."

"There are no strings," he adds as if I haven't spoken. "I hope that goes without saying."

I squeeze my eyes shut. I know I ought to say no. But another part of me is thinking, *Why not?* Already I can feel my energy levels coming back. The weight I put on is starting to come off. My skin is healing. And despite what I just said, I know I'm more than capable of playing this part.

This could be the opportunity I came to America for. I wasn't expecting it to be presented to me quite like this, but a break is a break.

And there's something else too. If this play is our story, putting it on together could be a chance to rewrite our relationship. For the real me, and the real Patrick, to lay our own hearts bare to each other. And this time I'll be on my home ground. My natural métier. The stage.

go back to Jess's for my stuff. I hear her gasp when I say my name over the intercom, and by the time I get to the apartment she's in the hallway staring at me, openmouthed.

"*Jesus,* Claire," she exclaims. "What the hell happened?"

"Things got—complicated."

"It's been *three months*. The university got in touch to ask why you'd dropped out of your classes. I had to tell them I had no idea. And your agent came around."

"Marcie came here?"

Jess nods. "She was worried about you. She said you have, like, this *history* of going off the rails."

"That's putting it a bit strongly," I mutter. "Still, it's nice of her to care. Can I come in?"

"I guess," she says, awkwardly.

"I suppose I owe you a lot of back rent," I say as I follow her inside. "We might have to come to some arrangement." Automatically I glance at the door of my room. A man's shirt in a laundry wrapper is hooked over the handle.

"Claire, I'm really sorry," she says miserably. "I had to rent it out. My dad insisted."

"Oh. Well, sure, I can see why you had to do that," I say, although I'd been half hoping she wouldn't. "Where are my things?"

"In storage. I nearly gave them to your brother."

"My *brother*?" Now it's my turn to stare at her. "I don't have a brother."

"Your foster brother, John. He came here a few days ago with his fiancée, looking for you—he'd gotten the address from the university. He was hoping to see you while he's over. They're only in the city for a week."

"Oh, that brother." No point in trying to explain to Jess that when you're in foster care, "brothers" are just more people who happen to share your life briefly. Still, John had been one of the better ones. "What was the fiancée like?"

"She seemed nice. Very down-to-earth. Anyway, I took his number." She hesitates, then says in a rush, "Look, I told him about the money. I didn't know what else to do—I mean, I gave my dad what he was owed, but I found the rest when I was clearing your room and I wasn't sure—"

"Oh," I say. "You found my money."

She nods. "I didn't know what to think."

"Maybe you thought I stole it from Stella Fogler," I say, because I know that's what she's really thinking. "The money that went missing when she was killed."

"No," she says. Meaning yes.

"I was working like crazy to get your dad his rent. Eleven hundred dollars in a month, if you recall."

"You couldn't work. That's what you told me."

"I told you the police had warned me off working for Henry. So I got that money on my own."

"I don't get it." Then she starts to understand. "Oh," she

says. "Jesus, Claire. *Jesus.* Why didn't you *say* something? My dad would have understood—"

"Oh sure," I say bitterly. "Your dad understood all right. Your dad understood *perfectly*."

"What do you mean?" she asks in a small voice.

"He came by a few times when you were at rehearsals. Checking the fuse box, fixing the sink we'd supposedly blocked with our girlie stuff, that kind of thing. So I thought I'd take the chance to talk to him. Get myself a bit more time, maybe. He turned out to be *really* sympathetic."

"Whoa." Jess is staring at me. "*Whoa.* If this is going where I think it's going, I don't—"

I nod. "A special discount for services rendered. To be delivered by installments, naturally. I said no, for what it's worth. Because that would be a bit weird even for me, screwing my roommate's dad. Maybe that's why he was so keen to get my stuff out of here."

"Oh God, Claire. I never realized—" She's gone very pale.

"Why should you? It wasn't your fault."

Jess starts to cry. "You should have said something."

"I was hoping not to fuck up your family dynamic. Something I now seem to have blown spectacularly." I sigh. "Blame it on the therapy. Sometimes I think truth is overrated. But they were pretty keen on it in the hospital."

She goes to the fridge and, shakily, pulls out a bottle of wine. "I think we'd better open this."

After that, of course, she wants to know everything that's happened since I left her apartment one morning with Frank Durban and a travel bag. She listens disbelievingly as I tell her about the undercover operation, my breakdown, Green-ridge. But it's the bit where I tell her I'm now living with Patrick and I'm going to be acting in his play that reduces her to stunned silence.

"So," I conclude, "I seem to have fallen on my feet. In love, in work, and still in the good ol' US of A. Triple word score."

She finds her voice. "You're in love. With a man who may have murdered the last woman who tried to leave him."

"That was just Kathryn's bullshit."

"I saw the press conference," she reminds me. Her voice has grown shrill. "We both did. That man was a *suspect*."

"I know what I'm doing."

"Says the woman whose only other experience of love was with a married philanderer on a movie shoot. Says the woman who just sprang herself from a psychiatric hospital. Jesus, Claire. You were safer when you went out and picked up random strangers in bars." She stares at me, shocked. "Or is that it? Do you secretly *like* the fact you might be sleeping with a psycho?"

"Patrick didn't kill Stella."

"Then who did?" she demands.

I don't have an answer for that, of course.

" think it's great. Properly staged, it could be spectacular. But a spectacle that poses a serious question: What responsibility do we have, as artists, for the effect our work has in the real world?"

Patrick has set up a meeting with Aidan Keating, a hot young director known for making risky subject matter his own. Last year he won a Tony for his revival of Ionesco's *Rhinoceros*. I'm trying hard not to be starstruck.

"With such a small canvas, though, casting really is everything," Aidan adds. Under his frizzy blond hair, his eyes flick in my direction.

I know what he's thinking. *If I let the writer cast his girl-friend, it'll be seen as a vanity project.*

Patrick says calmly, "Of course. That's why I immediately thought of Claire for Apollonie. She's an alumnus of the Actors Studio."

"I'm doing the Actors Studio course at Pace," I mumble. "I haven't actually completed it—"

"I know," Aidan interrupts. "No disrespect, Claire, but to make this play a commercial success, we need actors whose names are a draw. There's quite a trend at the moment for film and TV stars to take time out to do theater. This could be an attractive vehicle."

"Of course. I understand." I try not to let my disappointment show. "Whatever's best for the play."

"Claire's part is a given," Patrick says coldly. "I thought I'd made that clear. You'll have freedom over the rest of the cast, and the budget to lure big names if you need it, but if you can't accept my preconditions, you're not the right person for the job."

For a moment the two men lock eyes. Although neither moves a muscle, they both seem to grow more menacing—some subtle, subconscious adjustment of body language and breathing.

Aidan says challengingly, "And what about the script? I have notes, particularly about the second half. I loathe the Hollywood ending. Some of the dialogue creaks. Jeanne, in particular, descends into cliché every time she takes her clothes off. No self-respecting female actor will touch that part as it stands."

"As writer, I'll address any changes you ask for," Patrick says.

"I'd want job security built into my contract. I can't have you firing me because we disagree over the artistic direction of the play."

"That's hardly standard."

"These aren't standard circumstances. If you give me full control, a script I can work with, and a proper budget, I'll see Claire's audition. That's all I can promise."

"Audition her first," Patrick says curtly. "If you like what you see, we have a deal."

don't really want to see my foster brother and his fiancée, but halfway into the bottle Jess had started nagging me about him and, having spilled the beans about her dad, I didn't want to look like I don't care about my own family, even though I don't. So I promised I'd contact them.

Plus I was feeling a little guilty about the whole dad thing. The fact is, it might have been as much my fault as his. That is, it had occurred to me that having her dad make a pass at me, and me turning him down, might be useful leverage in our coming negotiations over the rent. I hadn't intended to tell Jess any of that, of course. I was just angry when I heard how he'd insisted she kick my stuff out. One moment the words had flashed into my mind, the next they were coming out of my mouth.

I seem to have become a more impulsive person since Greenridge. An angrier one, too. *Volatile* and *manipulative* even, to quote Dr. Banner's list of symptoms.

Or maybe it was just to do with the fact that Jess at least had a dad. Someone to buy her an apartment, to worry about her safety, to make a fuss over her.

Anyway, being Jess, she'd made me text John there and then, and now here I am waiting for him and his fiancée at a steak house just off Times Square. Next to me is Patrick. I didn't ask him to come, but he said he wanted to meet what little family I had. And I'd realized that, for my part, I wanted to show him off. To let John see he's not the only one who's been successful in love.

"Claire!"

They're here. I jump up and hug John a little overenthusiastically, then shake hands with his girlfriend, whom he introduces as "our Alice." I introduce Patrick, who congratulates them on being engaged. John gives Alice's shoulder a proud squeeze. She looks okay, I decide. I understand why Jess used the phrase *down-to-earth*. She's dressed for a hike in the country—sensible walking boots, jeans, North Face anorak, fanny pack—while John's carrying a backpack and wearing cargo shorts, despite the fact it's almost the end of September. He always wore shorts, I remember, even when it was snowing. Instantly I regret making so much of an effort. Patrick's told me to borrow any of Stella's clothes I want until I can get mine out of storage, but they're all a bit upscale for me.

"Eh, it's good to see you," John says as he sits down. He hasn't lost his Yorkshire accent, even though he tells me he's been working in London for the past three years.

"You sound like a Yank, though," he adds. "With some right posh English mixed in."

"The cabdrivers here mostly think I'm Australian."

"There you go—*cab*. That's how American you are. And how posh. Back home we say bus." He grins at his own joke.

Patrick tries to draw Alice into conversation but doesn't get much of a response. At first I think she's just quiet, but then I see her glance at John and I realize she's holding back, waiting for him to say something.

Eventually he comes out with it.

"It were Alice said I should try to track you down, Claire. She's got to know Ross and Julie quite well since our engagement, so she's part of the family now."

I try to place Ross. Then I remember that Julie, our foster mother, remarried.

"The rest of us—Julie's foster kids—have a WhatsApp group. Well, there's some who've fallen through the cracks, like you, but eight of us keep in touch, plus her birth kids of course. It'll be her sixtieth in a couple of months, so we're organizing a reunion. She's an amazing woman and we want to do something special for her. There'll be press and every-thing. Mebbe you'd think about coming home for it."

I stare at him. Even if I *could* go home—if I could afford the flights, if I could be sure of being allowed back into the United States—the idea that I would voluntarily go and spend time with that woman and my other foster siblings is, frankly, nuts.

John sees my expression and misunderstands. "She doesn't bear you any ill will, Claire."

"*She* doesn't bear *me* ill will?" I repeat incredulously. "After what *her* husband did to me?"

John glances at Patrick, as if he isn't sure whether he should say more. But he was always direct, even as a teen-ager.

"I meant, she doesn't bear you any ill will for lying about it," he says quietly. "Kids in care act out, she always says. Particularly when they've come from a bad place be-fore. It's social services she blames, for taking the word of a foster kid over her husband."

"So you think I was lying too," I say bitterly. "Just like she always did."

Next to me, Patrick has gone very still. Recognizing the warning signs, I put a hand on his arm. *I can handle this.*

"When you made that complaint about Gary," John says bluntly, "you made up a load of stuff that hadn't really happened. You know that, Claire. It were all part of your campaign to get into that stage school."

I glare at him.

"Do you really not remember what it was like?" I say. "How every summer, we were packed off to another foster home so Julie and Gary could go on holiday with their own kids 'as a family'? How they'd tell us not to leave our things in the living room, in case we forgot them when we left?"

"They had to have boundaries," John says. "At least they took us in."

"Oh sure," I say bitterly. "With the unspoken threat that, if we didn't behave, we'd be thrown out again."

You got used to that feeling, I remember, until it almost became a part of you. However welcoming people seemed, sooner or later they'd disappear, or break the news you were moving on. Inside, you were always waiting for the invisible sirens to go off and the formal procedures of separation to kick in.

John sighs. "So you won't come to Julie's party, Claire?"

"Wild horses wouldn't drag me there."

"Wow," he says, shaking his head. "You've changed. You were always a bit over the top, but you were fundamentally a decent person. What happened, Claire?"

I put my arm through Patrick's defiantly. "Yes, I *have* changed. I've got a new life. Things are going well for me here. As far as I'm concerned, none of that other stuff ever happened."

"I'm sorry you had to witness that," I say as we leave.

"Thank you for letting me be there," Patrick says. I look at him to see if he's joking, but he's serious.

"We obviously had very different experiences, growing up," he adds. "But we have this in common: However hard it was for us, at least we get to choose. We can choose our families, our hometown, our origins . . . We can be whoever we decide to be. And, even though it may be harder for us to give our trust to someone, when we do, we give it absolutely."

"Yes," I say, nodding. "It's one of the reasons I came to New York. It's the city where everyone's from somewhere else, isn't it? Where people reinvent themselves. And I certainly choose not to be part of that family anymore."

Patrick squeezes my hand with his arm. He doesn't say anything, but I know what he's thinking.

You have me, now.

68

Aidan auditions me at a small casting studio in Chelsea. He sits stony-faced behind a table with a casting director I don't know, a woman he introduces only as Mo. There's no chat, just a polite "What are you doing for us today, Claire?" and "Whenever you're ready."

Ignoring the fact that I want to throw up with nerves, I breathe, center myself, and begin. I've prepared Jenny's Epilogue from Leslye Headland's play *Assistance*. It's a loud, raucous monologue that has a bit of everything—drunkenness, dancing, pathos, comedy—so I figure it'll be a good showcase for my talents.

When I'm done there's a long silence before Aidan says, "Thank you."

I resist the urge to gush at him—*What did you think? What did you really think? Shall I do it again? Faster? Slower? Sadder? Funnier? What are you looking for? Do you like me?*

Kathryn Latham's words come back to me. *Although she tries extremely hard to hide it, she craves approval like a junkie craving a fix.* With a sinking feeling I realize my lack of confidence has just led me to do an audition that screamed *Look at me!*

What I did just now wasn't acting. It was showing off.

"I'd like to do something else as well, please," I say calmly.

Aidan glances at Mo, who shrugs, as if to say, *We might as well, we're here now.*

"All right," he says with a loud sigh. "What would you like to do, Claire?"

I dredge my memory for something that might be relevant to *his* play, to the part I'm trying to get.

And, intuitively, it comes to me.

You read it well . . .

Instead of a monologue, I do a poem. The poem I read with Patrick, the first time we met. Making my voice low, milking the rhythm.

> ME
>
> *I have more memories than if I had lived a thousand*
> *years . . .*

Halfway through I see Mo turn her head to glance at Aidan. His face gives nothing away. But, emboldened by her gesture, I trust my instincts and make the last few lines so still and quiet they're barely there.

> ME
>
> *Like some old statue of a half-forgotten god,*
> *Abandoned in the desert, starved of blood,*
> *Whose enigmatic, weather-beaten frown*
> *Lights up, for a moment, as the sun goes down.*

I finish, and Aidan frowns.

"Well," he says, "there was a lot about that I hated, particularly the first piece. But I think I can work with you."

He gets up, gives me a quick, professional handshake, and leaves. But not before I've seen the expression in his eyes.

He's angry.

He was hoping I'd be terrible, I realize. That would have given him the out he needed. Instead, he's got to work with an actress he hasn't chosen.

69

"So," Marcie says, reaching for her vape. "New York is talking about nothing else. Well, the small self-obsessed corner of it that's interested in fringe theater, any-way."

"It's very exciting," I say modestly.

"It's very self-indulgent, is what it is." Marcie blows a trumpet of vape smoke over my head. "But it changes every-thing as far as you're concerned. If a director like Aidan Keating sees something in you, everyone else will jump on the bandwagon. Is there nudity?"

"Some."

"Good. The reviewers will talk about it, and the bridge-and-tunnel crowd will come for it. Careers have been launched on less." She stabs the end of the vape in my direction. "Don't fuck this up, Claire. Second chances in this business come along maybe once in a lifetime. Third chances, never."

"I'll try not to. But even if it's a success, won't I still have the green card problem?"

She considers. "Realistically, yes. We can argue there's precedent for you to go through the exchange program now, but most producers won't bother for someone who isn't a big name." She studies me shrewdly. "How serious is it with this Patrick?"

"Pretty serious."

"Wedding bell serious?"

I blink, surprised, and she continues impatiently, "Yes, very good, but don't tell me you haven't thought about it. A wealthy U.S. citizen puts on a play just to see his favorite female actor in the lead role. Marry him, and you'll get a green card *and* a Gold Card."

"His last marriage didn't work out so well."

"*That* controversy won't hurt the play either, by the way."

"Which controversy?"

"They're saying one of you probably bumped her off. Which I always say is stupid. I tell them your destructiveness is generally directed at yourself."

"Thank you for that," I say drily.

She bats my words away with the vape. "The general consensus is, you did it together."

"That's absurd."

"If it makes them come to see the show, who cares?" She looks at me thoughtfully. "Have you heard who they're considering for the other parts?"

I shake my head. "Patrick doesn't know. Aidan insisted on full creative control."

"The word is he wants Nyasha Neary for Jeanne Duval."

I nod, impressed. Half Zimbabwean, half Irish, Nyasha was nominated for a slew of awards last year for her role in a harrowing slave biopic on TV. She has enormous eyes that can change expression from affection to withering scorn without a blink, and cheekbones so sharp she looks like a bust of Nefertiti. She's one of the most beautiful women on the planet.

"And Baudelaire?"

"They're talking to Laurence Pisano."

I stare back at her, speechless. Laurence. The actor I fell in love with on my first movie shoot. The man I believed I wanted to die for.

And instantly I see what Aidan's trying to do here. He'll have heard the stories about me and Laurence. Hell, Marcie probably told him herself. He couldn't refuse to cast me without losing Patrick's money. But by casting Laurence, he's hoping to force me to walk. Then he'll be able to shrug and say, *Well, it was her choice.*

"And who do they have in mind for Apollonie? After they've pushed me out, that is."

Marcie shrugs. "He'll have his pick. If you walk away."

"I'm not going to walk away."

Marcie's eyes glitter. "That's just what I told them, Claire."

70

And in the midst of all this, there's still me and Patrick. Coming back every day to his quiet apartment overlooking the cathedral. Getting to know each other the best way possible: working together on a play.

"Now that you've lived with her awhile, how would you describe the real Claire?" I ask one evening as he cooks us dinner. Patrick is amusingly obsessive about his cooking. Jess and I thought we were following a recipe if we had more than half the ingredients in some random list we'd found online, but Patrick even looks down his nose at Julia Child and Elizabeth David. Tonight he's openly debated which of two ancient French volumes to consult, Escoffier or Carême. He has a collection of knives no one else is allowed to touch, forged from razor-sharp Damascus steel and hammered like tiny samurai swords, and right now he's chopping crumbs of garlic like he's splitting the atom.

But I have to admit, a powerful man does look sexy in an apron.

Patrick thinks for a moment. "Mercurial," he decides.

"Messy. Loud. And endlessly fascinating. Just when I think I have a handle on you, I realize I don't."

"Maybe that's because there's no handle to get. Or," I admit, "because I'm still trying to impress you. I can't help worrying that when you know me better, you'll be disappointed."

"I doubt that very much."

"I'm not always nice, Patrick. Or kind. You saw that yourself, with John and Alice."

"Being nice all the time is for wimps." He hands me a spoon, to taste his sauce. "More pepper?"

"But *you're* nice," I say. I swallow the sauce and nod my approval.

He shakes his head, smiling. "Only with you."

As we eat, we discuss the rewrites Aidan's asked for. Some deviate from the facts of Baudelaire's life, and these Patrick is resisting; in all other respects, he's being true to his promise to give Aidan full control. In the latest version, for example, when Jeanne discovers Baudelaire has visited Apollonie, she flies into a jealous rage. Furious, she tells him she intends to visit a famous nude statue Apollonie modeled for, to spit on it. But when she gets there, she finds herself mesmerized by the other woman's beauty. The statue comes to life, and the two women make love. Only later do we discover the scene is in Baudelaire's head, a re-imagining of one of his banned poems on lesbianism.

"You don't mind?" Patrick wants to know.

I shrug. "Like you, I'm in Aidan's hands. But what about you? Will it be hard for you, seeing me like that on stage?"

He shakes his head. "I'm not the jealous type, Claire. I'll just be proud of you. Very proud."

Aware I'll be acting these scenes with a woman far more beautiful than me, I cut down on the French food and redouble my sessions on the gym machines. When that gets oppressive, I start jogging around the local parks. Morningside, the grass dotted with groups of students, and Riverside, with its spectacular views across the Hudson. That old feeling of *Wow, this is like a movie* replaced now with an astonished recognition that *Wow, this is for real.*

Wedding bell serious? Don't tell me you haven't thought about it, Marcie had said cynically. And of course I have, and do. Who wouldn't? But I'm trying to take each day as it comes, to give our relationship time to breathe.

Dr. Felix visits just once a week now. Gradually, our therapy sessions have become less about the police sting and more about my relationship with Patrick.

"I've always walked out on people," I tell him. "Or forced them to walk out on me. Already this is the longest relationship I've ever had."

"Are you waiting for someone to come and tell you it's time to go? For . . ." He consults his notes. "'For the invisible sirens to go off and the formal procedures of separation to kick in'?"

I've told him about meeting John and Alice. Dr. Felix took so many notes that session, he could barely keep up.

I wince at how melodramatic I must have sounded. "Of course not. Well, maybe just a little. I suppose I still feel like an imposter. Like I'm playing a part."

"Which some might consider ironic," he murmurs.

"Funnily enough, it's only when I'm acting I *don't* feel that. But being here, in Stella's apartment, even wearing some of her clothes . . ."

"Yes, tell me about that. Was that Patrick's suggestion, or yours?"

"His. But it's just a practical thing. My own clothes are still in storage, and somehow with the play and everything there's never been time to get them out."

He makes another note.

"I suppose I'm wondering whether this is really what love feels like," I say. "Or if I'm still doing what Kathryn Latham accused me of—getting too deep into the part."

"It's hardly surprising, given that for many years you were effectively forced to live both as part of a family and separate from it. It could even be why you were drawn to acting in the first place."

"Meaning I'll always feel like this?"

"I don't think anyone can say that. Perhaps being in love is simply a new and surprising thing for you, Claire. Just try to enjoy it."

And yet, if I'm honest, there's something missing between me and Patrick now.

"I have a confession to make," I tell him one evening.

I think how, once, those words would have set both our pulses racing. Not to mention our audience's, the invisible watchers and listeners crouched over their dials.

But Patrick only lifts an eyebrow. "Oh?"

"I miss our games," I say. "It was actually a thrill, not knowing if you were a murderer or not."

His lips twitch. "Would you like me to kill someone for you?"

"Probably not. But perhaps I'm like Apollonie in your play—I don't want to believe the poems reflect the real you. And yet, at the same time, a part of me hopes they do. Which is crazy, I know. You're no more an evil person than Baudelaire was."

Patrick stoops to kiss the top of my head. "You don't know me yet, Claire," he says lightly. "You don't know everything inside my mind. That takes a little longer."

71

Finally, we reach the first day of rehearsal, the table read.

I'm terrified, of course. Terrified of seeing Laurence again. Terrified Nyasha will show me up. Terrified the designer and the other department heads will know I only got the part because of Patrick.

Patrick seems almost amused by my nerves. He's never seen me like this, he teases, and really there's no need. I should just remember how good I am.

He and I get to the rehearsal room first. Aidan's next, greeting me with a hug that almost seems genuine but which I instinctively mistrust. The four actors with smaller parts, three of whom will also be understudies, turn up together. Laurence arrives ten minutes before the call time and makes a point of hanging out with the lighting team, joshing around, just one of the guys. His pretty, boyish face has barely changed, but I'm relieved to discover I feel nothing for him, nothing at all.

"Laurence, have you met Claire?" Aidan asks eventually. Laurence glances in my direction. "Yes, we met on *Tu-*

mult." He ambles over and gives me a perfunctory kiss on both cheeks. "How've you been, Claire? Really looking forward to working with you again." The smile that once melted my heart flicks on and off. And that's it. No acknowledgment we were once lovers. No apology, no mention of what I did. A simple word of affection or regret would have been all it took, but it seems I'm not even going to get that.

Doesn't Count On Location, darling.

Nyasha arrives precisely on time. She's dressed as if for a gym workout, in a gray tracksuit with a hint of crimson T-shirt showing under the zipper, a black baseball cap pulled down over her cornrow braids. It has the effect of dialing down her beauty, but nothing can dull the perfection of her cheekbones, or still her glittering eyes. She's smaller than you'd imagine from seeing her on TV. She shakes my hand politely, almost shyly, her expression serious.

Aidan claps his hands and conversation immediately dies. He starts by welcoming us to what is now, he says, a family, a community. He talks about the word *troupe,* an old and noble word to describe a traveling band of actors relying on one another for their survival. He talks briefly about the production—how it should have the raw potency of Baudelaire's own poetry, how it needs to challenge and provoke a modern audience, just as *Les Fleurs du Mal* challenged a century steeped in the sentimentality of Romanticism. And finally, he speaks about the read-through.

"Today's not a performance. And certainly not an audition. Focus on clarity, on revealing the words on the page. There'll be plenty of time for acting later. This is just us, as a group, taking a first look together at the project. No one here needs to impress anybody else."

We all nod. I wonder if that last note was aimed at me. Nyasha takes off her baseball cap.

My first scene isn't for a while, so to begin with I just listen. It soon becomes clear that, while Nyasha has heard what Aidan said and is simply reading the words out loud, Laurence has come along with some ideas of his own. Most noticeably, he reads Baudelaire's part with a French accent. Patrick's head goes up at the very first line, but Aidan says nothing for several pages.

"That's great, Laurence," he interjects at last. "I think let's just read it straight for now, and we'll come back to explore accents later."

"Okay," Laurence says. "Great." He resumes reading with exactly the same accent.

Once again, Aidan stops him. "Let's hold the accent for the time being."

Laurence frowns. I realize he's already directed himself in his head, and is now going to have a hard time letting go. When we resume, he manages to strip out most of the French inflections, but every so often one slides back in. As he reads, he pushes his hair out of his eyes with an impatient flick. Once, I used to think that gesture impossibly cute. Now I just wonder why he doesn't get a haircut.

Nyasha sits very still, scarcely moving, but her voice is a thing of beauty. She does almost nothing with it you could put your finger on, but I could listen to her for hours.

When it comes to my lines I try to follow her example and let the words speak for themselves. But my very first scene is the one where Baudelaire confesses that he's the author of the violent, anonymous poems I've been receiving for the past five years, and I allow just a little of the scorn I now feel for Laurence to seep into the way Apollonie speaks to

Baudelaire. I see Aidan look up from his script thoughtfully, but he says nothing.

Eventually we reach the end and applaud one another. Aidan tells us we're all terrific. But really, I think, it's the material that's good.

This could be something amazing, I realize. This could be my breakthrough. I can hardly believe my luck.

We all get up and stretch. Laurence makes a beeline for Aidan—I hear him ask if they can discuss some ideas he's had. Aidan says something polite but noncommittal.

Nyasha comes over and compliments me on my reading.

"This is going to be great fun," she says in her careful, serious voice. She's taken off her tracksuit top: The arms that emerge from her T-shirt are like slim black cables, woven plaits of hard muscle. Up close, I'm mesmerized by the otherworldly quality of her beauty.

She puts her hand on my wrist. "I hear you're with Patrick," she says quietly. "He seems really great." She lets her gaze travel from Patrick to Laurence—the latter still engaged in intense discussions with Aidan—and says no more.

But it's enough. We're allies now. And maybe even friends.

'm jogging around Morningside Park next afternoon, thinking about that morning's rehearsal, when I have a familiar feeling. It's a feeling every actor has when they're on stage: the sense of being watched.

Which is weird, because out here, there must be a dozen pairs of eyes on me at any time, and I don't usually feel like that. I shake my head and carry on.

As I do another circuit, I get the same feeling again. And in exactly the same part of the park. Involuntarily, the hairs lift on the back of my neck.

I stop and look up. High above me, on the steps leading down from the Harlem side, stands a figure.

Frank Durban.

At least, I'm pretty sure it's him. He's too far away to make him out clearly—it's more the way he's standing, the way he always stands: his big body braced against the balustrade, one shoulder turned in as if it aches.

For a long moment I don't move. Then I sprint toward him, dodging recklessly through the trees, jumping over a dog leash that threatens to entangle my feet. There are four

flights of steps, zigzagging up the steep incline, and I power
up them, my legs and lungs burning—

There's no one there. I stop, panting, and look around.

Maybe I imagined it.

All the way back to the apartment I keep turning around
suddenly. But no one drops to one knee to do up a shoelace,
or ducks into a doorway, or any of the other things you see
in movies.

By the time I get home I've convinced myself I *did*
imagine it. After all, why would Frank be interested in me
now? Given he's on sick leave, and Kathryn's vanished, and
Patrick is suing the NYPD—

I stop, brought up sharp by the thought that's just
crashed into my head.

What if none of that's true?

I only have Patrick's word for it that he's suing anyone. Frank's sick leave could be a cover story to explain his
absence on the operation. And Kathryn . . . She may have
vanished, but she's out there somewhere. I can *feel* it. Ma-
nipulating me. Playing her games.

With a sudden lurch of nausea, I realize what's really
happened here. *I've walked right back into their trap.* Sending
that desperate email to Patrick from Greenridge. I can just
imagine Kathryn reading it, tapping her lips thoughtfully
with her pen.

KATHRYN

It seems the operation may not be dead after all.

FRANK

You're not suggesting we continue to use Fogler? No way Claire will trust him now.

KATHRYN

Why not? It's clear from this she's still obsessed
with him. What if he swans into Greenridge as
her knight in shining armor?

FRANK

It'll never work. She's paranoid at the best of
times.

KATHRYN

So we need something to distract her with.
Something so tempting, she'll take any risks to
achieve it. What does Claire Wright want more
than anything else in the world?

FRANK

You're the shrink.

KATHRYN

An *audience*, Frank.

The play.

Just why did Patrick suddenly get a burning desire to
write his play? Out of love for me? Or was it simply the biggest, shiniest lure Kathryn could think of?

A brilliant, provocative role, written especially for me.
And a unique, almost unbelievable opportunity: the chance
to play it on a New York stage, alongside a professional cast.

Unbelievable . . . But like a fool I'd allowed myself to believe it.

I unlock the apartment door and step inside. "Patrick?"

There's no reply. But the quality of the silence seems different now. It may only be in my own head, but it feels like this place is listening to me.

I go into the bathroom and crouch by the washstand, feeling up the back of the porcelain like a cop frisking a suspect's legs. Looking for wires.

Nothing.

Feverishly I check the laundry cupboard. I pull out all the neatly folded towels, tossing them on the floor, but there's nothing there, either. No junction box squatting like some malevolent spider, connected by its web to a multitude of evil babies all around the apartment.

But, I realize, they wouldn't have made the mistake of putting wires anywhere I'd looked before.

I unscrew the light fittings one by one. Nothing. Nothing in the kitchen that I can find, either. Or in the master bedroom. Or the hall.

I glance at my phone where it lies on the coffee table. *Of course.* These days they can listen to you through the microphone on your smartphone. It's as easy as downloading an app, and you never even know they're doing it.

73

B y the time Patrick returns I've tidied up. The towels and sheets are back in the cupboard, neatly folded, the light fittings are reassembled, and I'm on the couch, learning lines.

"Hey," he says, coming over to kiss me. "How was today's rehearsal?"

"Pretty good," I say lightly. "Aidan talked about some possible inspirations. We watched some old footage of Stravinsky's *Rite of Spring*."

"The one that provoked a riot?"

I nod. "And we talked about whether or not art has a duty to self-censor. Things like, is it okay to show a suicide on stage if you might encourage someone in the audience to copy it." In most of these discussions, Laurence and Nyasha ended up on opposite sides, Nyasha being of the view that we all have to take responsibility for our actions, Laurence arguing we can't be held accountable for what other people do.

"It sounds very like one of my first-year seminars," Patrick says with a sigh. I watch as he goes to the kitchen area and starts taking ingredients out of cupboards.

"A lot of directors start like that. We'll move on to trust games next."

"Trust games," he repeats, glancing over at me with a smile. "You and I played some of those, as I recall."

"So we did. All suggested by Kathryn, I suppose?"

He nods.

"I saw Frank Durban today," I add casually.

"Frank? Where?" Patrick looks startled.

"Morningside Park. He was watching me run."

Patrick frowns. "That doesn't seem very likely."

"Well, I definitely saw him."

"How close was he?"

"Close enough," I answer, watching him carefully. If they've spoken about this, Frank would have played it down.

FRANK
She wasn't near enough to get a good look. Just
tell her she must have been mistaken.

"How strange," Patrick says, turning back to the fridge. "I guess the operation must be preying on his mind. What with the lawsuit and everything." He takes some tarragon out and starts chopping.

"Yes, how's that going?" I reply, equally casual.

"Like anything to do with the law, slow." He pauses, knife in hand. "Incidentally, Claire, my lawyer wants Dr. Felix to write a report on your mental health. Will that be okay?"

"Of course."

"It's obviously important to emphasize how much distress the NYPD caused you. But we should probably try to downplay any suggestion of paranoia."

"Oh, very clever," I say.

"What do you mean?"

"Your lawyer," I explain. "It's very clever of him to think of that."

"Well, that is what I pay him for." Patrick's frowning. "Is everything all right, Claire?"

"I know you're still working for the police," I say bluntly.

"What?" He looks genuinely baffled.

"The play. You wrote it as bait. To hook me in."

Just for an instant, he looks wary.

"It was Kathryn's idea, wasn't it?" I persist. "She thought I'd do anything for a role like that. And I have to admit, she was right." Scooping up my phone, I say, "Hear that, Kathryn? You were right."

"Claire," Patrick says, concerned, putting down his knife and coming over. "*Claire.* What's going on? You said before that you missed our games. Is that what this is— a game? Are you inventing something that isn't there, just to have more drama in your life? Or is it possible you genuinely believe this nonsense? Because frankly, you're scaring me." He takes a breath. "Yes, I wrote the play as bait—in one sense, anyway. I wrote it because I wanted *you.* Back here, with me. It was the only thing I could think of that would impress you. That's all."

Oh, Patrick, Patrick, I think. Even your beautiful name is slippery. Patrick the hat trick. Tricky Patricky. While I am Claire, lighter than air.

"*Prove* you're not working with them," I say.

"Dammit, Claire. How can I possibly prove a negative?" His face is tense with anger.

"I don't know," I say. "And that's the whole problem, isn't it? How do we ever trust each other again, when we both know how good we are at lying?"

74

In rehearsal, we move on to bonding games. The Wall Game, where you run at the wall blindfolded and rely on your fellow actors to catch you. Eye Contact, where you pair off and stare into each other's eyes with a look that has to flip among friendship, lust, and loathing.

Staring into Laurence's eyes, I think how incredible it is that he has no idea what I really think of him now.

And the Clay Game, in which one actor plays a statue and another has to sculpt them—moving their limbs, adjusting their expression—to display a particular emotion that the statue hasn't been told. Sculpting Nyasha to fit the word *languid*, I marvel at the way I can change the whole balance of her body with a simple push on her shoulder. She's like some finely made machine, everything in perfect counterbalance.

With Laurence, asked to model him into the word *pride*, all I can think of is to adjust his shoulders so he stands up straighter and lift his chin to make him more imposing. I see Nyasha smile at how absurd he looks.

Laurence grins back at her, and I realize he thought she was flirting. I feel a stab of anger. Not because of him, but because of *her*.

That's all I need, I think. A girl-crush on my costar. As if things aren't complicated enough.

At last we come to the text, and exploring our characters. One of the things that first drew me to the part was Apollonie's mysteriousness, the way the play never quite tells us what she's thinking. But that doesn't work in rehearsal. *I* have to know what she's thinking, or I can't make her convincing.

But equally, she might be lying to herself. Those are always the most interesting characters: the ones who deceive themselves. Because sooner or later, the deception always falls apart.

"I tell myself I want to believe in his goodness, while all the time I'm really being attracted by his darkness," I tell Aidan. "I'm like a moth being drawn to his flame, convincing myself it won't burn me because the alternative— pulling away—would be so disappointing."

He nods. "That works for me."

Later, when I tell Patrick this, he says, "Are we talking about the play, still? Or *us*?"

"The play *is* us. So to act it truthfully, I have to act the truth about us. And really, that's the sexiest thing of all, isn't it? Knowing the truth about someone." I hesitate. "And that's why, if you're still working for the police, you have to tell me."

"Claire," he says wearily, taking my hand. "This is my

fault. I've pushed you into performing too soon. While you're still fragile. It's not too late to drop out. You have an understudy, after all. You could step aside and let her take over."

"I'm not fragile," I retort. "I'm the very opposite of fragile. And I'm certainly not stepping aside."

At my weekly session with Dr. Felix, he brings it up.

"Patrick called me. He's worried about you."

I shrug. "I know."

"He thinks your suspicion of him is a sign you're becoming unwell again."

"So he says."

"What do *you* think, Claire?"

"I think it's like that old T-shirt slogan, *It's not paranoia if they're really out to get you.* I'm just trying to decide if they are. Out to get me, I mean. If it turns out they're not, I'll be fine."

He waits for me to expand on that. When I don't, he tries a different tack. "You have a significant professional challenge on the horizon, I understand."

"The play? Sure do."

"It's just possible you came off Dr. Banner's drug regime a little sooner than was strictly advisable. Of course, I had no idea at the time you'd be putting yourself under so much pressure . . . Perhaps we should think about reinstating some of those meds. At a much lower dosage, of course."

The question flashes into my mind, unbidden. *Is Dr. Felix in on it too?*

I shake my head. "I need all my wits about me right now. And I certainly can't risk getting pimples."

"Very well," he says uneasily. "In that case, why don't we go through your anxieties one by one, and see if we can unpick them?"

75

That evening, I tell Patrick I'm sorry.

"I just got a bit carried away with the idea you might be lying to me. But having talked to Dr. Felix, I realize I was overreacting."

"So we're good? You don't feel that way anymore?"

"No."

"Well, thank God, Claire. For a while there, you had me really worried."

Patrick is visibly more relaxed now that I've cleared the air. We go to bed early and start to make love. I don't actually say *I'm going to make it up to you,* but I do all the things I know he likes. That *all* men like, actually: Patrick's tastes are nothing if not conventional. I kiss him all over, pleasuring him for a while, then push him down and climb on top of him. But then I stop.

"Patrick," I say quietly, "there's something I have to tell you."

"What?" he says, smiling up at me.

"I'm tired of keeping it a secret," I tell him. "I killed her. I killed Stella."

76

For an endless moment he stares at me, stunned. "What is this?" he says at last, his voice hoarse with shock. "What are you saying, Claire?"

"I needed the money. I was broke. Jess was going to throw me out of her apartment and I had to pay for my acting classes . . . We'd argued, Stella and I, about how she was trying to blackmail you. And then, later that night, I decided she should be paying me a whole lot more than four hundred dollars, if that was what she was doing."

INT. LEXINGTON HOTEL, CORRIDOR—NIGHT

Stella opens the door to her suite, a glass in her hand. She's swaying.

STELLA
Oh, it's you. The girl who couldn't pick up my
husband. What do you want?

ME

We shouldn't do this out here.

INT. LEXINGTON HOTEL, TERRACE SUITE—NIGHT

ME

. . . You used me to try to blackmail your husband. And if he hadn't been such an honorable
guy, you'd have succeeded. Either way, that's
making me an accessory to a crime. I want another two thousand dollars.

STELLA

Or?

ME

Or I'll tell him exactly what you did.

STELLA

You little fool. You have no idea what you're
getting yourself mixed up with. You'd better
get out of here before I call the manager.

She goes to the phone beside the bed.

ME

Get away from that phone.

She turns—and sees I've pulled Jess's gun on her.

STELLA

What the—

ME

Turn around and face the wall. Wait—pass me
that overnight bag first.

"I didn't mean to kill her," I conclude. "That part was an
accident. She grabbed the gun when I took the bag from her
and I had to hit her with something to make her let go. But
once she was dead, there was no way I was going to leave
without her money." I look at him. "Patrick, I'm sorry. I'm
sorry for everything. But I'm not sorry it happened, because
then I met you. Can you forgive me?"

He's still staring at me incredulously. Neither of us
moves, a frozen tableau. Then I glance at my phone, on the
nightstand by the bed.

I see the realization dawn in his eyes.

"Oh Christ," he says disbelievingly. "You just said that
to see if I was telling the truth, didn't you? To see if the cops
broke in and hauled you away. Well, they're not going to,
Claire. There are no cops. Because I have nothing to do with
them anymore."

"I wouldn't lie about something like this—"

"Stop it," he says. "Stop this now." His expression is
fierce. "You've gone too far."

"I had to know," I say in a small voice. "I had to know
for sure. Please understand, Patrick. It was the only way I
could think of to prove once and for all that you're not still
working for them—"

"Oh, I'll prove it all right." He's angry now, as angry
as he was that time in the theater. He reaches up and puts
his hands around my throat. "If they were listening, they
wouldn't let me throttle you," he says between clenched
teeth. "They wouldn't let me do *this*."

I feel his fingers digging deeper, tightening. I can't breathe. I reach up and try to pull them away but he's too strong, his grip squeezing ever harder. The blood starts to pound in my ears. I claw at his hands. Fireworks pop and sparkle in front of my eyes. There's a moment of light-headedness and then I'm falling, falling down a tunnel.

I come to in his arms. His hands cradle me gently. My throat hurts.

"I'm sorry," I whisper.

"No. *I'm* sorry," he says quietly. He holds me tighter. He's shaking.

"Don't be. I deliberately provoked you, my love. It was a trust game. And it worked."

wake before dawn. Beside me, Patrick sleeps like a cat, his breathing so silent he might as well be dead. Even in repose his body seems coiled and watchful, a hair-trigger assemblage of muscle and sinew.

Quietly, so as not to wake him, I slip from under the covers and go to the kitchen for some juice. My throat's still sore, and we go off-book tomorrow—today, now. I can't risk losing my voice.

As I drink, I look out at the city. I love the way the big windows make these apartments feel like a stage set. It's like we're on show, a doll's house anyone can peer into, though actually this neighborhood is quiet at night and the street below is almost deserted.

I'm thinking about Stella.

In class once, Paul got us to play a game in which three people are given either a red hat or a black hat. They can't see their own hat, only the others', but the first person who can say what color they're wearing wins. It's an exercise in seeing a scene through other people's eyes.

That's what I'm trying to do now.

When I'd made my mock confession, Patrick had looked startled. And then baffled. Then angry. But not for one moment did he look convinced.

Because he loves and trusts me?

Because I'm not as good an actor as I think?

Or because he knows I couldn't possibly have done what I said . . . Because he was there himself when Stella died?

A cop car speeds along the empty street, lights flashing, its siren thoughtfully turned off to avoid waking the sleeping residents. On its way to another murder, perhaps. Another set of lives torn apart.

Unbidden, I hear Dr. Banner's voice.

DR. BANNER

It's not surprising you have these melodramatic delusions, Claire. They're a symptom of your disorder. Tomorrow you'll find yourself convinced of the exact opposite.

I have to know, I think. I have to know who really killed her. Not because discovering Patrick's a murderer would stop me loving him. But because, if he *is* a murderer, I don't want him to keep it hidden from me.

That's *my* dark secret: The simple fact is, my love for him is so all-consuming that even if I knew he'd killed Stella, it wouldn't change how I feel about him. But I couldn't bear for him to have done something as momentous as that and not share it with me.

Like Apollonie, I have to face into the darkness. To walk toward it.

I can't go to the police, of course. But there's something else I could try.

78

>>Victor?

>>Claire. I was hoping you'd come back to Necropolis one day.

>>Victor, I need a favor.

>>Anything, my angel.

>>You're not going to like it.

>>Try me. I'm surprisingly broad-minded, for a pervert.

>>I want to meet you. Properly, I mean. IRL.

There's a long pause. I can almost hear the hum of telephone wires, the buzz of interference, the whistles and clicks of distant exchanges as our silence bounces across satellites,

streaks from computer to computer, snakes down endless
fiber-optic cables—

>>Is this a date, Claire?

I think how many men I've led on, how many I've acted
for, become a delusion, a figment of their dreams.

>>No. Sorry. Just friends. But believe me, it's impor-
tant. You're the only one I think I can trust.

>>Where are you?

>>New York. You?

>>Near enough.

>>Where's good for you?

>>There's a cybercafé in the East Village, on
St. Marks Place. I could meet you there at noon.

>>How will I recognize you?

>>Log onto the site. I'll tell you then.

>>Thanks, Victor. I wouldn't ask if it wasn't impor-
tant.

get to the café fifteen minutes early and choose a computer in the corner. Beside me, a Japanese student is engaged in earnest cyber-chat with his girlfriend. Nearby, a heavyset businesswoman types a report, banging her keyboard energetically with two fingers. A teenage boy is playing a computer game. A giggling Italian couple are uploading pictures of their honeymoon.

There's also a middle-aged guy in a raincoat, fiddling with an empty Starbucks cup.

I log onto Necropolis.

>>You here, Victor?

>>I'm here, Claire.

>>Here in the website? Or here in the café?

>>Both. Tell me what you look like.

>>I'm twenty-five. Dark hair. I'm wearing a cashmere twinset that used to belong to someone else. I'm at the computer in the corner.

>>You didn't mention that you're beautiful.

I look up. The businesswoman smiles at me rucfully.

80

"**B**ut would you ever actually hurt anyone? *Really* hurt them, I mean?"

Victor, whose real name is Corinne, shakes her head. "In my fantasies, I dream about sexual domination. But I also dream about world peace, living with a supermodel, and being a professional musician. I acknowledge my obligations to society, Claire, and that means that like anybody else I have to regulate my wants." She shrugs. "Good submissives are hard to find, particularly if you're a fat old dyke. But my straight friends don't seem to have it much easier."

"Okay. I get that."

"Tell me what this is about," Corinne suggests.

I explain about the police sting, my theory that it might somehow have been linked to Necropolis. I have to stop myself from sounding like some crazy woman. "It was the police psychologist who suggested I go on that site in the first place," I finish. "If it hadn't been for her, it would never have occurred to me to take my character in that direction. And then of course Patrick appeared to be into all this weird stuff too, even though he wasn't really."

"Speaking as someone who's into that weird stuff myself, I'd say that's pretty generous of him."

"Sorry—I didn't mean—"

She waves away my apologies with a smile.

"So what I'm wondering is—why Necropolis?" I say. "Why would a psychological profiler be so interested in a perfectly legal BDSM site?"

Corinne hesitates. "There may be more to Necropolis than meets the eye. At least, that's what some users say. There's talk of a part that's hosted on the Dark Web—a part even members can't access unless they've been invited. That's where the heavy stuff happens."

"What do you mean, *heavy stuff*?"

"Trading. Images and videos, I understand."

"Illegal images?"

Corinne nods. "From what I hear. I never asked for details. That's not my thing."

I'm not surprised to discover that the website Kathryn Latham pushed me toward was part of something illegal. But where does Patrick fit into this?

"*An old desk full of dead ideas / Is not more full of secrets than my aching head*," Patrick had said to me the first time we met, his voice thick with conviction. Was that a clue? Was this the secret he was obliquely referring to, using Baudelaire's words as a screen to disguise their deeper truth?

If he was buying images on Necropolis, and Stella came across them, that might explain why she was talking about leaving him; even, perhaps, why she was so agitated that night.

And that, I realize, is the difference between us. What

she was frightened of, I'm intrigued by. If Patrick *was* doing something like that, I won't be shocked. Quite the opposite: I'll welcome the chance to show I can accept that part of him. To deepen our intimacy. Like a moth drawn toward the flame.

81

When I get to the bar where we've arranged to meet, Henry's already ordering his second beer. He was there early, he tells me. Since Stella's murder, the law firm has cut back on spousal work and he's been reassigned to debt collection.

"Computer searches, mostly. The boring stuff. My guess is they'll be pushing me out soon. My particular skill set's not much use to them anymore."

"What if I had some freelance work for you?"

He raises his eyebrows. "You want me to check out your boyfriend?"

For a moment I'm almost tempted, then I shake my head. "This isn't a person. More like a thing."

Briefly I explain what I've learned about Necropolis. "I need you to take a look at it. See if you can get into the hidden part, somehow."

"You know," Henry says thoughtfully, "there were a couple of things about Stella's murder that always seemed strange to me. You recall how jumpy she was that night?"

I nod, remembering. She'd been pacing up and down by the windows as I entered.

STELLA

You will be careful, won't you? Promise me you'll be careful.

"She had a USB stick—a little metal thumb drive on a keychain," Henry continues. "She kept twisting it around, remember?"

I think back, picturing it. The way she'd wrung her hands. Squeezing something that for a moment I'd thought was a rosary, before I'd seen the glint of a keychain. And how, when she'd warned me about her husband—*He's like no man you've ever met*—she'd glanced down. Almost as if it was the proof of what she was saying.

"This is a long shot, but if we're talking illegal images, maybe that's what was on the stick," Henry adds, reaching for his drink.

"Did you mention it to the police?"

"Sure. But they said nothing like that was found when they searched her suite. They thought either I was mistaken, or the killer took it with him."

I sit back, thinking. "Stella said the whole point of having me entrap Patrick was to get some leverage over him. In which case, maybe the thumb drive was leverage too. But if it was missing, how come Kathryn Latham already knew about Necropolis when she briefed me?"

"Perhaps she was FBI."

I glance at him. "Why do you say that?"

"First, because it would explain why she was using a false name—that's standard for FBI agents on field operations. Second, because it's the Bureau's job to keep tabs on illegal websites. If they were already aware of this Necropolis thing—monitoring it, even—that might be how she got involved. There's an electronic questionnaire cops have to fill in after a murder for something called VICAP—the Violent Criminal Apprehension Program. Most times, it's a pain in the ass—thirty pages of questions, just to find out if your crime matches another one that hasn't been solved yet either. But just occasionally, you'd hit 'Send' and get an automated message telling you to call a number at Quantico. If the computer thought there was a link between Stella's murder and something on that site . . ."

"Which there was," I say, nodding. "Baudelaire. That's why it's called Necropolis. The people on that site are into Baudelaire. And not in a nice way, either."

82

"I spoke to Henry today," I say.

"Who?" Patrick doesn't look up from his book.

"The ex-cop I used to work with. I wanted to ask him about the police investigation."

He does look up then. "I thought we agreed we weren't going to rake that up again."

"No. *You* agreed that. I never agreed anything. The point is, Henry told me something interesting. Stella had a thumb drive. The killer took it, but it's just possible it contained images from a website called Necropolis." I pause. "I need to know if that name means anything to you."

Patrick looks at me steadily, his face expressionless. "Yes," he says at last. "It does."

I exhale. "You've been on the site. You bought their images."

"No." He shakes his head. "Some thumbnails just arrived in my inbox one day. That was the domain name they were sent from—Necropolis."

"But why were they sent to you, of all people?"

"They were digital photographs of imagery relating to

Les Fleurs du Mal," he says quietly. "Re-creations, if you like."

"Why?" I'm puzzled.

"In the old days, connoisseurs' editions of poetry would sometimes have plates—illustrations of the poems by well-known artists. If the subject matter was erotic or obscene, the editions would be created in tiny quantities, for private collectors." He indicates the bookshelves that fill one whole wall of the apartment. "I have some rare illustrated volumes of *Les Fleurs du Mal* myself."

"And that's what these were? Illustrations of the poems? Only photographed, rather than drawn?"

He nods. "I thought they were ridiculous—so obviously Photoshopped that the whole effect of Baudelaire's verse was lost. I replied, saying so. I never heard from Necropolis again."

"Do you still have the images?"

"No." He glances toward the bookcase. "Well . . ."

"Patrick, please. It may be important."

He sighs. "I kept one. Just one. The cover. The least unpleasant."

He goes over to the bookshelves. Pulling a single sheet from between two volumes, he hands it to me. Involuntarily, I gasp.

The photograph shows a woman's flat stomach, her skin tone somewhere between brown and black. A downy rosette of hairs surrounds her navel, catching the light from a source out of shot. Another neat line of fuzz leads downward. Because of how it's been cropped, together the navel and fuzz resemble a flower. It's a delicate, tender image—except for the way the words LES FLEURS DU MAL have been gouged above the belly button, deep into the skin itself. It doesn't look Photoshopped to me.

"My God," I whisper.

He nods. "I know. The others were in a similar vein."

"Were they all . . ." I stop, aware how incongruous this will sound about something so gruesome. "Were they all this *beautiful*?"

"I suppose they were, in a way," he says quietly.

I stare at the picture, unable to tear my eyes from it. "Beauty from evil."

"Beauty from evil," he agrees.

"Did the email contain anything else?"

"Just a very brief note. Something like: 'Another flower from the same seed. Another transfiguration. From an admirer.'"

"What does that mean?"

"It's a reference to something I said in my introduction. The job of a translator, I wrote, is not just to transcribe from one language to another, but to transfigure—to make the poems come alive again in a new century, a new medium."

"And here he is, doing just that. Only where you use words, he's making photographs. He's doing it for *real*."

Patrick frowns. "Perhaps."

"Did you tell the police?"

"I told them there'd been some emails, yes. They didn't seem very interested."

"The regular cops wouldn't have made the connection. It was Kathryn Latham who did that, much later." My eyes keep being drawn back to the image. "*Another flower from the same seed*—it's almost as if he imagines *Les Fleurs du Mal* sprouting and multiplying. The evil spreading. And you're the person who inspired him." I realize something else.

"That's what's behind the second act of your play, isn't it—where the prosecutor asks Baudelaire how he'd feel if someone was inspired to commit an evil act by one of his poems. That's the position you're in. You have fans. *Followers,* even. And one of them, when you were rude about his work, killed Stella."

"It's a possibility," Patrick says uneasily. "Let's not jump ahead of ourselves."

"But Patrick—don't you see what this means? This play—we're charging straight into some nutcase's private fantasies. How's he going to feel about what we're doing?"

"Why should he feel anything?"

I look at the picture again, repulsive and strangely alluring at the same time. "I don't think this man thinks of himself as just some sick pornographer. I think he sees himself as an *artist.* If he doesn't like the play, he won't just write a bad notice in the *Times.* He'll take it more personally than that."

"I don't see why he should. But if you're worried . . . Do you want to back out?"

For a moment, I'm almost tempted. But as Patrick said, this may all just be some wild theory. And I'm not about to throw away my big opportunity because of something that happened before I even came on the scene.

"Of course not," I say. "But perhaps we should start being careful."

83

And then, jogging around Morningside two days later, I see something on a bench. Someone's left their paperback behind.

As I get closer, I see it's a copy of *Les Fleurs du Mal.*

I go and pick it up. As I do so, a photograph falls out. A photograph of me. The headshot Marcie had me do for her website, printed out on cheap computer paper.

The poem it was marking is called "The Ghost."

> *Like an angel with bright monstrous eyes,*
> *I shall come to where you sleep,*
> *Gliding toward you silently*
> *In the shadows of the night.*

I feel a lurch of nausea. But I keep reading.

> *And I will give you, my dark beauty,*
> *Kisses cold as moonbeams,*

Caresses soft as the touch of snakes
That crawl around a tomb.

Where some might woo with tenderness
Your loveliness and youth,
I mean to reign over you with fear.

84

"And you didn't see anybody?"

"No one. That is, there were people around. But no one out of the ordinary. And I had that feeling again—the feeling of being watched."

Patrick turns the book over in his hands. It's the standard edition, the one with his own translations, unremarkable in every way. "The university bookstore is only two blocks away. It could be one of my students—"

"With a photograph of me in it?" I interrupt. I can hear the stress in my own voice. "Why?"

"You're appearing in a play about Baudelaire. Maybe they'd Googled you. Maybe it was just a reminder to buy a ticket—"

"I don't believe that's all it is."

"Just as you didn't believe I wasn't collaborating with the police," he says gently. "Just as you believe you saw Frank Durban."

"Maybe I overreacted then," I admit. "But I'm not overreacting now. That book was left for me to find. It's as clear as day—'*I mean to reign over you with fear.*' He wants me scared." I pull the book out of Patrick's hands and throw it across the room. "It's *him*. It must be. The man who made those images. He's following me. Sending me messages."

"Do you want to go to the police?"

"They're hardly going to take it seriously, are they? Like you say, it's just a book. And you're not their greatest friend right now."

"What, then?"

I think. "Why don't I ask Henry if he'll act as my security? He could escort me to and from rehearsals."

Patrick nods. "That's a good idea. Anything to keep you feeling safe, Claire."

But I notice he stops short of saying he thinks I'm right.

85

At our next rehearsal, Aidan makes an announcement.

"You may've noticed we have extra security, and that you've all been issued passes to get in and out. This is because Claire may have a stalker. You'll also notice she has a bodyguard when she leaves the building. Please cooperate fully with the new procedures. They really are for everyone's protection."

Across the room, I see Laurence frown as he doodles on his script. I can just imagine what he's thinking. *Here we go again. Drama queen in the house.*

Screw you, I tell him silently.

Even Henry is skeptical.

"Stalkers tend to do weirder shit than leaving books around," he tells me. "Usually it's love letters to begin with. Then they get pissed you don't respond, and the obsession flips to anger."

"I don't think this guy is a stalker in the usual sense," I say. "This is more like a hunter stalking prey."

"If so, why would he risk alerting you?"

"I don't know. But I think it's all part of his plan, somehow. Messing with my head. Playing mind games."

"If that's all he does, maybe we shouldn't worry too much."

"You didn't see the images. He's killed before. He won't stop at sending poems. Eventually, he'll want to reenact them."

"*If* it's the same guy. Speaking of which, I hung out on Necropolis last night. Made it pretty clear I found the stuff on the regular site way too tame. Nobody took the bait."

"They will," I say. "Necropolis is the key to this whole thing. I'm sure of it."

86

All the sex scenes are meticulously choreographed, just like a stage fight. We rehearse them fully clothed to begin with, first at half speed, then three-quarter, until they become more like an exercise in dance or gymnastics; precision rather than passion.

"If at any point you feel uncomfortable, just say so," Aidan tells us. "Respect your fellow actors and yourself. There's nothing wrong with having boundaries."

Of course, I never do say anything. Partly because I don't want to be the person whose limitations hold back the show, and partly because I never saw a boundary I didn't want to cross.

"These are the only scenes where you never, ever improvise," Aidan emphasizes. "Nothing unexpected on the day. It's all about trust."

I have three such scenes: the one where the statue of me comes to life and Jeanne and I make love; the one where Baudelaire and I spend our single night together; and the very last scene of the play, the climactic new ending Aidan's had Patrick write, in which Nyasha, Laurence, and I perform a waltz with three human skeletons, a danse macabre that gradually turns orgiastic. The skeletons will be worked by puppeteers, hidden in the rigging above the stage. The first time we try it, we get hopelessly entangled, so that's the scene we spend the most time on. Only when it's working do we turn to the others.

My scene with Nyasha is relatively easy—I'm required to be passive at first, a statue lying on a plinth, then gradually more aroused, until I freeze, immobile, in the same ecstatic pose in which I was sculpted. The scene with Laurence is more problematic. No one's quite sure how it should be played, not even Aidan. In some ways, it's the most important scene of the whole play, its central mystery, the scene that pivots Baudelaire from adoring Apollonie to rejecting her. We discuss a series of options. Was he impotent? Ecstatic? Terrified? Tearful? Patrick's script doesn't say. Everyone thinks that's a cop-out, but we can't agree what should fill the void.

At Aidan's request, Patrick comes in to workshop some ideas. We try a few things, but it's still not working.

Patrick says diffidently, "Can I suggest something?"

"Of course," Aidan says.

"If she's on top of him," Patrick says. "On top, and then she deliberately takes his hands and puts them on her throat."

"What's her purpose?"

"It's ambiguous. Either she's inviting him to prove he isn't the person the poems depicts . . . or she's inviting him to prove he is. The point is, he gets angry. And we won't know if his anger is because she still doesn't believe him, or because he can't help but lose control."

"Ambiguous is fine for the audience. But for Apollonie?

What does *she* want, right at that moment?" Aidan turns to me. "Claire? It's your role."

"I think she wants him to be true to the poems," I say slowly. "When all's said and done, she wants him to be authentic. And she's scared, because she doesn't know where it will take her—where it will take *them*. She knows this is breaking a taboo. But that's what she truly desires, at least in this moment—the intimacy of sharing his deepest, darkest secrets. And he goes along with it. *That's* why he rejects her. It's right there, in the letter he wrote her the next day: *I have a horror of passion, because I know too well the abominations to which it can tempt me.* Baudelaire's frightened himself by what he's revealed."

I look at Patrick. He holds my gaze. After a moment, he nods.

"Okay, that works," Aidan decides. "Let's block it."

87

Eventually we get to the undress rehearsal, as we've dubbed it: the first time we're to rehearse the nude scenes without clothes. The session is closed, with only Aidan and the choreographer allowed in. It's hard to know how to approach it, tonally—serious and respectful, or humorous and bantering? Both options, though, are silenced by the sight of Nyasha disrobing. It wouldn't have mattered how many miles I'd jogged: I could never compete with her whipcord-hard body, her perfect breasts, the stomach that's as flat and taut as a tennis racquet. I take my own robe off in silence.

It feels awkward for about two minutes, then I completely forget I'm naked.

When we're done and the set is open again, a runner comes up to me. "Flowers for you, Claire. I've put them over there."

In the sink is an enormous bunch of black lilies. From Patrick, I guess immediately. He knows I was nervous about today.

There's no name on the card, just a few typed lines.

> *How I would love to see the happiness*
> *Chased from your sweet eyes*
> *And your heart in horror drown.*

I call him.

"Did you send me flowers?"

"No," he says. "Damn—I should have."

"It's not that—I've been sent another poem." I read it to him. "It's from *Les Fleurs du Mal,* isn't it?"

"Yes—from a poem called 'Sad Madrigal,'" Patrick says slowly. "Addressed to the White Venus. He says many men have made her smile, but he wants to be one of the privileged few to have made her weep."

"'*And your heart in horror drown . . .*' It's him again." I'm trembling. "Book guy. It must be."

Patrick's silent for a moment. "But a bouquet can hardly be construed as a threat, Claire. It could just be someone saying congratulations, your talent's been spotted at last."

"It's flowers, Patrick. *Black* flowers. Flowers of *Evil.* He's doing exactly what he said he'd do—trying to scare me." *And succeeding, too.*

But even as I think that, there's a part of me that's almost grateful. *Use that.* When Apollonie was sent that same poem, anonymously, opening the handwritten letter that simply arrived at her house one day, the ink only just dried on the sheets, she too had no way of knowing who it was from, or why she had been singled out for this man's attention. Whether it was from an admirer, a stalker, or—as it turned out—someone who was actually a strange mixture of both. I'd always known she must have been scared, but now I really *feel* it.

"You don't think you might be reading a significance into those words that isn't really there?" Patrick says quietly, and I know then that he too has researched the symptoms of Histrionic Personality Disorder.

88

As I'm leaving, Laurence comes up to me.

"That was pretty wild earlier," he says with a boyish smile. "You really went for it."

"Thanks," I say. I'm distracted, still thinking about the flowers. I just want to get home.

He lowers his voice conspiratorially. "You know, I'd forgotten how amazing you are in bed."

"I'll take that as a compliment. Look, I need to go—"

"Wait . . ." He puts his hand on my arm. "How *are* you, Claire?" he asks quietly. "It's been hell, trying to pretend there was never anything between us. But don't assume that just because I can fake it for *them*, I don't feel anything for you."

I stare at him. "To be honest, Laurence, I *had* assumed that."

He ignores my sarcastic tone. "Actors, huh? We never know what's real and what isn't. Look, would you like to meet up for a drink? I'm staying at the Mandarin Oriental."

"Okay," I say slowly. "Sure. I'll be there at eight. Just for a drink and a talk, okay? To get things straight between us."

"Of course. Just a drink. That would be great."

I look at his eager, beautiful face and realize that what happened between him and me isn't over.

89

That evening, halfway through his second martini, Laurence confesses how turned on he got earlier, rehearsing our sex scene. "I'm not sure how I'm going to cope, doing that with you every night," he adds with a boyish smile. "And would I be right in saying, you were also getting into it just a little more than was strictly professional?"

"Maybe just a little," I say, blushing.

Halfway through the third martini, after we've flirted a bit, he asks me up to his room.

We flirt some more, and then I say, All right, let's go upstairs. He has a suite on the top floor, with a view over the park. It must be costing Patrick a fortune.

He opens a bottle of champagne. As he pours the first glass, I tell him I'm not going to sleep with him.

"You're not?" he says lightly. He clearly doesn't believe me. Not many women say no to Laurence, I imagine.

"I'm not," I repeat.

He's still smiling. "Then, if you don't mind my asking, why did you agree to come up to my room tonight, Claire?"

"I just wanted to see the view."

I walk out of there and go home. I go back to Patrick and show him the video, the one I made with the camera hidden in my bag. The one I'm going to send to Laurence's wife, just as soon as the production closes.

"You are a crazy, evil woman," Patrick says, staring at me.

"You don't know how crazy," I promise him. "You haven't seen anything yet."

Next morning Henry picks me up as usual and walks me to the rehearsal studio. I'm still buzzing from the thrill of entrapping Laurence. But when I enter the rehearsal room, everyone's standing around looking shocked. Louise, my understudy, is crying. Laurence has his serious-but-sensitive expression on. He doesn't meet my eyes.

"Claire," Aidan says, his voice somber. "We've just heard some terrible news. About Nyasha. There's no easy way to say this . . . She's dead."

For a moment, his words refuse to make sense. "What?"

"The police informed us twenty minutes ago. She was staying in a serviced apartment over on Columbus. When she didn't come down to her car this morning, the concierge went up to check on her." He looks around at all of us. "The police didn't say much, but I'm gathering there was foul play involved. They want us all to stay here so they can ask us some questions."

We sit around in stunned silence. Nobody wants to ask what this means for the production. Someone asks about Nyasha's family but no one knows much. She was an intensely private person, I realize.

Three detectives turn up to take statements. I get a woman who introduces herself as Detective Ferelli.

I have to tell her everything, I decide. For Nyasha's sake. So I explain about the stalker, the flowers, how I'd assumed those messages were meant for me.

"The first time, he marked a poem called 'The Ghost.' It's about breaking into a woman's bedroom and assaulting her. I thought it was aimed at me, but actually he was doing exactly what Baudelaire did. He was sending me the poem, but the action it describes happened to the *Vénus Noire*."

Detective Ferelli blinks at me, uncomprehending. Impatiently, I go and pull the book from my bag.

"'*Like an angel with bright monstrous eyes, I shall come to where you sleep,*'" I read. "In other words, Nyasha's apartment. '*Gliding toward you silently in the shadows of the night*'— well, that's clear enough. '*And I will give you, my dark beauty, kisses cold as moonbeams'*—That's when I should have realized. It's 'my *dark* beauty.' He means the *Vénus Noire.* Nyasha was his target. Not me."

"You're saying the circumstances of Ms. Neary's death may resemble a scenario in this poem," Detective Ferelli says slowly.

"That's *precisely* what I'm saying." I almost tell her the killer will have taken photographs too, but that means explaining about Necropolis, and once we go down that path, I'm going to start sounding really crazy.

Her lips tighten skeptically, but she writes something in her notebook.

"How did Nyasha die?" I persist. "It was like the poem, right? While she was asleep? And it involved a knife or broken glass—some kind of mutilation?"

Detective Ferelli looks at me with distaste. "We won't be sharing any details at this time, Ms. Wright. For operational reasons." She makes *operational reasons* sound like *Not with ghouls like you.* "Now, can you describe your own movements after you left this building last night?"

"I had a drink with Laurence Pisano—that's him, over there—at his hotel, the Mandarin Oriental, between eight and nine."

She cocks an eye at me. "In the bar?"

"Yes . . . and in his room too. Briefly."

She writes this down without comment. Something makes me add, "We didn't sleep together."

"Well, that's none of my concern, Ms. Wright. Just the times. And after that?"

"I went home—I live with Patrick Fogler, the writer. The Enclave building, on One Hundred and Thirteenth."

"Okay." She snaps her notebook shut. "At the present

time, there's no reason to think Ms. Neary's death has any connection with her professional life. So try not to alarm yourself."

It takes me a moment to understand what she means. "You don't believe me? You don't think the stalking has anything to do with it?"

"We'll keep an open mind," she says neutrally. "But the fact someone left a poem for you, and you received some flowers, doesn't support any line of investigation we're currently pursuing."

92

Aidan tells us to stay as long as we want, then take the rest of the day off. Louise, the understudy, finally stops crying. She goes off with Laurence, who has his arm around her. The rest of us disperse silently, each wrapped in his or her own thoughts.

I call Henry so he can escort me back to the apartment. By the time he drops me off, Aidan is there with Patrick, talking through the implications for the production. The news is already trending on social media, apparently. I go into the kitchen area, but I can't help but overhear.

"I've talked to Faith," Aidan's saying. Faith is Nyasha's understudy. "She's ready to step up. We'll just have to do a small rewrite to take out her existing part."

"Won't the public expect us to cancel?" Patrick asks.

"I don't think so. It's rare for an actor to die during rehearsals, but not unheard of. Everyone knows the show must go on."

And *you* know the publicity will help ticket sales, I think cynically.

"We'll put out a statement," Aidan adds. "*We're mourn-*

ing a dear friend and a brilliant talent. Nyasha's sudden loss is a terrible tragedy and she will be sorely missed. And we'll get the cast back into the rehearsal room first thing tomorrow. Faith will need intensive run-throughs."

"He seems remarkably calm about this," Patrick says after Aidan's gone.

"It's his job. The cast will be looking to him for leadership now."

"And you? Are you all right?"

I hesitate. "Can I tell you something terrible?"

"Of course."

"When I heard," I say slowly, "when Aidan told us . . . my first reaction was shock, obviously. I was horrified. And so sad for poor Nyasha. But then I felt . . ."

"Go on," Patrick says.

"There was just a tiny, tiny part of me that was disappointed. Because this is the final proof, isn't it? The proof Kathryn was wrong all along. Most likely Stella was this killer's victim too, just as all those other girls were. Even though a part of me had hoped . . ." I stop. "I'd still half hoped it was you. That you had this terrible dark secret that, one day, you were going to share with me."

He looks dumbfounded. "You can't be serious!"

"You wanted to know the real me. Are you shocked?"

"But this *isn't* the real you, is it?" he says slowly. "It's her—Apollonie. Your character. You've gone in too deep again—"

I shake my head. "I based her character on me—you know that. This is always who I've been, Patrick. It's just taken a long time for me to trust *you* enough to share it with you. I might wish I had more empathy or compassion or whatever, but the fact is, I'm just not wired that way. Blame it on being a child nobody wanted, or on being a bit border-line, or whatever the hell you want to call it, but I'm not like other people. I'm just not."

93

We resume rehearsals the next day. Faith is professional enough not to change the role Nyasha's created: She keeps everything the same, right down to the same pauses, the same movements and blocking, so the rest of us don't have to start from scratch. It's almost as if Nyasha's back in the room. It shows how talented Faith is, I think. It's what they always say: Today's understudies are tomorrow's stars.

A few times, I even catch myself calling her Nyasha by mistake. Laurence pointedly calls me out on it.

Of all the cast, only Laurence gives interviews to the media, telling them how much he admired Nyasha. I think about letting some blogger somewhere know *she* thought he was a buffoon, but I don't. I have enough on my plate, and the Internet is awash with enough theories about her already.

After two days of intensive rehearsals, and with just five days to go before opening night, the entire production moves from the rehearsal studio into the actual theater. The set—which until now has been colored tapes on the studio floor—is suddenly a physical reality. As well as scene run-throughs, we have costume parades, tech calls, cue-to-cues for the lighting team. Advance ticket sales are excellent, apparently. The first two weeks are already sold out. But then, who could resist a show about Baudelaire in which there'd already been a murder?

I'm given my own dressing room, a cramped, dusty space in the backstage warren that would have been Nyasha's if she hadn't died. It has a dressing table, basin, mirrors, even a tiny daybed. I love it. Every time I walk in I stop and inhale the smell. Scenery paint, stage dust, and moth-eaten velvet. The perfume of the magic kingdom.

Soon it starts to fill with flowers. From Patrick, from Aidan, from Jess, from Marcie.

None from Laurence, I note.

And then a bouquet arrives that immediately catches my eye. Long-stemmed black roses, wrapped in a tall cone of paper bearing the logo of one of Manhattan's most expensive florists. When I unwrap it, my heart thudding, the bouquet falls apart. The blooms have been mutilated; sliced from the stems, which have been shredded.

The typed note says:

> *Sometimes I punish flowers*
> *Simply for daring to bloom.*

I recognize the quotation instantly. It's from "To One Who Is Too Cheerful." One of the poems Baudelaire sent to Apollonie Sabatier. The poem that was later banned for obscenity, in which he described how he wanted to kill her.

94

"You can't think I'm imagining this now," I tell Patrick. "He's saying it's still not over. That Nyasha wasn't the end of it."

He frowns. "I'm going to call the florist."

He hangs up looking troubled. "They say the flowers were fine when they left the shop. But they were delivered to an Internet locker, not the theater. Whoever did this must have shredded them before redelivering them to you."

"Did the florist get a name?"

He shakes his head. "An online order. Paid with Pay-Pal."

"So I *wasn't* being paranoid."

Patrick busies himself opening a bottle of red wine. As he hands me a glass he says carefully, "Not paranoid, no. But there are other possibilities besides a stalker, aren't there?"

"Like what?" I say, bemused.

"A practical joke."

"*What?*" I begin, but he cuts me short.

"Laurence, for example. He would have seen how freaked

out you were after you got that first bunch. Maybe this is his revenge for that little stunt you pulled on him."

"Which completely ignores the fact he didn't send me the first bunch. And he still doesn't know I have that video."

"Aidan, then. Directors have been known to deliberately frighten actresses, haven't they?" He hesitates. "Particularly actresses they don't think are up to the job. Hitchcock did it with Tippi Hedren—"

"It isn't Aidan. Patrick, it *isn't*. He didn't want to cast me, but once he did, he's been nothing but professional." I push my wine away, untouched.

"Claire . . ." Patrick falters.

"Yes?"

"I have to ask you this," he says quietly. "Did you send yourself those flowers?"

"You're joking," I say disbelievingly.

"I would understand." He looks into his glass. "If it was a way of getting yourself into the part. Of feeling as Apollonie must have felt, when Baudelaire sent her the poems. But if it is, you must tell me."

"You cannot possibly think I would do that."

"I know you're capable of some amazing things. I know you throw yourself into your roles. It's one of the things I love about you. I just don't know how far you'd take it."

"I didn't send myself those flowers, Patrick." I reach for my glass after all and take a long swallow. "It's *him*. He's doing this."

That night, I call Jess and ask her for a favor.

"finally managed to get on the site," Henry tells me as he walks me to the theater the next morning. "The hidden part of Necropolis."

"And? Did you find anything?" There's a street kiosk on the corner of 116th, just where it becomes College Walk. I stop to buy a copy of the *Times* to see if there's any news about Nyasha. I flick through quickly. There doesn't appear to be. Just yet more speculation, along with several mentions of the play. *Ms. Neary was playing opposite the actor Laurence Pisano, along with up-and-coming British newcomer Claire Wright.* It's the first time anyone's used the phrase *up-and-coming* about me.

Henry shakes his head. "It's a reciprocal thing—unless you upload, you don't get to see the downloads."

"Oh," I say, disappointed. I'd been so sure that would be the answer.

"But I could read the titles of the available pictures on a list."

Something about the way he says it makes me look at him. "How does that help?"

"'The most recent one was titled 'The Ghost.'"

"That's Nyasha," I say immediately. "It must be." I feel almost light-headed at the realization I was right.

"There's something more, Claire." He hesitates. "There was another image—one that didn't exist yet. It was titled 'Coming Soon: *My Heart Laid Bare.*'"

"The name of our play."

He nods.

"Henry, you have to tell the police."

"Theoretically, I agree. But realistically, what are they going to do? The whole reason people use those sites is because they're anonymous. You and I both know it could take the cops months to find out who the users are." He reaches out and squeezes my shoulder, clumsily. "Listen, Claire. Don't worry, okay? I've got your back. I'll keep you safe."

step into my dressing room and close the door. The technical run-through has gone well. Now there's just this evening's dress rehearsal. The show opens tomorrow.

More flowers have arrived. Flowers come every day now, so that's nothing out of the ordinary. But even so, my heart is pounding as I go and read the note.

It says:

My Heart Laid Bare.

Nothing else, no signature or name. I unwrap the bouquet fearfully. But the flowers are beautiful, and intact. The blooms haven't been mutilated in any way.

Perhaps, I think, these have been sent to everyone, and the florist simply wrote the name of the production, instead of the sender.

I lie down on the daybed and run through some sense memory exercises, trying to recharge my batteries ahead of the dress. But it's difficult to concentrate. Henry's words earlier keep running around my head. *I'll keep you safe.*

And something else, too. His touch. The way he'd squeezed my shoulder. Maybe I'm overly sensitive to male attention, but there'd been something odd about it.

And then, suddenly, everything rearranges itself, like stage scenery shifting on fly-lines around my head.

Henry.

I remember how, the very first time I was interviewed by the police, I asked if they'd questioned Henry. Frank said they had. But as an ex-cop, Henry would have known exactly how to handle himself in that situation.

How to throw suspicion away from himself . . . onto *me.*

He said himself, he'll probably lose his job soon. He needed Stella's money too. And as someone who'd worked undercover, he'd have had the necessary presence of mind to rig the crime scene, make it look like more than just a robbery.

Was I just the fall guy for Henry's murder of Stella?

After all, I was perfect. The law firm was about to ditch me because of my supposed criminality. He could use Rick the scumbag lawyer's allegations to paint me as a skilled liar as well as a thief.

He even got me to come and meet Stella beforehand, so it looked as if I'd had time to plan it. What was it Stella said to him that night? *I knew this was a mistake.* As if this was all something he'd persuaded her to do.

Some guys, the gray takes hold of them, and they can't make it let go . . .

I shake my head, freeing it of these thoughts. The police checked Henry out, just like they said they would. That clumsy hand squeezing my shoulder was because he felt protective, nothing more.

And maybe because, if I'm honest, Henry has fancied

me a little ever since I first auditioned for him, when I pretended to flirt with him in that bar.

Henry's keeping me safe. I've got to stop being so paranoid.

There's a knock. "Who is it?" I call.

"Hair and makeup."

I open the door. A young man is standing there. He has well-groomed short hair, a big smile, and he's wearing a discreet amount of eye shadow. Over his shoulder is one of the ubiquitous folding cases makeup people keep their stuff in. He's wearing a theater security pass on a lanyard, just like all the staff have been told to.

"Hi," he says brightly. "I'm Glen, Ms. Wright. How are you doing today?"

"Oh—hi." I know Laurence and Nyasha insisted on having hair and makeup assistants written into their contracts, but I'd been assuming I'd do my own. "Come on in. And please, call me Claire."

"Pleased to meet you, Claire." He unslings the case from his shoulder and pulls it open. The top section ladders out into a series of trays crammed with brushes and makeup pencils. "Shall we get right to work? You'll need to put on a robe."

"Sure." Aidan wants my whole body pale for the statue scene. I turn away from Glen, take off my top, and pull on a bathrobe. As I do so, I glance into the mirror.

He's watching me.

Which is, on the face of it, unprofessional. But perhaps he's just looking at what he's got to work with. *Mustn't be paranoid.*

I sit. Together, we examine my face critically in the mirror. "If you can do anything about this . . ." I say, pointing to a pimple high on my forehead. Even though it's ten weeks since I stopped taking Banner's meds, my skin still breaks out.

"No problem," he says, taking my head in his hands and tilting it this way and that. His fingers, through the thin white rubber gloves he's pulled on, are cold. "By the time I've finished with you, you'll be the most beautiful corpse this theater's ever seen."

I flinch. I can't help thinking of Nyasha. "Strictly speaking, I'm a statue. And only for one scene."

Glen reaches down to his case and pulls open another layer, selecting a colored concealer from one of the compartments. "Love the show, by the way. I just caught the tech. Everyone was good, but you were terrific."

"Thank you," I say modestly.

He rubs the concealer on my forehead skillfully, working in small circles toward the pimple. "To be honest, I have quite a thing for Charles Baudelaire." He pronounces the name the way Patrick does, with a French accent. *Sharler Bod'lair*.

Pausing what he's doing, Glen looks at me in the mirror and quotes dreamily:

> *"Let us now be tranquil, O my sad and restless soul.*
> *You wanted evening: see, now it is here.*
> *Dusk has engulfed us in its dark embrace,*
> *Which brings some people peace, but others, fear."*

I glance down at my arms. I've got goosebumps. "You speak it very well."

"Thank you . . . Do you know how that one ends?"

I shake my head. "Patrick's the Baudelaire expert, not

me. You should really talk to him." Though even Patrick, I suspect, won't relish the attentions of this superfan.

"Oh, Patrick. The *translator*." Glen waves the concealer at me in the mirror like a wagging finger. "To the true aficionados, some of his translations can seem a little *free*. Not that one, admittedly. It's almost like a lullaby, isn't it? A lullaby of death."

His eyes still on mine, he continues:

> *"The weakened sun slips out of sight:*
> *Death, triumphant, sweeps in from the sea.*
> *Listen, my love, listen, to the sweet approach of night."*

It's always in the eyes.

That hint of satisfaction as Glen said the word *triumphant*. Why? What does he have to be triumphant about?

He reaches down to replace the concealer in his case. That's when I see that the lower levels are full of steel implements: scalpels and needles and ugly hooks that look as if they'd be more at home in a dentist's office.

Suddenly everything clicks into place.

The images. The flowers. The poems.

My Heart Laid Bare.

Not Henry. Not Patrick. Not anyone I know, after all. But this gentle-looking stranger with the groomed hair and the gleaming smile.

"Could you hand me my script?" I say. "It's over there."

"Sure." He turns to reach for it. In that moment, I'm on my feet. But the chair topples to the floor and his head snaps around. He grabs at something in his case and comes up with a scalpel.

I jump back, but the dressing room is tiny and I stum-

ble against the daybed. The wall's at my back. There's nowhere to go.

The expression on his face as he comes at me is one of
sheer joy. Like a kid on a theme park ride.

Reaching down, I fumble for Jess's gun under the daybed's mattress. I assume that when he sees it, he'll stop. But
he doesn't. And now I have a split second to decide. A split
second that lasts an eternity.

Don't think. Act.

So I do.

97

They closed the theater.

They didn't really have a choice. Even those who say the show must go on can't ignore the practical requirements of a forensic team conducting a detailed examination of the scene of a killing. Plus there were all the police interviews to deal with.

I'd broken laws, of course. Even in America, foreigners can't carry guns without a license. But the fact it was self-defense gave Patrick's lawyer some leverage.

My attacker's full name was Glen Furman. He was a trainee mortician, the police quickly discovered, which was how he knew enough about makeup to pass himself off as a hair and makeup assistant. He was also obsessed with *Les Fleurs du Mal*. They found a dozen copies, heavily annotated, in his apartment.

In his makeup case was a digital camera, set to upload images directly to Necropolis.

By the time the police were done with me, it was the next day. Exhausted, I went and joined the rest of the cast in the rehearsal studio, where they were deciding what to do next: whether to try to put the production on somewhere else, or cancel.

Laurence thought we should cancel.

"If you think about the play's central question," he argued, "it's the one the prosecutor puts to Baudelaire at the trial: What if your poems inspire even one person to do evil? What's your responsibility then?" He looked around at the rest of us. "What if, by staging the play, we help create another psycho like Furman? How could we live with ourselves then?"

"Claire?" Aidan said quietly, turning to me. He too looked tired. "What's your view? You're the one who's been most affected by this."

I didn't answer for a moment. For some reason I had a sudden, vivid memory of the day I first arrived at Gary and Julie's house. I'd been thrown out of my previous foster home after just a few weeks, and everything I owned was in garbage bags. Because, while there was always money for social services to pay for a taxi to get me from one foster family to another, there was never any money for suitcases. Even though traveling—moving on—was what I mostly did, as a kid.

I remember lifting one of the bags and realizing that, if they could, social services would have put me in it too, and thrown the whole lot away. Because that's all I was to them. Garbage.

"I think we should do it," I told Aidan. "We'll never get another opportunity like this. At least, I won't."

I could see them all looking at me. As if I was some kind of monster. But the fact is, I was right. Whereas Laurence was just mouthing platitudes he'd probably read on Twitter.

Aidan put it to a vote. I was the only one who wanted to go ahead.

Patrick took me home. And that's when I finally collapsed, retching and crying, replaying the shooting over and over in my head. Because it turns out that the one thing they never get right in movies is death. Human beings don't just clutch themselves and lie still so the action can go on around them. The body doesn't want to die. It won't give up until long, long after the point where you know it's going to have to. The body bleeds and twitches and gasps for breath. The body fights, even harder than the paramedics who are rushing to save it. The body refuses to accept the inevitable.

Who would have thought the old man had so much blood in him? I spoke those words on stage once, when I was sixteen. I had no idea back then what they really meant, even though people said my performance was brilliant.

Of all the images looping in my head, the one I can't free myself from isn't the moment I shot Glen Furman the first time, because that barely slowed him down. It's the second time I pulled the trigger, when he sank to his knees in front of me. His lips moved—he was trying to say something, but my bullet had punctured his lung and his voice had no pressure behind it to speak the words: It was just an empty hiss, like air escaping from a balloon.

That's what I feel like now—empty, hollowed out, as if there's nothing left inside.

98

"We'll go to Europe. I'd like to show you Paris."
All I want to do is sleep, but I can't. "You forget, I came from Europe. I went to Paris on a school trip when I was fourteen. Me and another girl bunked off to spot ladyboys in the Bois de Boulogne."

"This is different." Patrick strokes my hair tenderly. "I'll show you where I hung out as a student. When I first discovered Baudelaire. It'll be good to get away. We can talk properly then. There's something I want to ask you. But I don't want to do it here."

Something about the way he says it makes me think he means more than just idle chitchat. But that's okay. One consequence of Glen Furman's death is that Patrick and I are finally free of any suspicion of each other.

Besides, I think I can guess what Patrick wants to ask me in the City of Love.

"Well . . . That does sound nice."

His hand continues to smooth my hair. "What did it *feel* like, Claire?"

I don't pretend I don't know what he's referring to. "Honestly?"

"Honestly."

"I felt proud, first of all—proud I'd reacted so fast. That was because of Paul's improv games, I think—going with the moment, not stopping to analyze the situation. I thought—" I glance up at Patrick's face, almost ashamed to say this, but I know now that he loves me for *me,* that I can trust him with the very worst things inside my head. "I pulled the trigger and I thought, *I played that well.*"

"And afterward?"

"Afterward, I was horrified—both at what I'd done, and my own reaction. But that didn't last long. And then I felt . . ." Again I stop, wondering if I can really tell anyone this.

"Yes?" he prompts gently.

"I felt *real,*" I say. "After I killed Glen Furman, I felt more real than I'd ever felt before."

Being truthful, with someone you trust. There's no feeling like it in the world.

99

F ive days later, we fly to Paris.

"There's something I need to tell you," Patrick says as he drives us to the airport.

Something about his stillness, the way he doesn't take his eyes off the road, tells me this must be important.

"Yes?" I say, when he doesn't immediately continue.

"A long time ago, when I was in college, I had a girl-friend. She was beautiful and intelligent and I worshipped the ground she walked on. Or at least, I thought I did."

He stops, gathering his thoughts.

"Then, one evening, I saw a girl. Standing there, beside the road. A prostitute. Something made me call out to her . . . It was a revelation. Suddenly I was free to do all the things crammed inside my head. And she matched me. Anything I dreamed up, she pushed me to go further. I was obsessed by her."

We're passing through a tunnel now, the sodium lights overhead strobing his face. He doesn't appear to notice them, his eyes fixed on something far back in the past.

"Go on," I say quietly.

"One night it went too far. An accident. She knew the risks we were taking. She just got—unlucky."

His hands on the wheel are rock-steady, his speed unwavering. But I can see the tension knotting his shoulders.

"She died," he says.

I can't speak. *Get in touch with your feelings,* Paul used to say. But what if you don't know what you feel? What if it's all too much?

"I'm telling you now," Patrick adds, "because I don't want there to be any more secrets between us. And because you have a choice. In my bag, along with two tickets to Paris, there's a one-way ticket to London. If you want, you can fly straight back to your old life. Or you can stay with me. It's up to you, Claire. But before you decide, know that I love you."

We exit the tunnel. For a long time I stare out of the window, at the endless urban sprawl as it flickers past.

ME

I want to stay with you.

And I smile at him, happy. Because it turns out the only thing better than sharing your own worst secrets is when the person you love shares his with you.

100

Patrick's booked us into a tiny hotel near the Arc de Triomphe, a quiet haven of eighteenth-century elegance. I unpack, then relax in the vast white bath while he goes out.

When he comes back, he refuses to tell me where he's been. "Making arrangements," he says cryptically when I try to press him. I think I glimpse the square outline of a ringbox in his pocket, and don't ask again.

The next day he takes me on a tour, his own personal itinerary of Baudelaire's life. The Hôtel de Lauzun, where Jeanne and the poet lived together. Clésinger's nude statue of Apollonie at the Musée d'Orsay. Les Deux Magots, the famous bar where Baudelaire and the other bohemians gathered to drink and argue.

In the afternoon we visit Patrick's haunts from his student days—the Left Bank, the Café de Flore, and, best of all, the tiny cobbled streets of Little Africa, where we eat couscous and drink rough red wine from unmarked carafes. There are hookahs in the café windows, their mouthpieces tipped with silver foil, and in one he shows me how to pull the hot tobacco through a bubbling bath of arrack, leaving me dizzy and light-headed.

"Wait here," he orders, and goes to the back. When he returns, it's with an unmarked bottle.

"Absinthe," he explains, pouring two shots of lurid green liquid. "Just to complete the experience. It contains a mild hallucinogen." He takes a spoonful of sugar from the bowl, dips it into the liquid, then holds it over the candle. It starts to bubble, and he stirs it into the absinthe.

"Will it give us a hangover?"

"Of course. But, unlike Baudelaire, we have access to ibuprofen. *Salut!*"

"*Salut,*" I echo. The rest of the afternoon is a blur; a vague recollection of pulsing colors, roller-coaster vertigo, Patrick reciting the poetry he loves while my heart expands seamlessly, like helium.

That night, he tells me to dress warm.

"Why?" It's a sunny evening, much warmer than the chilly fall we've left behind.

"We're going somewhere cold." He picks up a backpack.

He tells the taxi driver to take us to the cemetery at Montparnasse. After the cab drops us off, we walk through a pair of massive stone gates into a park, neatly laid out with roads and avenues of trees. But the graves between the avenues—more than thirty-five thousand of them, Patrick tells me—are a riot of different styles, from gothic to art nouveau.

Patrick leads the way to a quiet spot near the center.

"Baudelaire has both a grave here and a cenotaph—a burial monument," he explains. "This is the cenotaph."

It's a white marble sculpture, eight feet high. An ambiguous figure, half angel and half devil, stares down at an effigy of the poet on his deathbed. Scattered across the stone are a dozen or so Métro tickets, each one weighed down by a pebble.

"This is how people here pay their respects. To show they've made a special trip." Patrick slips our boarding passes from his pocket and stoops to add them to the pile.

Next we visit the simple grave where the poet's remains are buried beside his mother's, then leave the cemetery and continue along the Rue Froidevaux, stopping at a small gate of rusty iron bars set into a wall. Beyond it are steps that look as if they lead down into some kind of cellar.

Patrick produces a key and opens it.

"We're in luck. I was worried they might have changed the locks." He takes two flashlights from his backpack.

"Where are we going?" I ask as we step inside.

"Into the catacombs." Carefully, he relocks the gate behind us, then clicks his flashlight on and gestures for me to go ahead. "There are dozens of entrances like this. They're kept locked, but keys are available on the black market. Students sometimes hold parties down here."

I descend the steps. A faint cool breeze wafts from the darkness, bringing with it a smell of dry, musty decay. And an absolute, whispering silence. "I can't hear any parties."

"You're unlikely to. These tunnels stretch for over two hundred kilometers."

By the light of the torch I see a rock ceiling overhead. There's a kind of gray, chalky gravel underfoot. The only sounds are the crunch of our footsteps and the dripping of water.

"These were quarries originally, some dating back to Roman times," Patrick's voice says behind me. There's no echo, the sound somehow absorbed by our surroundings. "It was only in the eighteenth century that they had the bright idea of moving the cemeteries down here."

He shines his torch at the space we're passing through. At first it seems quite narrow. Then I jump. What I'd taken for walls are actually piles of human skulls, blackened with age.

"There are the bones of six million Parisians in this part of the tunnels," he adds. "It was one of Baudelaire's favorite places."

We walk through cavernous stone chambers as high and broad as churches. Gradually we leave the boneyard behind. At last Patrick stops.

"This way," he says, gesturing.

We're near some more steps, carved out of the rock. Below us is a pool of crystal-clear water, perfectly still. Patrick leads the way down, then scoops up a handful, letting it dribble through his fingers.

"When the quarrymen needed to clean themselves, they simply dug down to the water table. It's purer than Evian. And twice as old." He takes a small silver candelabra, a towel, and a bottle of champagne from the backpack.

"Are we going to bathe?" I ask as he lights the candles.

"Yes. But not yet. There's something else I want to show you first."

I pick up on the tension in his voice. This is more than a sightseeing trip, I realize. It's a kind of performance, and I'm the audience. I allow myself to go along with it, to empty my mind of everything but the unfolding of his ritual.

Leaving our things, we walk down increasingly narrow passageways before coming to more steps. Again we descend. We're in a kind of cul-de-sac now, a cavern the size of a chapel, hewn out of the rock, with several smaller chambers leading off it. It's utterly silent. By the light of the torch I see two more backpacks, propped against the wall

"Are those for us?" I ask.

He nods. "Provisions."

"Is that what you were arranging last night?"

"In a manner of speaking." He shines his torch around the vaulted rocky ceiling. "We're directly under his grave now. I'm glad you're here, Claire. This is a very special place to me."

He goes into a side chamber. It fills with warm yellow light as he lights a gas lamp.

"Well, I think it's great," I say, looking at the bare walls. "Very *hygge*."

There's no reply. Then I hear a noise. It sounds weirdly like a sob.

"Patrick?"

There's no reply. I walk through to the far chamber.

"Hello?" I say cautiously. "Hello?"

Suddenly, without warning, two hands scuttle from the darkness toward my feet. I leap back, gasping. The hands are gone, back into the shadows. But not before I saw they were bound together with a strip of cloth.

Patrick appears noiselessly behind me, holding the gas lamp.

"Patrick, what's going on?"

He lifts the lamp. It illuminates a woman, young and

dark-skinned, crouching on the floor. Her legs are tethered, the end of the tether attached to an iron bracket in the wall. Another strip of cloth is tied across her mouth.

"Oh my God," I whisper. I feel dizzy. There's only one possible explanation for what's happening here, but my brain's refusing to process it, to accept that everything I thought I knew was wrong.

"It wasn't only Glen Furman who met like-minded people on Necropolis," Patrick says calmly. "It's a surprisingly thriving community. Our interests may be niche, but the Internet has allowed us to find one another. And, sometimes, to help one another. I have friends in Paris who were only too pleased to make this arrangement for me."

"Who is she?" I say, horrified.

Patrick doesn't even look at the shaking girl. "Her name's Rose, I believe. She's nobody important. Except to you."

"What do you mean?"

"She'll be your first," he says simply. "Just as that girl beside the road was mine."

"Oh no," I say, horrified. "You can't possibly think—"

"It was a similar test that Stella failed. I loved her so much, you see. But she couldn't accept me once she found out. She wasn't as strong as you are."

"You killed her," I whisper. "You killed her because of what she knew."

"Yes, I killed her. But not because of that—I knew she was too frightened to go to the police. I killed her because of someone I met that night. A girl, in a bar. She read with me, one of the poems. And her voice . . . It was a perfect moment, so full of promise, of possibility. That was when I knew Stella had to die." He takes a step toward me, his pale eyes fixed on mine. "I knew as soon as we met that you were someone extraordinary, Claire. The one I might share everything with. But now you have to prove it. To show me you can do this."

"I can't. Patrick, I can't—"

"But you already did," he says reasonably. "You killed that poor, deluded boy. You said yourself, it made you feel *real*. I'm offering you that feeling again. But you can't imagine how much more intense it will be this time."

"Patrick, please . . ."

"So now we have to play the ultimate trust game," he continues as if I haven't spoken. "You have to kill her. And if you don't . . . Can you see the risk I'm taking, Claire? That I might have to lose you. Just as I had to lose Stella."

feel sick. I've been so stupid. I'd thought Patrick was bringing me here to propose. But all this time, he was bringing me here to kill.

"Patrick, I can't," I repeat.

But already a small, terrible part of me is thinking, *Can I?*

"You can, my love. You can. I know what you're capable of." His voice is low and calm, hypnotic. "I've watched you. *Tested* you."

"Patrick . . . I need time to think about this. Please?"

He considers for a moment. Then, turning to the girl, he speaks to her in French. Her terrified eyes widen. Desperately, she nods.

"Good." He pulls out a knife and cuts through the tether tying her to the wall, leaving her hands bound. Then he places the knife a few feet in front of her.

"I just told her that if she wants to get out of here alive, her only option is to kill you," he says matter-of-factly. "So now you really have to make a choice, Claire."

Rose is edging toward the knife.

"You know, there's a poem by Baudelaire about this very conundrum." Patrick takes a gun from one of the backpacks and holds it out to me. "He describes a menagerie, a zoo filled with every kind of vice. And he poses a riddle: Who is the monster even worse than these? The answer is you, the reader, who can enjoy the horrors in his poems without having to bloody your own hands."

"Don't pick up the knife, Rose," I say desperately. She doesn't appear to hear me. I don't even know if she speaks English.

"Well, now you have to bloody your hands," Patrick tells me.

Rose hesitates, then lunges for the knife, scrabbling to pick it up with her bound hands.

Reluctantly, I take the gun.

"Good," Patrick breathes. "Now, my love. Do it now."

To kill or be killed. It has the unreal clarity of a dream. I can't even begin to process the emotions—revulsion, terror, disbelief—flooding through me.

And something else, too: a terrible realization that this moment was always going to happen. That at some level, I always knew.

I *wanted* this.

102

Every child in foster care is there for a different reason. Some have parents who are alcoholics or users. Some are orphans. Others have been neglected or abused.

I used to tell people I was an orphan. But that wasn't true. My parents had been going through what people call a bad patch. There were fights that went on all night. Once, my dad marched into my bedroom and woke me up to yell at me about my mum—he wanted me to know what a whore she was, wanted me to know *the truth about this so-called angel who thinks she's so much better than me.* I remember glimpsing her behind him as she tried to pull him off me; the way he wheeled around with his arm flung out, as carelessly as if he was scattering seed. The way his hand connected with her face and she spun to the floor. To a child, it looked as seamless as a dance.

Once, he broke all the furniture in the living room and used a table leg to beat her unconscious. Time after time she threw him out, but he kept coming back, always with the same mantra: This is *my* house, *my* daughter, and you're not going to deprive me of them.

I used to hide under the bed when they fought.

That was where he found me, that night.

"Come on out, Claire," he said. "Mummy's hurt herself."

"I've got to go away now," he said when I was sitting on the bed. "Let Mummy rest, okay? Mummy needs to sleep, then she'll feel better. And in the morning, can you get yourself dressed and go to school? If anyone asks, don't tell them about Mummy being in bed. Just say she's fine. Can you do that? Can you pretend? For me?"

I nodded. "Yes, Daddy."

"Good girl. I love you. Do you love me?"

"I love you loads," I said.

At his trial, they offered to let me give evidence by video or behind a screen but I didn't want that. I wanted him to see me telling everyone out loud all the things I'd had to keep secret before.

The judge told me I was one of the bravest witnesses he'd ever had in his courtroom.

Then he sentenced my dad to life for murder. I never visited him in prison, not once.

103

INT. CATACOMBS, PARIS—NIGHT

Patrick speaks to me calmly, soothingly.

PATRICK
You've been here before, Claire. You pulled the trigger then. You remember how easy it was? Trust me. This will be easy too.

As if I'm simply in a scene we're rehearsing, I turn. I aim the gun. I shoot. I shoot Patrick. The monster I love.

pull the trigger. The gun clicks. Patrick sighs.

"When I say I'm trusting you with the gun . . . I was speaking metaphorically. It wasn't loaded."

He takes the gun from my hand and loads it with bullets. Then he points it at Rose, plucking the knife from her grasp. She sobs despairingly through her gag as he fastens the rope back to the hoop in the wall.

"Come," he says to me, ignoring her.

"Where are we going?"

"I don't know. Nowhere. Everywhere. I didn't want this to happen, Claire. I wanted you to do it. To understand me. To share my world."

We retrace our steps toward the pool chamber. The candles Patrick lit earlier have burned low now, guttering and flickering in the faint stale draft, their flames gouging shadows into the rock.

He takes a bottle from his backpack. "Drink this. It will numb the pain."

I take a long pull. Absinthe.

"And read for me," he says softly. "Read one aloud. Like you did that first time."

I take the book he hands me and in a flat toneless voice begin to read.

> *"I have more memories than if I had lived a thousand years . . ."*

There are tears on Patrick's face. I let the book fall from my hands, reciting the rest from memory.

> *"An old desk full of dead ideas*
> *Is not more full of secrets than my aching head . . ."*

He puts his hands around my neck.

"Constantinople," I say.

"What?" Patrick says, frowning.

"My safe word. The one I said I couldn't remember. It meant come and get me. Now. Constantinople."

"So, Claire?" he says disbelievingly.

Something tumbles into the chamber. A round, metallic object. Out of the corner of my eye I watch it roll along the ground. It hits the wall and stops.

For a split second, nothing happens. Then there's an explosion of white light. Noise follows a moment later, a percussion blast so powerful it knocks us both off our feet. A high-pitched ringing fills my ears. Torch beams slice through the smoke-filled darkness as shadowy figures in black uniforms storm the cavern from all sides.

One of them kneels beside me and lifts his visor.

SWAT TEAM LEADER
Claire! Claire—are you okay?

I feel his hands dig gently under my shoulders as he lifts me into his arms.

"Frank," I say. "You came."

105

a Martine, just outside the city of Lyon, has a long and checkered history. Originally a lunatic asylum, it was later used by the Gestapo for interrogations. Now it houses some of Europe's most high-security prisoners. Because of its proximity to Interpol headquarters, it has become the nearest thing there is to a prison of the world.

Kathryn Latham comes here one frosty morning in December, as so many have come before her, to conduct an interrogation. She's shown into a small, pastel-colored room where, once upon a time, the questioners used lengths of rubber hoses, baths full of shit, truncheons, thumbscrews.

She's brought a pen and paper, a small recording device, and a pack of French cigarettes.

Patrick Fogler is led in. He's wearing the standard-issue prison uniform: loose-fitting jeans and a denim jacket. His wrists are cuffed.

"I brought you some cigarettes," she says as he sits down. "I'd heard you were smoking now."

"Everyone smokes here. It isn't like America."

"Are they treating you well?"

He shrugs. "What do you care? It's tolerable."

She pushes the cigarettes across the table. "I have a proposition for you, Patrick."

"Ah, yes," he sneers. "The fearless academic in her quest for the truth. Not to mention professional advancement. The pressure to publish is so intense these days, isn't it? No doubt you're hoping to get a nice fat monograph out of me."

"Your relationship with the other users on Necropolis," she says calmly. "I want to know more about how it worked. Who fed off who? Did you and Furman see each other as competitors, or as fellow artists collaborating in different media? Would some of your own desires have remained unrealized if it hadn't been for the images he created? Or did you always hope the translations would find followers like him? There's a lot of material here, Patrick, and it's all new territory for us. If you cooperate, I might be able to do something for you in return."

"Somehow I don't think there'll be a plea bargain in my case, Dr. Latham."

"That's not what I'm offering. More like a trade. You answer my questions . . . and I'll answer yours."

"What makes you think *I* have any questions for *you*?" he says witheringly.

"Oh, I think you do. One question, anyway."

She's got him, and he acknowledges it with a grudging nod.

"You want to know how much of it was real," she adds. "Whether Claire meant a single word she ever said to you. Or whether she was simply doing our bidding all along."

He sits back. "So tell me."

"She's a remarkable person, Patrick. And a remarkable actress. When we found her, she was studying a kind of act-

ing that involved immersing herself in the part with absolute commitment. It was her suggestion that she do the
same with the role we were asking her to play."

INT. KATHRYN LATHAM'S OFFICE—NIGHT

Kathryn's briefing me.

KATHRYN

You need to become a more extreme version of
yourself. And you need to live that character
twenty-four hours a day, week in, week out—
even when it seems the people you trusted the
most have betrayed you the worst.

ME

I can do that.

KATHRYN

There's something else . . . Something you're
going to have to do, if this is going to be believ-
able.

ME

I know.

"I told her she had to fall in love with you," Kathryn says
simply. "And I told her she had to follow the logic of that
emotion wherever it took her. No matter how disloyal or
crazy or dangerous it seemed."

Briefly, Patrick closes his eyes. "So it *was* a lie. All of it."

"You're missing the point. For her, there's no difference.

She loved you. She *made* herself love you. That was what we needed from her."

"'Yet all my lady's virtues are a mask,'" Patrick quotes softly. "'Her beauty just a painted face.'" He gives Kathryn a sharp look. "And Necropolis?"

"What about it?"

"You'd infiltrated it somehow, hadn't you? The FBI. But instead of shutting it down, you just sat there and watched us. *Studied* us. Like we were crawling around some glass-sided ants' nest in a lab. I'm even willing to bet it was you who sent me Furman's images in the first place." He leans forward. "You do know you're complicit in every one of the murders that took place after that? Stella's included. Poor Stella. I may have killed her, but it was you who set those events in motion."

Kathryn presses a button on the Dictaphone.

"Interview with Patrick Fogler," she says. "Tape one."

106

INT. DELTON HOTEL BAR, W. 44TH ST.,
NEW YORK—EARLY EVENING

sit in a quiet corner of the bar, a drink in my hand, trying to make it last. You'd probably think I was waiting for my date.

But then you'd see the burly middle-aged man who drops into the seat opposite me, and revise your opinion.

I smile across the table at him. "What kept you, Frank?"

"Paperwork. You need to be a fricking touch-typist to be a detective these days." He waves the waitress over and orders a beer, then turns back to me. "You okay?"

"I'm . . . okay," I say. "Thank you for asking."

"I meant, for a drink," he says gruffly.

"I know. And yes, I'm okay."

Frank nods. He reaches into his jacket, pulls out an envelope, and slides it across the table. "Here. You just need to sign it and mail it in. Should have your green card within a week."

I look at the envelope. But don't pick it up.

"I might be going back to England, Frank."

He raises his eyebrows. "Oh?"

"My foster mother's having a birthday party. I should be there. And then, all those things I was running away from . . . They don't seem so scary anymore. Not by comparison with . . ." I leave the sentence unfinished.

"I guess not," he says quietly. Then: "Well, if you ever need anything . . ."

I smile. "Just say *Constantinople?*"

He grins back. "Right. And I'll come running. With a SWAT team and a couple of stun grenades."

I look at him with affection. At this man I've shared so much with. My guardian angel. Crouched over his monitors, headphones pressed to his ears, listening through the crackling static for the magic word, the one that would bring the whole illusion tumbling down around our ears.

Even when the weeks turned into months, not once did I doubt that when I needed him, he'd be there.

I'd known from the start they were going to spring a twist, something to help me break through Patrick's secrecy and paranoia and make him trust me. They'd offered to tell me what, but I hadn't wanted to know. I'll react in the moment, I told them. Using whatever you give me. It'll be more authentic that way.

Even I never imagined quite how far I'd take it. But I was drawing on my only previous experience of love for my affective memory, and there was only one place my instincts were taking me. *Three relatively shallow lateral incisions in the left cubital fossa. It would have taken you hours to bleed out.*

Same when I glimpsed Frank in the park that day. Not reacting as myself, with a smile or a wave, but asking, *What does my character think about that?* Using it to make Patrick believe I was still suspicious of him. And, therefore, that he had no reason to be suspicious of *me.*

Giving him tiny glimpses into a mind almost as twisted and sociopathic as his own. But always, always, following the through line, the one overarching truth that drove my character ever deeper into his arms.

"I still love him," I say softly.

"Who?" Frank frowns, not understanding, then: "*That* creep? Why?"

"It turns out Kathryn was right—you can't just take it off along with the makeup. I made myself go inside his head. And a part of me's finding it hard to get out."

He studies me for a moment. "Tell me something, Claire. How far would you have taken it? If we hadn't been there, I mean. Could you have pulled the trigger on that girl?"

"I guess that's the question, isn't it? Where does the acting stop?" I shake my head. "No. No, of course I couldn't."

I say it so smoothly that even I'd be surprised to discover it's a lie.

Because it isn't the right question. It isn't the right question at all.

What Frank should have asked is what I'd have done if Patrick had been the one to kill her. Whether I'd have broken character and died at his hands as a result. Or whether we'd have made love beside her still-warm corpse.

Frank's sentimental, like all Americans. The Hollywood ending I'm providing him with will keep him satisfied, like a box of buttered popcorn.

Who is the real Claire Wright? The one sitting here, with her precious green card permit in front of her, exchanging pleasantries with the man who provided it? Or the one who fell for the darkness she sensed deep inside the only man she couldn't seduce?

Which is the performance: Who I was then? Or who I am now?

Some guys, the gray takes hold of them, and they can't make it let go . . .

Frank's looking at me a little strangely. "Maybe you should remember that thing they say on movie shoots, Claire."

"Yes?" I say. "Which thing is that?"

"Doesn't Count On Location."

"Right," I say, smiling. "Doesn't Count On Location."

I raise my glass and touch it to his, a toast. The strange look he just gave me—concern mingled with fear—gets put away somewhere, deep in the filing system.

I'll use that, someday.

And the invisible camera in my head slowly pulls up and away, releasing us, our voices fading into the background chatter of a New York bar at night, as the words THE END fade up and the credits start to roll.

ACKNOWLEDGMENTS

Seventeen years ago, under another title and another name, I wrote a novel about an actress given a role in an undercover operation. It received some favorable reviews, was published in a few countries, and then—like so many books—failed to sell. I was left with a nagging sense of frustration—not with the publishers, who'd done all they could, but with myself. I felt I'd thrown away an interesting idea by not writing it well enough.

Fast-forward almost two decades, and the success of my novel *The Girl Before* made it possible for me to get the earlier book republished. But I didn't really want to bring that flawed offering back before the public. I wanted to start again, and rewrite it from scratch.

So that's what I've done. This book, although built around the same idea as the earlier one, and containing some of the same scenes, is completely different in plot, characterization, and structure.

The translations of Baudelaire's poems are my own. In many cases I've taken the liberty of omitting or condensing verses to make them fit the demands of a thriller. In no cases, though, have I substantially changed the meaning.

In my original afterword, I acknowledged the help of Professor Chao Tzee Cheng, Michael Ward, Clark Morgan, Anthea Willey, Mandy Wheeler, Ian Wylie, Sian Griffiths, Brian Innes, Sam North, and my agent, Caradoc King.

To those names I'd now like to add Kate Miciak, Denise Cronin, Kara Welsh, and the whole team at Penguin Random House, along with Millie Hoskins and Kat Aitkin at United Agents. And Caradoc King—for a second time.

My thanks, also, to Tina Sederholm and Dr. Emma Fergusson for invaluable advice on an early draft.

In the original, I gave the name Durban to the most decent, loyal, and steadfast man Claire encounters, and dedicated the book to my friend and colleague Michael Durban. Seventeen years later, for the same reasons, I dedicate it to him again.